HELL CAT

VIC SHAPESHIFTERS NOVEL

YVONNE REDIGER

I0524542

Published by Brown Wolf Publishing

Dedication

Thank you to my family and friends.

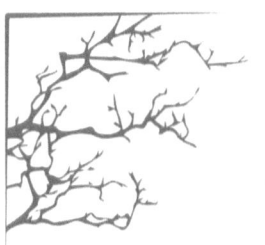

Chapter One

William Conall sat at a shadowy table in the far corner of the bar with his back to the wall. He was nursing a drink and watching my every move.

I could feel his dark eyes on me even though I hadn't looked at him in over an hour. I could detect his scent and it tantalized me, making me extraordinarily aware of him. It also made me think about the last time we were together, and I had to squash that thought without mercy. I had a job to do.

There was no way I was going to avoid having a conversation with Will. The more I thought about it, the more I welcomed the idea. I was glad he had found me. Maybe we'd finally get a chance to clear the air. Possibly, we could save our professional relationship, if not our personal one. Although, I knew I would have preferred the latter.

Most of the Kicking Horse's patrons didn't notice the tall dark-haired man in the corner. He wore snug jeans and a black T-shirt that hugged his hard, lean body, and over it all, he wore a black leather coat. I knew that under the clothes his arms and chest were scarred, but he was fit and well-muscled.

I had run my fingertips over that hard body. I still remembered the texture of his skin and the heat that burned within me as we lay side by side, skin touching.

The clothing did help to conceal him, but Will had a talent for making people ignore him. Eyes seem to slide right off of him. I couldn't really explain how it worked, but it did. Mine didn't. I could see Will quite clearly, but then I was a shapeshifter and we had excellent eyesight.

"Get your head back in the game, Helly," I muttered to myself.

I kept the beer and hard stuff coming for the waitresses at the Kicking Horse. It was a rougher than average watering hole in an industrial section of Edmonton.

Jimmy was the bar manager and my current boss. He kept the guys sitting at the long wooden bar lubricated while he pretended to clean the scarred surface.

The majority of our clientele were males. I avoided serving the regulars sitting at the bar as much as possible—to avoid unwanted attention and the need to break any bones. Many of these guys were old enough to be my father, and that alone made me cringe. Some were too young to bother with and I was pretty sure most of them didn't own a mirror.

There was also the fact that, in the late evening, a few of them would try and tap out the Breathalyzer machine. It was a game they played to see who was the drunkest. Now there's a recommendation for you.

I used my Aunt Rita's line on most of them at one time or another. "I don't shit where I eat." It made them laugh and also let them know I wasn't interested. Words could be powerful weapons when used correctly.

I listened to them and collected rumors about the bar robberies that happened before I got here. I sorted information from their conversations. Some of what they said was even useful.

"Hey, Alice," Belinda slumped against the bar, plunking her damp cork bottom tray down next to her.

I used Alice Munro as my name for this contract. Nobody at the bar asked if I was the Nobel laureate for literature, but then I hadn't expected anyone to.

Belinda's breasts were bulging out of her V-neck tank top with the aid of an industrial-strength push-up bra. Her tiny denim shorts were riding up her ass showing a considerable amount of cheek. Belinda was well tipped for her efforts. Her brassy blonde hair with the odd splash of green and too much makeup took most of the attention, and thus the heat, off me. My natural blonde hair looked washed out in the dim lighting, but Belinda blazed, and I was good with that.

Jimmy didn't have a dress code. The waitresses decided on their own how much harassment they wanted, versus how high they expected their tips to be.

I stuck to jeans and T-shirts and, with my assets, I did okay. Especially if the looks I was getting from Will across the room were anything to go by. It was all for appearances anyway, I wasn't here for the tips.

"Hey, Belinda, what do you need?" I gave her a commiserating smile. We only had another forty-five minutes to go and we could close down for the night.

"Fifteen minutes to last call and table six wants a dozen tequila shots and two pitchers of Purple Plank."

"Purple Plank?" I asked to make sure I had heard her right. "Nobody likes it." That was an understatement. It was one step below swill. It was the cheapest draft beer you could get. I had looked it up.

"I know, Jimmy isn't going to re-order it, we're supposed to get rid of it as fast as we can." Belinda pushed bright green bangs out of her eyes. "I told them there was a discount on it tonight. You know, like the featured beer? Not to worry, they aren't too choosey and probably can't taste much right now anyway. Most of them are having trouble standing."

"Ah, smart." I nodded as I continued pouring out the dozen shots. I'm afraid I've had too much practice at this.

I'd hired on as a bartender to investigate the robberies. Unfortunately, since I started, no one from any biker gang had materialized to hold up the place. At least while I was here, the building owner got his rent on time.

I gathered up the shots between my spread fingers and deposited them on her tray. "Do they have a designated driver?"

"They have a van coming for them at closing. Don't worry. I don't want any of these guys on the road when you and I are driving home." Belinda winked at me.

"I appreciate that," I said, filling the second pitcher from the tap.

"That guy in the corner has been keeping tabs on you all night," Belinda commented glancing over her shoulder and looking at Will.

He ignored her completely I noted when I glanced up. His eyes locked on mine for a second, and then I broke the contact.

"Yeah, I know," I said as I took the money she offered me. Jimmy didn't let anyone run a tab. You paid up for each round or you didn't get served.

"Do you know him, or should I have Donny roust him out?" She offered to involve the bar bouncer to protect me as she gathered up her tray. "Or, better yet, let me take care of him," she said as she gave me a sly smile and laughed at her own joke.

"No, it's okay I'm acquainted with him, but thanks for the offer." I smiled at Belinda as I gave her back change for the fifty she had handed me. I was sure it would all be tip money.

"He looks like trouble with those dark eyes and that body." Belinda grinned at me. "I hope he shows you a good time." She turned away to head back to deliver the order.

I didn't have time to comment. Sindy was waiting for her order to be filled, and I knew Mattie would be back shortly, too.

"Last call!" Jimmy's bellow cut through the country western music and conversation like a hot knife through butter.

After I placed the pitcher of beer on Mattie's tray and added two rum and Cokes to Sindy's, I could feel eyes on me, so I glanced over at the bar manager.

Jimmy gave me a wordless frown from his end of the bar and tipped his whiskered covered chin at Will in the corner. I was touched that our grizzled, grouchy old boss was concerned that Will was eyeing me.

I shook my head and gave Jimmy a thumbs-up. He narrowed his eyes at me but, as usual, didn't say anything. Jimmy was a man of few words.

I returned to my section of the bar and did a fast cleanup of the surfaces before Belinda made a return trip with one more order. I still had a beer keg to change out too.

Will Conall took a shallow sip of the room temperature Glenlivet from the short glass. He'd been slowly turning the tumbler between his hands for the past few hours. It was a younger whisky than he usually drank, but it was the only thing the bar served by way of a decent brand.

His server Sindy, ambled over again as she had every half hour.

"Can I get you anything else?" she leaned on the table, giving him a good look at her considerable cleavage. She cocked one hip so her painted on jeans tightened. The girl was pretty enough with her fuchsia pink hair and her heavily made up dark brown eyes, but Will didn't care.

"No thanks, I'm good," he said, shaking his head and turning his eyes back to the lean, hard-bodied blonde behind the bar.

"Okay." Sindy looked him over one more time, gave a little sigh, and moved on.

There was only one woman in this establishment Will was interested in. When her charade of a job was done for the evening, he would corner Helly Cooper.

Helly had only looked up at him three times all night, and each time those blue eyes rested on him, he'd felt them strike him right in the heart.

Her expression had remained blank when she saw him. No reaction at all. Like looking at him was the same as looking at one of the grubby oil-patch workers. She hadn't given him any sign of recognition. She'd acted like she could have cared less that he had been sitting here since nine o'clock, waiting for her.

Stupidly, he had hoped for some emotion. Whether Helly had intended it or not her attitude had gotten under his skin. They had known each other a long time, but Helly was a cool one. She always had been.

Will had stopped being angry with her months ago. He had to admit he had driven her away. She hadn't cut all her ties to him and Security and Protection Services on a whim. It was his fault, even though admitting it to himself still stuck in his throat.

He'd to concede he was the one who had crossed the line. It was past time to do something about it if he was ever going to get her to come back to the company.

He had reconciled himself to the fact that he couldn't be with Helly, not like she wanted. He couldn't, not with his issues, but they could still work together and, for him, that would be enough.

We got through last call and Donny only had to pour two people into cabs. No one argued with big Donny.

True to their word, table six had a van pick them up. It was nice to see people were occasionally doing the smart thing. I figured they must be from one of the bigger drilling companies.

Horizontal drilling was the new hot technology for oil and gas companies. The technology allowed access to pockets of the resource previously too expensive to go after. Now that the price of oil had gone back up, Edmonton was back to feeling like a boom town. The Kicking Horse patrons had the disposable income to prove it. I knew Jimmy pulled in several thousand each night, a tidy sum for a dump like this.

By the time I had finished running all the dishes through the dishwasher and stacked the trays of glasses, the bar was almost empty.

Jimmy was cashing out and shoving wads of bills into the deposit bag. The rest the staff were cleaning up and wiping down the tables. I was faster than usual at this task because I wanted to get out on time. I wanted to get Will out of here. Why had he felt it was necessary to sit for hours scrutinizing me while I poured drinks? He hadn't come up to the bar and tried to talk to me. He could have left me a number to call him later, but maybe he thought he'd lose me again. He had to know I had been expecting him to track me down for the past couple of weeks. I had stopped covering my tracks as well as I had in the beginning. I was getting tired of being alone.

I hadn't seen Will in over ten months, and we hadn't parted on the greatest of terms.

I knew he wasn't comfortable working with me anymore, so it had been time for me to move on. I left SPS after working for them for almost nine years and hadn't been in contact with him or the company since.

That being said, something compelling must have made him find me. I knew he wanted to talk to me because he had stayed seated at his table as I worked my way over to him. I glanced over at him now, and we exchanged a watchful look.

He was waiting. Like a predator stalking his prey.

Every time I met his dark eyes, I felt something. It was hard to describe, but even after ten months I still had feelings for that man.

I was spraying cleaner on a worn table top when the front door of the bar slammed open, hitting the wall.

I cut my eyes to the entrance.

Three men walked in wearing dark windbreakers, dark jeans, and ski masks, each carrying a weapon. The last one across the threshold paused by the door to close it and to throw the dead bolt.

Donny was still outside.

From the corner of my eye, I saw Will get quietly to his feet.

"Nobody moves," ordered the male leading the three new arrivals. He was wearing a navy windbreaker with a splash of white paint on the sleeve. He raised his pistol in a one-handed grip and walked up to the bar, no doubt trusting the hand gun would freeze us where we stood. He leveled the pistol right at Jimmy's face. "Hand over the cash and keep your hands on the bar."

He couldn't know about the shotgun Jimmy kept loaded under the bar. Probably it was just as well, if Jimmy went for the rifle, Jimmy would be dead.

The taller guy at the door swung a rifle up and pointed it at the waitresses. Who brings a hunting rifle to a robbery?

"Get over to the wall," he growled at them.

They scurried to the wall by the kitchen doors and froze like deer in the headlights. Each one of them clutched a tray of dirty glasses like it was a shield.

The third guy advanced farther into the room and held a rifle as well. He didn't have it braced correctly against his body and waved it around like an idiot. He clearly wasn't sure who he should cover—me or the two old guys to the left of Jimmy, still seated at the bar.

At least Jimmy's cronies were following the bar manager's example. They each kept one hand flat on the bar and had a death grip on their beer mugs with the other. They weren't moving, but their eyes were bulging pretty good. To these thieves, it must have looked like a nearly empty bar with a few old guys and some women.

Easy pickings?

That almost made me smile. They hadn't counted on me or Will. They certainly didn't look like members of a biker gang, so this had to be something else.

I knew Will would take out the guy at the door first. I would have to go for whoever seemed like the most imminent threat. I was almost equidistant between the leader and his idiot sidekick. I watched both of them carefully. With my shapeshifter abilities, I would be on my target before he knew it.

I could move faster than standard humans, not faster than a bullet, but close. We shapeshifters considered ourselves human too. But we were enhanced, where regular or standard humans were not.

None of the gunmen had noticed Will. I could pick him out by the back wall in the gloomy light. He made his way effortlessly across the room to the door. He soundlessly skirted the tables and chairs and got behind his target.

Will moved quickly and efficiently as he grabbed the guy by the door. He wrapped his arm around the guy's neck and squeezed off his air. Will grabbed the rifle with his other hand as he eased the gunman down to the floor with almost no noise.

It was a practiced move, and Will did it fluidly. Had I been facing the opposite way, like the others, I wouldn't have known anything was going on either. One down, two to go.

I turned my body toward my target as I prepared to make my move, now that we were down to two. I would take the guy at the bar because he was their leader. Cut the head off the snake so to speak.

Idiot here, waved his weapon between me and the bar regulars. If I took out the leader, this guy would probably fold without a fuss.

The kitchen door swung open and Juanita, Jimmy's wife and the bar cook, shuffled into the room. She was completely unaware we were in the midst of a robbery.

Idiot was startled and swung his weapon toward Juanita. He fired his rifle at her. Everyone snapped their heads in his direction.

Juanita shrieked, the waitresses screamed and dropped their trays. Juanita threw her arms over her head, turned tail, and ran back into the kitchen. Thank God the shot went wide and hit one of the wooden posts, splintering it.

With the commotion, I changed direction. I ran toward the idiot and, before he could turn on me, I grabbed the gun stock and pushed the barrel up and away from everyone. Then I pulled him into me, easily landing a punch to his throat.

He gagged, his throat was constricted. I pulled the weapon out of his hands and swung the rifle at him. I cracked him in the jaw with the butt, effectively shutting out his lights.

He dropped to the floor as well. I flipped the gun around and pointed it at the leader. Will had beaten me to him. The leader of this ragtag crew was lying unconscious on the floor at Will's feet. I dropped the barrel down and away from Will.

He flicked one eyebrow up at me before he returned his attention to the weapon in his hand. He ejected the clip from the pistol, checked the breach to make sure it was clear, and then laid the pistol on the bar.

Will had the tall guy's rifle that, from here, looked like a Remington 700. He cradled it in the crook of his arm as he leaned down and pulled the balaclava off the robber's face.

Will's eyes met mine, and he gave me a slight shake of his head. No one we knew. Which meant the leader wasn't on any list SPS would have been aware of such as a Canada-wide warrants. He was probably a local.

Will straightened and turned to Jimmy. "Call nine-one-one," he ordered the stunned bar manager.

In the four weeks I'd worked at the bar, I had never seen a look like that on Jimmy's face, he was at a loss for words. Yeah, seeing Will work would do that to you.

"Jimmy?" I prompted to get him moving.

"Yeah, I'm calling." Jimmy growled and reached for the phone under the bar as he aimed a scowl first at Will then at me. I ignored him and turned back to Will.

"I'll go check on the bouncer," Will was already moving. "Have you got this?"

"Yeah, all good," I said. I flicked my eyes over to Mattie, Belinda, and Sindy. "One of you, go to the kitchen and check on Juanita," I ordered.

All three scurried into the kitchen. They paused only briefly to avoid the broken glass and trays in their path. I couldn't blame them for being scared, but the danger was over.

One handed, I flipped my assailant on to his stomach. His weight was nothing to me. I nudged his hands away from his sides with my booted foot. I needed to keep an eye on all three of the gunmen while Will was outside.

My old boss wouldn't have asked for the police if he had killed the guy by the door. There was no smell of death either. If he had, we would be calling SPS for a cleanup crew. They would handle the body and scrub the vicinity.

The front door swung open again and Will had his shoulder braced under the big bouncer's armpit. He helped Donny through the door and down onto a chair.

"Did he get shot?" I asked, looking at the blood running down Donny's forehead.

"No, he took a blow to the head," Will put a hand on Donny's shoulder so he wouldn't slide out of the chair.

"Belinda!" I yelled to the kitchen. "Donny needs the first aid kit."

Will returned to the entrance and grabbed the tallest gunmen's left ankle. He dragged him over to where the idiot was laying prone next to me. I rolled him onto his stomach as well. This was so that, if any of them regained consciousness and were sick, they wouldn't choke.

He also dragged the leader over to the other two thieves, again by his ankle, to complete the set, and I flipped him over too.

It was Juanita who came bustling out of the kitchen, carrying a first aid kit and apparently unhurt. She called over to Jimmy and he waved her off dismissively. So she turned to Donny and began fussing over the bouncer.

I frowned. Juanita seemed to have regained her equilibrium remarkably quick.

Jimmy was on the phone with emergency services dispatch, explaining what had just gone down. He rolled his eyes at me as he listened to the dispatcher's instructions.

I leaned down and removed the ski masks from the other two guys. I lifted their heads by their hair to get a good look at their faces. Nope, nobody I recognized. Well, that sucked.

"Have you got cuffs?" Will asked as he gave them a cursory look as well.

"I have riot cuffs." Will had the Remington in his hand and the Ruger now lodged in his belt at the small of his back.

So I dropped the Winchester's barrel to point at the floor. "Give me a second to get them."

I walked behind the bar and dug my shoulder bag out. I extracted the white plastic restraining cuffs. The cops could trade the plastic cuffs for real ones at their leisure.

Both of the regulars left at the bar took the opportunity to head to the men's room. The older one stumbled a bit as they made for the restroom. His friend grabbed him by the arm to lend support as they wobbled unsteadily out of the room.

"This was amateur hour," Will said quietly as he drew each man's hands behind their back and I secured their wrists.

"Yeah, when they walked in, I was hoping we would nail someone from a biker gang tonight. Maybe we should see if we can get anything out of navy windbreaker here."

The former leader of the awesome trio was making groaning sounds. He had a serious bruise on his jaw were Will had clipped him.

I went through his pockets. "No wallet or ID," I commented. That was what I had expected, but I had to look anyway.

I tried idiot's coat pockets and, running true to form, idiot had ID on him. "Percival Jenkins," I said reading his license. The photo matched, but anything could be faked. "Who names their kid Percival?"

Percival was coming around too. He was fairly young, maybe eighteen. The other two were older, between twenty and twenty-five.

All three had average builds with Percival on the skinnier side. They had medium brown hair and unremarkable features. Upon closer inspection I could tell the clothing was cheap, worn, and several years out of date. Possibly, from a thrift store.

"Are you seeing what I'm seeing?" Will asked.

"I think so," I said.

Will leaned close to Percival's ear and said in a low tone, "Hey, Percy, what's your big brother's name?"

"Alvin or Marvin?" Percival asked. His voice was hoarse and groggy as his eyelids fluttered.

Will and I shared a grin.

"I need ice for Donny, *cosa dulce*," Juanita called over to me as she cleaned up Donny. The bouncer hung his head and hadn't moved from his seat.

I raised an eyebrow at Will. "Is Juanita talking to you, sweet thing?"

"Funny," Will said dryly, even though there was humour in his whisky-colored eyes. It had felt good to work together again. I had missed this.

I left Will to keep an eye on the idiot squad. He was going through the third guy's pockets as I went behind the bar. I found a clean towel, dampened it slightly, and added a scoopful of ice.

"Who's that guy?" Jimmy asked me as I replaced the scoop in the ice bin.

I knew who he meant so there was no point in pretending. "He's a friend of mine. He does security." Will was much more than that, and so was I, but I didn't think it was necessary to give Jimmy all the details. Will certainly wouldn't thank me for it.

Jimmy grunted at my answer as I brushed a strand of blonde hair off my cheek. The hair must have been dislodged from my pony tail when I took out Idiot Boy.

I looked steadily back at Jimmy, but he didn't say anything about Will, even though I could see he wasn't happy. Instead, he changed the focus to me. "That was some punch, Alice. You have some experience taking guys down?" It wasn't really a question and I had already tipped my hand.

"Some," I said. My expression told him that was all he was getting out of me.

"Yeah, I'm still here," Jimmy said into the phone, but his eyes bored into me.

Dispatch wouldn't let him off the line until the uniforms got here. I raised my eyebrows at Jimmy. He shook his head and turned his back on me. I took it our conversation was over. I headed back around the bar to take Juanita the iced towel for Donny.

The idiot squad were all sitting up, though still on the floor with Will standing to one side and keeping an eye on them. All three looked embarrassed, and scared, I noted as I passed them.

I handed Juanita the towel, and she gently placed it on the left side of Donny's head, where his bald patch started, covering the swelling.

Flashing blue and red lights hit the window. "Cops are here!" Sindy called from the kitchen.

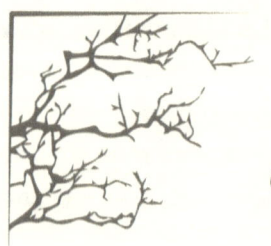

Chapter Two

I t was coming on to five in the morning when Will and I made our way to the parking lot and over to his black 1998 Dodge truck.

"Thanks for the help," I said as I walked beside him, falling into the same gait as Will.

"I enjoyed it," Will said as he flashed a grin at me. "Just like old times."

I couldn't help smiling back. Over the past few months, I had had no one to watch my back. It had been good to work with him again, someone I trusted.

Will had made it plain he wasn't leaving without me after the cops arrived. The police took a while to get to us, but finally, we gave our statements and contact information to the Edmonton Police Service, and we were free to leave.

Not that the contact information we left would be any good to them. We were not the type of people that were easily accessed.

Will's phone number would ring through to a handler, who would either divert the caller or forward them on to someone else. It depended on the instructions Will had left.

For myself, I gave a false number to go with my false name. The police didn't need me. They had several other people they could talk to about the attempted robbery. I would be just another old employee who had moved on. If Jimmy suspected something, there wasn't much he could do about it now.

I looped the strap of my leather bag over my shoulder and zipped up my gray hoodie against the cold November air. I was glad I'd added a down-filled vest over my top. I wished I had added gloves to the pockets. I wasn't like a wolf that thrived in the winter. I could handle it, but as a cougar, I'd rather be warm.

Usually, I took the bus to the bar and cabbed it home. The bar was right on the edge of the Warehouse District. Which meant all the old industrial brick buildings were in the process of being converted to pricy condos. Parking was at a premium around here, although this area did have excellent bus routes.

The shabby bar was one of the last holdouts to sell to the condo development. The owner had hired me to look into a few things. One of those things was Jimmy and his financial situation. He complained he was cash strapped due to several robberies over several months. As a result, he couldn't pay his lease. Jimmy told the building owner a biker gang was pressing him for protection money. So, I looked into that, too.

I wasn't sure if my client was more worried about the crime rate and his condo development or losing the lease money. I did suspect that one way or another the owner wanted Jimmy out. I bet Jimmy wanted to put the screws to his landlord before he moved on. It didn't matter to me, it was a job.

I paused behind Will briefly as we reached his vehicle and he popped the truck locks.

"Why don't you spend some of that huge pile of money you've squirrelled away and buy yourself a decent ride," I said as I climbed into the cab and buckled my seat belt.

"Look who's talking, where's your car?" Will countered with that sexy half smile I had missed seeing over the past months.

"Okay, point to you," I conceded with a nod.

"There are no CPUs in these old models. That means I don't need a computer to be hooked up to my vehicle to run diagnostics. It's not necessary. I can figure out why I have an oil pressure light and fix it myself," he said turning over the motor. "No chips, no tracking either."

As I sat beside him, I breathed in his scent. It filled me with a yearning for opportunities missed.

"Does that save you money?" I was searching for something to say so as not to appear to be off balance. I had fallen back into my old habit, hiding my feelings for Will.

"A bit, but mostly it gives me peace of mind. I know who worked on my brakes."

Our eyes met briefly. "Ah," I said in understanding.

"Breakfast?" Will asked.

He wasn't looking at me now. Will was focusing on the empty street and automatically scanning the area. He was taking everything in. This behavior was one of the things we did without a thought. It was the way we were trained.

Will had something on his mind. Hearing him out over breakfast was not an undesirable way to find out what he wanted. Well, and I'd get fed.

"Absolutely, head down Fourth Avenue, and take a right after three blocks. There's a good breakfast place six blocks on. They open early for the truckers."

"How do they fix their hash browns?" Will put the truck in gear and we rolled out of the lot.

"Real potatoes, diced, boiled, and fried in butter with green onions, salt, pepper, and a dash of paprika."

"Sounds like a keeper."

Good food was one of the few pleasures we could enjoy in the field and, like many organizations, we ran on the fuel we took in. Better fuel meant better performance. However, I reminded myself, I was no longer a member of SPS and that status still felt odd.

Will followed my directions and, in the light early-morning traffic, we arrived in minutes.

We were seated in a retro vinyl booth with menus that we didn't need. Strong coffee in large white porcelain mugs sat in front of each of us.

I waited until our waitress took our orders and then figured enough was enough, I was done with waiting.

"So, what brings you here all the way from the west coast?" I sipped my scalding coffee while I watched Will's brown eyes consider me. I loved the way gold flecks shimmered in their depths.

He finished his own sip and put his mug down with deliberation before answering. "I need you back." He looked directly back at me, he wasn't playing games. "I can't wait any longer for you to return to SPS on your own so I came to find you and ask you to come back in person."

I stilled.

His eyes were sincere. I breathed in, and his scent said the same. I had to force myself not to react. But wait, in what context did he want me back? It was too much to hope for that he needed me for personal reasons. It was also long past time for that. And yet, I wanted confirmation from him. I had to know where I stood.

"I need to know why. I hate to drag up ancient history, but when you woke up next to me, you made it pretty plain that you didn't want that to happen again. I also couldn't leave town fast enough for you." There, let's cut to the bone shall we?

"I never said I wanted you out of town because we shared a night together." He dropped his eyes as he fiddled with his coffee spoon.

"Is that so? You said, and I quote—" I hooked my fingers in quotation marks. "—'this never happened.'" I dropped my hands into my lap and leaned back. "When the next assignment came in, it was mine. I was packed off to North Africa to deal with a team I had never met, let alone worked with before." Saying this made me realized his attitude toward me back then still hurt now.

"You did a great job." Will spread his hands with a how-can-you-complain air. "Your team brought back the victim in one piece. The kidnappers were caught and dealt with by MI6. The ransom was returned to our client with a hefty bonus for SPS. Of which, you received a very large cut."

"Hugh would have been the more logical choice to go instead of me," I said evenly. "He had history with the required team members. His knowledge of the geography was superior to mine. Hugh also fit in better because he had contacts and a network to draw from."

"He shared all that with you?"

I read Will's tone to mean he hadn't expected me to have spoken with Hugh McAvery. Not about who should have been assigned to the job anyway.

"Of course he did," I said derisively. "Hugh was a big help to me. He shared detailed intel on the political situation in the neighboring countries. Especially ones that foster terrorist activity even passively. Info like that sometimes gets missed. But that's not the point and you know it."

I folded my arms over my chest, raised my eyebrows at him, and waited.

"All right," said Will after a long moment with a sigh of resignation.

He ran an aggravated hand through his thick dark hair. "I'm sorry I sent you away," he said, returning his eyes to me. "I don't want you to think I sent you on that assignment to get rid of you. It wasn't because you and I spent the night together. It wasn't about that."

"You have trust issues," I said, relaxing a bit. It felt good to get some of this off my chest. It was good to hear him apologize, too.

"Like you don't?" Will tossed back at me.

"Duh, we all have issues. Why else would we be in this line of work? Well, besides being adrenalin junkies." I uncrossed my arms and reached for my coffee cup.

Will compressed his lips.

He didn't like my bluntness. Tough, you came looking for me.

"Okay maybe it was a little about putting some distance between us. We're professionals, we can't get personal. I have to stay detached and so do you. If we don't, there's a chance we could put our teams at risk. You know this."

I was silent for a bit. I could see the issue upset him. I had no idea why.

"It was just sex," I said, testing to see if he agreed.

"No, it wasn't." Will shifted his eyes. He poured us more coffee from the plastic carafe our waitress had left, along with silverware and napkins.

So, it was like that, was it?

"Best secret Santa ever," I said, taunting him with the words I had used on him before I left his apartment.

Will had about as much of a sense of humor right now, as he had then. None.

"I can't get personal with you," he said, soberly. He hit me with those intense eyes of his, and I could see he was deadly serious. I could tell my teasing bothered him.

"Stop it. Please, Helly."

His words contradicted what his scent was telling me. He wants me. "How are you going to make me? I don't work for you anymore, remember?" I tipped my head to one side, giving him a flirty look from under my lashes, daring him.

Will narrowed his eyes as he considered me for a moment. "Cut it out, or I'll release the details of your real identity to the rest of SPS."

My lip curled. "Heloise is not on the table," I said, leaning forward. I hated my given name.

"It is if I put it there." He was adamant about telling my friends and former coworkers my real name.

I swallowed and asked the question I was afraid to hear the answer. "Is it because I'm a shapeshifter?" I needed to know. "Is that why you don't want to get involved with me?"

"Don't be ridiculous, of course not," Will said, giving me that 'don't be stupid' look. "I don't care that you're a shapeshifter." Again, he sounded sincere.

"You know, being with someone like me, a shapeshifter, can add an element of danger to the relationship. A lot of guys would jump at the chance," I said lightly. "We are exceedingly open to new experiences and very flexible." I all but purred at him.

Will gave me his thousand yard stare.

"Fine," I said dropping the flirty tone. "I'll forget about it if you will." My ego was a bit bruised by his attitude.

"Oh, I have," he assured me. He looked relieved when he turned and smiled at our approaching waitress. She deposited our huge breakfasts in front of us.

Steak and eggs for me with a side of fresh fruit and rye toast, heavy on the butter. Will opted for back bacon and eggs. Also, his previously mentioned hash browns, and whole wheat toast, again heavy on the butter.

We dug in. I ate as I examined my feelings and Will's relief regarding my assurance we would never mention our indiscretion again.

So he wanted me for work only. Fine, his attitude wasn't going to stop me, I decided, as I gave him a calculated look.

His scent called to me. It always had. Some things were meant to be and it didn't matter to me that he was a standard human. Shapeshifters had fallen in love with standard humans before. My situation wasn't unique. It would mean a few restrictions but I could deal with that.

I had been in love with Will since forever. It also didn't hurt that he had a great body. He was not too tall, just shy of six foot, and extremely fit. He had a nice square jaw. It was currently darkened with whiskers that matched his thick wavy hair and eyebrows. How can a girl pass up a guy like this without a fight?

While reflecting on his many attributes my favorites were Will's hands. His were capable, and I found capable sexy. I'd seen him handle every type of weapon or tool you could imagine. He could knock the bullseye out of a target or fix a piece of tech when it broke. He was faster than me at hot wiring a truck when under fire. He was also a good commander.

I liked his attitude about trying something new every chance he got, and stuff he liked, he stuck with. Like scuba diving or kayaking. I wanted him interested in starting something with me. Will paid attention to detail and he was a gentleman. That was probably the reason nothing happened between us. Not before, and not that night after the Christmas party.

I had been pretty drunk even with my shapeshifter metabolism and so had Will. We simply didn't progress that far. But it had been close, obviously too close for Will. I had left his place, thinking we had done the deed, but it had all come back to me after my head had stopped pounding.

We'd been the last to leave the restaurant. Everyone else had headed off to see family, or they were going on a vacation in the sun. The office was closed for the holidays, except for emergencies.

We had taken the on-call position for Christmas and Boxing Day. In case something happened over the holidays. Our team was on stand-by and ready to respond if required. Will and I also didn't have any family to speak of so that wasn't a problem. We both had always felt it was better to work during that time of the year. I never minded spending the time with Will.

I glanced at the heavy watch on Will's wrist and looked at the date indicator. Tomorrow would be a eleven months since that party. Huh.

Will had invited me to his place for one more drink before he would send me home in a cab. Or that had been the plan.

It was the first time I had ever been to Will's apartment. He rarely invited anyone to his place. I think I only knew one other person we worked with who had been to Will's condo. He kept his private life private.

Will poured us some twenty-five year old whisky, and it had gone down too smoothly. We had talked. A lot. He told me a little about his growing up in foster care. I had told him about growing up with my brother and parents outside of Rocky Mountain House, Alberta. Until all the bad crap had happened.

We realized we shared some common ground, and it opened us up. I was not the type to cry on other people's shoulders. I was pretty self-sufficient and so was Will. So talking about our pasts with someone that didn't lay on the sympathy too thick had been good.

Since we didn't have anyone waiting for us, and the on-call didn't actually start till Christmas Day, we drank too. A lot.

Being that toasted, Will invited me to crash at his place. While he had made it sound innocent, we both knew where it was headed.

I had shimmied out of my dress and shoes, and tossed them on the floor. Then slid into Will's king sized bed and watched him strip. While I'd seen Will in various stages of undress over the years, this had a different feel to it.

I only had on my tiny black laced panties when I stretched out beside him. I remember how his eyes had burned as they slid over me. I also remembered how good I felt when his fingertips had followed.

In turn, I ran my hands over his scarred abs and chest. He closed his eyes and sighed with pleasure as my hands moved over his body. He felt so warm and smelled so good, like coming home—comfortable, safe, and warm. The last thing I remembered was resting my head on his shoulder. Then we had both dropped off to sleep.

By morning, it all came apart and Will couldn't get me out of his bed fast enough.

What an opportunity I had missed. Ah well, water, bridge, history, move on, Helly. I couldn't help but wonder what it would take to get close to Will. To see if I could trust these feelings I had for him.

"Why do you need me back?" I asked. I had to think about something else. "I have to warn you, I have a pretty good thing going on with being a freelance contractor."

"I'll bet you do. Tell me about this contract." Will finished off his eggs and moved on to his hash browns. He saw me looking at his plate. "What?"

"You eat weird, mix it up for heaven sake." Why had I never noticed this idiosyncrasy before?

"I like to finish one food at a time. Deal with it. The contract?" He slid his fork in to the crispy golden-brown potatoes and green onions.

I shook my head and returned to dunking my rye toast into my egg yolks. "I was hired to look into the shake downs the Kicking Horse manager said he was suffering. His bar was being victimized by a biker gang called the Pendejos. Or at least that's the story Jimmy was feeding my client. If there were shake downs, I was to stop them. But that's not what was happening."

"Wait, the Assholes?" Will laughed.

"Yeah," I said grinning back at him. "Anyway, while I've been working at the bar, I tried to get a line on the Pendejos. Find out if there is a connection between them with the bar robberies. The place has been knocked over three times in the past five months. The Pendejos are into organized crime, and I can find areas where they have been dealing in drugs. There was evidence of some black market gun sales as well, but I haven't seen

No matter what Jimmy says."

Will was trying to keep a straight face but every time I said Pendejos, he snickered.

"Stop it," I said, trying to frown at him, I guess it was a bit funny.

"I'm trying to stop, honest." He gave me his best innocent look and waved his fork at me. "Please continue, this is fascinating," he said. "I assume Jimmy is the bar manager?"

"Ass," I said, pushing my plate away. I was stuffed. "Yes he is. Anyway the more I looked, the more I was pretty sure no one was shaking down the Kicking Horse. Nor were they robbing it as a tactic to get Jimmy to pay up. Multiple robberies are not usually the way these things go anyway. By now there should have been an arson attempt or something similar."

"So what's going on?"

"Jimmy told my client that the money he should be paying for the lease of the premises was being stolen by this biker gang. He also told the landlord he can't pay any of his other bills. And, he is only barely scraping enough money together to pay the staff. But that isn't true. I looked into Jimmy's finances and everything is fine. He has no leans or credit issues, his bills are paid on time except for his lease. I also found an impressive savings account off-shore that belongs to Jimmy."

I slid my coffee mug in front of me and wrapped my hands around it to absorb the warmth. I noticed absently that my bruised knuckles had completely healed.

"That means Jimmy is pocketing the lease money. And of course he has reported the robberies to the police, but they haven't been able to find anything either." Will finished, filling in the blanks.

"Exactly," I said, nodding. "It helps that during the other three robberies, Jimmie and Juanita were the only people in the bar. Obviously, there isn't anyone to catch. Chances are good that the Jenkins brothers were hired by Jimmy. Perform a robbery while there were customers inside so his story sounded more believable." I leaned back in the booth. "If I had access to at least one of the Jenkins brothers, I could sweat it out of him. But, all I need to do now is to let my client know what's going on with Jimmy's finances and leave it at that. It will all come out in court anyway. I'm sure the Jenkins brothers will come clean to the cops before their case goes to the Crown Prosecutor. I'm also sure whatever Jimmy is paying them isn't enough to take the fall for him."

"You've about wrapped up this gig." Will had polished off the rest of his breakfast. His plate was clean except for the orange rind from the garnish.

I let my eyes drift over his lean muscled upper body. I didn't have to wonder where he put it and not gain weight, I knew. We had worked out in the gym together before. We had been partners and worked in the field together on many occasions, before he moved up the ladder to become a handler. Will was a real physical guy.

When I looked at this man, it reminded me of some-thing Belinda had said. "Men think every woman's dream is to live happily ever after with someone they love. The truth is we actually want to eat and not get fat." We had shared a laugh over that.

I wouldn't get fat eating a big breakfast. My metabolism would take care of the calories. If anything, I needed to make sure I got enough calories. I would also never get a chance at living and loving Will happy ever after, he would never permit it. Or at least he thinks so.

"Yes I'm about done." I sighed, coming back to my-self. Rubbing my tired eyes, I pushed strands of hair off my face and back into my pony tail. "I have to write my report for the client and bundle up the information I've uncovered on the Pendejos to send to the cops anonymously."

Will's chiseled lips quirked.

I frowned at him to contain his snicker. "And get paid, then I'm done," I finished.

"Is there anything else keeping you here?" Will asked. He accepted the bill from our waitress.

"Other than the amazing bison burgers you can get here, no." I had to admit it I was intrigued by what Will had to offer me. I assumed he had a contract from SPS for me. "I'm not saying I'll take what you have to offer. I kind of like being my own boss."

"You'll want this one," Will said confidently as he dropped money on the table. "Come on, we need to talk and not risk being overheard." He stood and slid his arms into his leather jacket.

From under my lashes I watched his muscles flex as he moved. "You won't tell me now?" I said, sticking my arms into my vest and zipping it up over my hoodie.

"No, I can't, not here. We need some privacy." Will's tone had dropped back down to a gravely serious level and that made me frown. Usually, there was a hint of excitement in Will when he offered me a new mission.

"All right," I agreed. I grabbed my bag and then led the way out of the restaurant. "It must be bad."

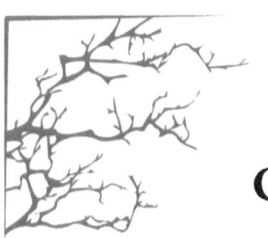

Chapter Three

"Where to?" Will asked as he unlocked the truck.

"To my hotel please." Helly climbed up into the truck and gave Will precise directions.

He watched Helly as they drove through Edmonton, grabbing glances of her now and then as he navigated through the early morning traffic. The city was slowly waking up to a frosty November morning.

Will had been hungry for the sight of Helly for months. It had almost driven him crazy when she had walked away from SPS, but he would never admit that to her or anyone else. She had walked away from him as well, and he had completely deserved that. He knew he should have handled the situation better. No, they hadn't had sex, but the close call was ever present in his mind. Along with regret, something else he would never admit to her.

It had been bad when she was across the pond in North Africa, assigned to rescue Frake Industries' CEO from his terrorist kidnappers. as Helly's handler on that operation. He had let Hugh McAvery run the operation so Will wouldn't make the situation worse by micromanaging every detail.

Although he hadn't been hands-on, that didn't mean he hadn't lived for every one of her infrequent He read everything she had sent back. He made sure all her requests for resources, hardware, and support were all handled as quickly as possible. Hugh had given him a hard time about it back then.

Of course, Will had expected Hugh to share intel with Helly. Every piece of data, as well as his contacts, or any-thing else he knew that would assist Helly on the Op. Will wanted to make sure Helly had every advantage he could give her to ensure her safety and the safety of her team.

It had been hard. She had collected her last paycheck, said her goodbyes to the team, and left without a forwarding address. She hadn't stopped at his office, and no one had told him she was even in the building. He hadn't spoken to her, not then or since. Not until today.

Will had looked for her for months and found nothing. Helly covered her tracks well. He hadn't taken Helly's leaving at all well. He wasn't proud of that fact, but he did acknowledge it. He worked the SPS research team relentlessly until they found her working in Edmonton.

For the first time in his life, Will had hesitated making contact. He had no idea what he would say to her, telling himself that he only needed to know she was okay.

Then he had seen her again, working at that rundown bar. While it was true she was a resource SPS sorely needed back, he couldn't lie to himself any longer. He wanted her back for himself. Even if that meant all he would get to do was see her work and keep her safe on her assignments. At the time, Will thought it would be enough. Now, he was having doubts.

And Helly was good, one of the best. Her talent and leadership abilities were hard to come by. Will knew that if she didn't want to be found, she wouldn't be sitting here next to him right now.

"You were expecting me," Will guessed, glancing briefly at Helly.

"I figured you'd find me as some point, if you wanted to."

He breathed in slowly, taking in her scent. Will always had an acute sense of smell and Helly Cooper had always smelt like a tantalizing, tasty treat. Now his reaction to her was stronger, more visceral. He wanted her to smell like she was his.

Will blinked. Where the hell had that thought come from? He ran his hand over his face. He was tired, that's all. It had been a long chase finding Helly.

Focus, Conall. He told himself he had to fix thing He had to get her back into the SPS fold.

Will let his eyes linger on her for a moment before cutting them back to the street. She looked good, her creamy skin was a bit paler than normal, but not much else had changed. She still had that incredible hair that shifted from bronze, to tawny gold, to white. The many layers of her hair color fascinated him. She could change her hair color, dial back the attractiveness of her features, and make her appearance dull and uninteresting. it was not so much trade craft as her shapeshifter abilities.

Her blue eyes changed too.

Sometimes they were dark navy and, sometimes, the same light blue as a Siamese cat's eyes. But they were always penetrating. He felt them go deep, right to his soul when she looked at him. He knew she saw everything and was fooled by nothing.

Helly's nose twitched, and she slowly turned her head to look at him. She studied him for a moment. "Where are you staying?" she asked.

"I haven't gotten a hotel room yet. I came straight to the bar as soon as I hit town. I knew you'd be there." He watched from the corner of his eye, and he could see her set jaw. This could be trouble.

"You can stay with me, I have a spare bed," she said and turned away. Helly looked out the front windshield again, a smile twitching the corners of her full lips.

Will raised his eyebrows, but said nothing about her offer. Maybe she was daring him to accept. He knew he had to distance himself from her emotionally. He had to get them both back on a professional footing. But first, he had to get her to agree to come back to SPS, whatever it took. "Okay, thanks," he said after a pause.

"This building is all executive suites for contract workers," Helly said as she unlocked the deadbolt and they entered the short hallway. "Usually, the suites are filled with information technology geeks and oil workers. We all mostly avoid each other."

"Nice setup, no one is interested in their neighbors, like a hotel. Paid for weekly?" Will followed her inside and wondered why he was saying such inane things.

"Yes, it makes it easier to come and go." She glanced over her shoulder at him. She could no doubt feel his eyes on her as he watched her move around the suite. She turned on the lights and gave him another little look over her shoulder. Shapeshifters were sensitive like that.

He should probably move his eyes higher, but Helly filled out her jeans so nice. He had been watching her for most of the night but it was still hard to take his eyes off her. Looking couldn't hurt.

Will finally shifted his eyes before she noticed him eyeing her figure and dropped his bag by the door. The apartment was set up like a hotel room. It offered minimal comfort boasting generic furniture, mundane carpeting, and the ubiquitous floral mass All the walls were painted in shades of pastel pink. Apparently, hotel decorators thought that was a soothing color scheme.

"It also makes it easy to move on to the next job," Helly said as she moved into the kitchenette. "There's beer and water in the fridge. Do you want anything else?"

"No, I'm good." Will accepted the cold bottle of water she handed him. "Thanks."

Helly walked over to the couch and tossed cushions onto one of the arm chairs. "There's only one bedroom and bathroom. We'll have to share the bathroom but the pull-out couch is fairly comfortable." Helly grabbed the handle and easily pulled the bed out of the frame, letting the legs unfold. The bed was already made up.

Will liked watching Helly move. He found her She was like a predator. His thoughts drifted back to the bar and how she had handled herself. breathtaking.

Helly looked over at Will as she tossed two pillows on to the bed. "So?" she said with finality. "Please end the suspense. Why are you really here?"

There was no point in stalling any further now that he had her alone. "I got a call from your sister-in-law, Lasha Cooper. She said she couldn't find you and neither could their security guy so she called me to pass on a message for you."

"And?" Helly asked with her fists braced on her hips as she looked at him, waiting.

Will noted that Helly's eyes iced over at the mention of Lasha Cooper. No love lost there obviously.

"Mrs. Cooper said that they had discovered who You should call her when it's convenient and she would explain."

Helly stared at Will for a heartbeat or two. The fine hairs on the back of his neck rose, and he felt locked in place. She was so focused on him, he couldn't break her stare. That was when he saw the electric green color roll over her eyes. He knew that shapeshifter tell, but it had actually never been aimed at him before.

The rolling color communicated the shifter was about one second from changing shape and ripping your throat out.

Then Helly blinked and looked away.

Or maybe not. Not if said shapeshifter had sufficient control over herself.

Will allowed himself to breathe again. He wasn't afraid of Helly or how close to the edge she held herself sometimes. If anything, he was more attracted to her. That thought made him frown.

"So, he was murdered. I figured." Helly crossed the room and pulled off her vest and hoodie. She dropped them on a chair by the door and sat down to pull off her well-worn cowboy boots. "I'm going to take a shower. You can have the bathroom in about fifteen minutes."

She walked to the bathroom and quietly closed the door. A couple minutes later, Will heard the shower "Wow," he said out loud as he cracked the seal on the water bottle and took a drink. That had been pretty in-tense. He thought she might be more emotional about this news. It was the reason he hadn't told her in the Apparently, he had worried for nothing.

Helly had incredible iron-clad control over herself. He knew how that felt to some degree. emotions and impulses locked down, especially in her presence.

Will knew Helly's brother had died a little over a year ago, and it had affected her. She was alone now. were already deceased. A hunting accident was what her dossier said. However, being shapeshifters, a hunting accident could mean a whole wealth of things. Will hadn't pried. If Helly wanted to talk about it, she would. Maybe she needed time to process the information.

She'd never openly discussed being a shapeshifter with Will. It wasn't something that was documented Those were the type of cards you kept close to your chest and SPS believed the same thing.

Will knew the agency had a few more shapeshifters working for them other than Helly. Only their team members and handlers knew who was and wasn't a shapeshifter. Well, except for Drayton. Miles Drayton was a retired Canadian Armed Forces colonel and All of the agency's staff went with the belief that Drayton knew everything. Your ass was chewed out less frequently that way.

However, until Helly had come onboard, Will had only ever worked with Zavier Koering. Zav was a wolf, which was the most common shapeshifter as Will understood it.

Helly was a cougar. He'd seen her use her abilities to scout and track some of their targets when they were in the field. She was a very efficient hunter.

Will took another pull from the water bottle, set it aside, and removed his own boots. His were thick soled, insulated hiking boots. November in Alberta could be unpredictable, and he'd dressed for the worst case SPS didn't have a "how to train your shapeshifter" course or handbook. It was known what these special field resources could do and they were assigned jobs The existence of shapeshifters in SPS ranks wasn't widely acknowledged. The agency kept that in-formation off the books with regard to individual not known much about shapeshifters either. Zav had told him some. He'd learned more from the SPS research people in order to educate himself. Zav had come to them over a decade ago. He and Will had been partners until SPS had hired Helly Cooper.

The agency was employed by the federal government to carry out clandestine operations all over the globe, wherever Canadian interests or citizens were at risk. And sometimes, they did favors for trusted allies. Most of the resources working for SPS were retired and former Path-finder or Joint Tactical Force operatives from the Will was a former Pathfinder member and a veteran of the Canadian Armed Forces. He had spent his military career in some of the worst places in the world. He had gathered information on terrorists or stopped terrorist It was all to make the world a safer place. His job description hadn't changed much since moving to SPS thirteen years ago. Except for the fact he was paid much better now.

SPS functioned with only the most accurate and up-to-date information gleaned from civilian law enforcement, intelligence circles, and military. So, it wasn't surprising SPS knew about the various packs and clans across There were even rumors of shapeshifters in Africa and Asia but nothing concrete as far as Will knew. Not that it meant anything.

The agency had recruited a few more shifters over the years. Their skills and abilities were finely honed and It was easier to be a covert ops agent if that was your natural mind set. Shapeshifters were a good fit, Human orphans like him were also good at the job too. They both took risks without hesitation, and both had nothing to lose.

Will dragged his bag over and rooted out his toiletries and some clean clothes.

The bathroom door opened and Helly came out The soft material was not thick. It clung to her curves in a way that allowed Will to clearly see she was naked underneath.

He had seen Helly in various stages of undress over the years. But this felt like something else entirely.

She sat down across from him in the other arm chair as she began to gather her wet hair into a clip.

Will knew he shouldn't let his eyes linger as they He took in her bare feet which were nicely shaped. Up trim calves to her sculpted knee caps. To her firm thighs that disappeared under the material of her robe.

Shapeshifters didn't think about nakedness the same way as most people did. He knew this. But he should probably stop staring at her breasts, which were heavy and full. They were pressing against the soft white Will forced his eyes up. He let them travel over her long sleek neck and finally up to look at her face.

Helly had one tawny eye brow cocked at him as she secured her wet hair. She knew what he was looking at. He was pretty sure she knew his body was reacting to everything he was seeing too.

Get a grip Conall, he reproached himself. He actually had to swallow to clear his throat.

Helly lowered her arms to lay them in her lap now that her wet hair was secured and off the back of her neck.

"Was Lasha's message all you came to tell me?" she asked steadily.

"No," Will focused on Helly's eyes. "And?" Helly said, prompting Will to continue.

"A member of the VIC pack, Geoff Howard, murdered Julian. It wasn't a legitimate Challenge. Julian was poisoned. The people responsible are a middle-school chemistry teacher, John Foggle, and his lab tech wife, Cheryl Foggle. Howard befriended the couple and manipulated them into doing his bidding. This was all done when he was a beta on Lasha and Julian's security team."

Will watched to see if Helly would react to any of this information. But she merely waited, pinning him with that steely blue regard. Now he knew what Helly's targets felt like.

"Geoff Howard was the brains behind the plan and the Foggles were merely his tools. He orchestrated events to bring about Julian's death. He covered up the murder by threatening Charles Hector. He threatened the doctor with exposing his lack of data security, when it came to private information about the pack. Hector was gullible. He knew he had allowed the data to be accessed by Cheryl Foggle. Probably not intentionally, however, the Foggles used the information against the pack. The cause of death for Julian was—"

"Burst appendix," Helly interjected, her tone was completely devoid of emotion.

"Yes, it was. And while it was true his internal organs had failed, that may not have been what killed him."

"Our organs regenerate fairly quickly," Helly said. "It shouldn't have killed him."

Will nodded and plowed on to the new information. "This all came out when Foggle poisoned Dylan Cooper, your nephew."

"Is Dylan dead, too?" Helly's eyes rolled green as they narrowed. Finally, she reacted.

"No, Dylan was certainly sick, but he pulled through and he's fine now." Will detected obvious relief in Helly's reaction to Dylan being okay. He knew Dylan was one of her last living blood relatives. "I don't have a lot of details about Dylan's sickness. The information is kind of sketchy. There were references to some work John Foggle was doing on blood typing shifters. He was trying to find a way to differentiate them—you—from other humans."

"I know the pack's history pretty well. I'm sure I can get more information about what happened to Dylan from my sister-in-law." Helly waved that away. "What else?"

"Geoff Howard was turned over to George Mathieu. He was transported to the VIC's incarceration compound up Island. It was the judgement reached after a hearing by the senior council. Where, by the way, Howard confessed to everything." Will braced his hands on his knees and gave Helly a steady look. "A couple days ago Howard escaped. He took a handful of other prisoners who are also rogue shapeshifters from other packs, with him. Together, they have attacked the compound twice and killed one of the guards. The shifters running the facility believe Howard will keep attacking. He and his crew could take control of the compound eventually."

"He wanted to remove Julian to take his place as alpha, but didn't have the balls to challenge Julian. Not with Lasha backing up her mate. That's probably still his goal. To create his own clan and rule it as an alpha," Helly surmised. "It might explain his attacks on the facility."

"Probably," Will agreed.

"So, you came here to tell me I have a murderer to capture."

"I thought you would be interested in finding and bringing in your brother's killer. He needs to be re-incarcerated and face the consequences of his actions. That at least, would be some kind of justice."

Helly shook her head. "It doesn't really work like that, but you're right, I like this one. I'm in." Helly stood up and Will got a brief glimpse of her inner thigh. "The bathroom is all yours, and there's still plenty of hot water and fresh towels." She went into her bedroom and closed the door.

Will stood and collected his stuff and headed into the bathroom.

When he closed the door, he was bombarded by Helly's personal aroma. She hadn't turned on the bath-room fan to rid the small room of the steam from the shower or her tantalizing scent.

Will flicked on the fan and rethought the plan to sleep in the same apartment as Helly tonight. But leaving wouldn't help his long-term goal. He needed to fix the rift between them and bring her back. He couldn't do that if he avoided her on a personal level.

It was going to be hell if he stayed in her company for long. It was going to be worse than hell being this close to her and not acting on it. Especially with the way his body was reacting after only a few hours in her presence.

Will sighed and shucked his clothes. Hot water was the least of his problems, he thought as he turned the tap to cold and stepped under the shower spray.

in and out as deeply and as slowly as I could manage.

I stared at the far wall and saw nothing but red. I knew I had color rolling over my eyes, and I had to re-establish control of myself. Julian, you careless asshole. I was seething. My brother let himself get killed by a stupid beta—so typical of him.

And Lasha, what a moron, she was so incompetent. How could she fail to protect her mate and her child? It had been obvious when I first met her, she wasn't pack alpha material. She would probably have been fine run-ning a wolf clan, but the whole pack was another story.

The problem with the VIC pack was that it was made up of multiple types of shifters—bears, wolverines, cats, and wolves. This combination made managing it much harder and not something I judged Lasha could have done.

I let a snarl flow from my throat. It was either that or destroy something.

Neither of my parents had been that experienced with their animal forms. They hid their shifter sides and ran a hardware store in

Rocky Mountain House, south west of Edmonton. They had raised my brother and me and we had a quiet life—mostly.

My parents were a mixed marriage. Our father was a wolf and our mother was a cougar. We lived outside the Wild Rose Pack territory to avoid the politics. Back then, mixed shifter species marriages were, at best, frowned upon. At worst, forcibly broken up. I never met or knew my grandparents on either side because of that. Only my mother's sister, Rita Fisher, had visited once before my parents were killed.

Some hunters thought they found the cougar This had been one of the few times my parents had used their abilities to track down the real culprit. It had all gone wrong.

The hunters and conservation officers had trapped my mother in a tree and shot her, ending her life. In response my father had attacked, and they had shot him too.

The authorities thought the whole incident could be explained by rabies. At least until the animals reverted back to their human forms upon death.

SPS had shown up and covered up the whole episode. The official story was a hunting accident between my parents and the others. No one wanted the knowledge of shifters to be public.

At least not back then. No one had even been sent to jail. No one had paid for killing our parents.

Julian had rebelled after our parents passing. He had been fifteen and had never listened to me. I was younger by two years, but I was the more mature of the two of us. Julian never tried to make anything easy. He was always trying to figure out how to get out of everything. The trouble he caused, the chores he was assigned, whatever. He generally didn't take any responsibility for himself or his actions. He was always trying to shift the blame or accountability to someone else, usually me.

Poor Julian, no one understood him. He was sick, he was grieving, and no one cared about him.

Right. Where was I? What about me? I had lost my parents, too. I was the younger sister here. Did anyone give a crap about me? The social services lady had been kind but useless.

It had been a Godsend when the alpha from the Wild Rose Pack came. He brought our Aunt Rita and took charge before we could be put into foster care.

He had told us we were going to be sent off on ex-changes. Julian would go to the Vancouver Island Clan which was predominantly wolves. I was to go to the big-ger Wild Rose Pack with our aunt, where there were other cougars.

Aunt Rita lived in Bonnyville, which was part of the Wild Rose pack territory. I would be away from Julian and his self-centered neediness. At first, being thirteen, I welcomed this. But I still missed Julian. He was my brother after all and the last of my immediate family. Even now I wondered if maybe it would have been a Because we were minors we fell under the authority of the alpha and I suppose he meant well. It was all moot now anyway.

I breathed in slowly.

Julian seemed to straighten out on the Island. George Mathieu was a strict alpha. His daughter Lasha, who was a couple years older than Julian, decided he would be her Chosen mate and husband.

I breathed out slowly.

Lasha would have what she wanted. I met her at the wedding when Julian was nineteen and Lasha twenty-one. Anyone could see she was the dominate alpha in the pair. Julian liked to be taken care of and, even though he may have had the alpha title, the real ruling alpha was Lasha. It didn't matter. Julian was completely besotted with Lasha. I was happy for him. He had found someone to spend his life with. He would be safe and I wouldn't have to worry about him.

I breathed in slower still.

Lasha also didn't let Julian get away with anything, so I figured it could work and it did for many years.

I breathed out.

They had had a kid, Dylan. Julian seemed like a good father. I heard from him once in a while. I sent regular emails. In turn, he would send me one-line answers and pictures of Dylan. But, apparently, Lasha didn't know how to protect Julian or Dylan properly. I breathed in and out again. The wall was starting to fade from red to pink.

There were no Challenges, and it was a seamless transition as far as I knew.

I hadn't thought too much about it. I was outside pack politics and liked it that way. I determined my own path, even if it went against my shapeshifter nature. We give our loyalty to the pack. The pack was everything. Without a pack, I gave my loyalty to SPS and Will.

I pulled my thoughts away from that disappointment.

Julian had been a pain in the ass, but he was still my brother, my blood. Now he was gone and his killer was free.

Well, I would have to remedy that. There was no real decision to be made, it was a no brainer. I would go and take care of Geoff Howard and, after that, I would deal with the areas of my life I had been avoiding.

I would ensure I met Dylan too. He should know who his Aunt Helly was. He also needed to know that if he ever needed help, he could come to me. I would be there for him.

The wall was fading from bright pink to the light pink it was actually painted as I gained control again

The fan and the shower were running.

I smiled and thought about Will having to deal with my scent in the bathroom. It might have been unfair of me to do that to him, although, he sort of had it coming.

Will Conall was my priority for the moment. I needed to deal with this situation between us. I had had enough of letting things happen and drifting from one contract to another.

I knew what I wanted out of life and no one was going to give it to me. It was time to take it for myself.

It was a fact I'd acted like a coward and that was not me. I wasn't proud of the last few months. It was past time to step up, on all fronts. time to lay the ground work with Will.

First, I stripped off my robe and pulled on a pair of soft pink cotton panties. They were more lace than any-thing, and I added a pale pink Lycra camisole that stopped at my midriff. The neckline dipped low and hugged my generous breasts. My taunt stomach and belly button were exposed, and my ass cheeks were almost completely uncovered.

I walked out into the living room and strolled into the kitchen for a bottle of water. When I heard the bathroom door open I walked back into the living room. Will was standing outside the bathroom door as he turned off the light. His eyes locked on me and burned.

For a moment, I paused in front of him and saw a muscle flex in his jaw. His eyes slid over my body slowly and I could feel the heat of his eyes consume me.

"What are you doing, Helly?" Will's usual controlled tone was a hoarse whisper, like he was coming to the edge of his control.

With a slow smile, I cocked one hip and placed my hand on it. "Just showing you again what you turned down last year."

Will swallowed. I raised my chin.

I watched the muscles of his jaw work. He was bare-chested, and he looked as amazing as I remembered. Along his wide shoulders and muscular arms I could see the pale ridges of scars on his skin. Some of those scars he took when we worked in the field together. I had bled with him and patched him up more than once.

I dropped my eyes lower. To follow the light dusting of dark hair that trailed down over his insanely ripped abs. His belt was undone and dangling from his belt loops. The top button of his jeans was open.

What an invitation. I could feel moisture gathering in my mouth and elsewhere as I looked at him.

I lifted my eyes to meet his. They were dark and smoldering. He was breathing deep and slowly, like he was forcing himself to stay in control. Good.

With a tip my head I reached up to release my long golden hair and dropped the clip to the carpet.

Will's eyes flared.

I sauntered slowly over to him, and the closer I got, the darker his eyes got. I stood in front of him, within reach.

He shifted his bare feet. I could see he was reacting fiercely to me so I let my eyes drop and linger on the Then looked back up again into his molten eyes, I slid the tip of my tongue out and over my bottom lip.

"Helly," Will breathed a hoarse warning as I stepped inside his personal space. The items in he was holding hit the floor and then his hands were on me, pulling me against his naked chest.

His hot mouth came down on mine, and I eagerly opened to it. He felt and tasted so good. I ran my tongue along his bottom lip.

He groaned and I answered him by grazing my teeth over his lip.

Will's hands were pressing me against him, molding my softer breasts against his hard muscle.

I dropped the water bottle. It might have bounced on the carpet, but I didn't hear it. My senses were focused on other things. I felt the hard force in his jeans brush firmly against my mound. I moaned as I ached to feel more of his touch.

Yes, finally, I thought. I ran my hands over his back and up into his thick dark hair and then downward, going lower, teasing, touching.

Will groaned again. His scent was extremely strong, his need so apparent.

I slipped three fingers into the waist band of his jeans, ah, no underwear. Excellent. I nudged the material down a bit and that was the cliff's edge for Will.

He walked me backward to the sofa bed. We went down on the exposed sheets, his kiss devoured me, and I was completely pliant and willing. I loved the feel of his body pressing me down into the mattress.

Will broke our contact briefly to remove his jeans and then he was naked. His hands were lifting my camisole and exposing my breasts to his eyes. He gently stroked his fingertips over them.

I closed my eyes as ripples of pleasure coursed through me, and I arched against him. Ran my hands down that scarred chest and over his ribs to his back. I just couldn't touch him enough.

"Look at me, Helly," Will whispered.

I opened my eyes and let him see how much I needed him.

"Do you really want this?" he asked softly. His eyes were so hungry it was almost painful.

"Yes, I do. I've wanted this for a long time," I I breathed in his musky scent along with soap and mint toothpaste.

"All right," was as all he said, even though I knew he wanted this as much as I did.

He kissed me again, his warm mouth moving over mine, his tongue dipping inside. I welcomed it as I touched it with mine. His hands continued to stroke my breasts, with his thumbs concentrating on my nipples. His massage made me gasp and ache with need.

"I don't have any condoms," he whispered as he re-moved my camisole and placed hot kisses on my breast. His touch made me arch my back again to get closer to the source of the pleasure.

"We don't need any," I whispered as I closed my eyes. I could feel the heat of him against my thigh. "Shapeshifters and standard humans rarely conceive off-spring." I wasn't going to mention I hadn't been with Yes, I still had trust issues.

I simply wanted to enjoy this one night together. I would think about the consequences later, but hopefully by then, I would have a strategy. Right now I wanted to live in the moment.

"Good to know," Will said, dipping his head and tak-ing my nipple into his mouth. His fingers slid my panties off. Then he touched me, and I went up in flames.

I'd barely come down from the last extraordinary ex-perience, when a delicious heavy fullness slid into me, and we began the climb to ecstasy, this time together.

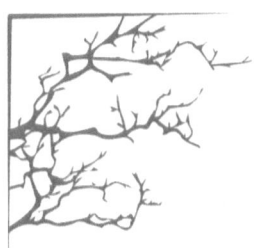

Chapter Four

Slowly, I became aware of my surroundings and opened my eyes. I squinted uncertainly at the bright sunlight. It had to be late morning, close to noon.

Soft snoring met my ear and the sound belonged to the hard, warm back and I couldn't help the smile that curved my lips. I was with Will Conall. He had come for me. I had made him work for it, but he had found me.

He used the excuse of my sister-in-law's information on my brother's death as the reason for looking for me. While that might have been part of the reason he had made the effort, I knew there was more.

A shapeshifter gave off a strong scent when they were emotionally involved with another shapeshifter. It was a warning to all others to back off. We couldn't hide it or disguise it.

Humans couldn't hide the scent they gave off either when their emotions were affected. My nose told me Will was more than interested in me. His scent was distinct and intense. I only needed to give him a nudge in the right direction to make him realize it.

Well, okay, maybe more than a nudge. He did have this mental road block about getting involved with any-one. I thought it had something to do with losing his mother when he was young and never knowing his father. Who could say? Getting the guy to open up was literally like pulling teeth without the right equipment.

I had waited a long time for him to be receptive to my attention. Last year with the invitation to his apartment, I had thought I had finally gotten somewhere.

Will was an alpha, even if he was a standard human. I guessed it was referred to as a type-A personality. You didn't manipulate alphas. To me, it was completely logical that we should be together.

What was the point of being alone and miserable? It wasn't like I was expecting a home and a family. Both of us knew we couldn't have those things, not with the life-style we led. Forget the fact that humans and It was a billion to one chance. It had happened once or twice, but those cases involved a shapeshifter male, and a standard human Not that that mattered, we were both "the job." We liked the challenge of taking on near impossible tasks and seeing them through to the end. It didn't hurt that we're both addicted to the danger. However, that didn't mean we couldn't have some kind of relationship besides a working one.

The truth was that any job he brought me, I'd have taken. I was getting bored with these small-time con-tracts. I wasn't challenged.

Finding Julian's killer felt right. I had suspected there was foul play in his death, but there had been no proof.

While Julian could be a pain in the neck, he was my pain in the neck. He had a son and a wife who loved him. He belonged to the VIC pack and to his family.

I could feel the anger rising again. I forced it back into its cage and slammed the door shut. I didn't have time to allow myself a pity party.

Finding this Geoff Howard and making him pay for my brother's death would give me closure. spirit would rest easier too.

I savored Will's aroma. His scent said "mine" to me in twelve-foot-high glowing letters. I felt this intense right-ness with Will. It was hard to describe but it was like my heart was connected to him.

No, deeper than that, like my shapeshifter magic was, at some level, deeply connected.

If he was a shapeshifter, I'd say it felt like we had the mate-bond between us. Maybe it was because we'd been through some hairy-scary situations together and come out alive. All the same, a definite linking was there, at least for me.

Will may not completely understand or acknowledge it yet, but he and I were meant to be mated. It didn't matter that he was a standard human. My blood and my magic pulled me to him. Will was the only person I had ever experienced this deep primal shifter-based attraction for. He would be my Chosen.

I knew it would be a challenge to convince him we be-longed together. While it may be partly true he thought he was too damaged to be able to function in a long term relationship, I didn't think so. I also knew it would be difficult because he was a standard human and he didn't hold magic like a shapeshifter did. There were things about me he would never know or understand.

The magic part about shapeshifters was not known to standard humans at all. , discuss it with them. I had to be careful with that information. I trusted Will but that knowledge involved all shapeshifters. Each of us carried magic that allowed us to change from one shape to another. We had our human form and the animal form we were blessed with.

For some of us, who had the right kind of magic, we could hold a half form or a half shape, which was part human and part animal.

It was considered an art to attain that level of shifting and use it to fight. Not all of us could attain it. We rarely showed that shape, it was the stuff of nightmares.

It was also how we were generally portrayed in movies and television and those ideas help feed the myths about us. One myth was that if one of us bit a standard human, that human would become a shapeshifter.

Nope, it didn't work that way. You needed to have shifter parents to be a shapeshifter yourself. were part of what the two packs who had gone public were fighting to dispel.

On the other side of the spectrum, there were non-shifters. Even though we all carried the capability to shift, some were not physically able. The theory was that a shapeshifter's magic had to be strong enough and deep enough, to enable them to change form.

Some of us had deep pools of magic, deeper than the average shifter. Those people became mages. Most of them didn't shift at all. This was because their magic was channeled in a completely different direction—the manipulation of creation power.

I'd only heard of two cases where a mage had levels of magic strong enough to enable them to shift into their animal and also wield mage powers. One was in the last century in the Ukraine, and the other was currently residing with the Vancouver Island Clan. Julian's old pack.

Will's broad back was pressed against my nose, and I breathed him in. He was starting to wake up. I knew when he woke, he would regret that we had allowed our-selves to become intimate.

I bit my lip and frowned. I would have to go slow with him.

My arm was wrapped around him, and he held my wrist in a firm grasp against his chest. I spread my fingers and lightly brushed them against the silky mat of hair that feathered his chest. Touching him was habit forming.

I bet it would be a while before he lowered his guard and allowed this to happen again. between us, at least for now. It had to be his idea to take this further. He knew I was willing; the next move had to be his.

Still, I couldn't let it be too easy for Will. He still had to chase me a bit more. If he didn't, he wouldn't come to the conclusion on his own that he needed to have me in his life.

Helping him to discover this was my ultimate goal. Yes, it bordered on manipulation, but I preferred to think of it as seduction.

I flexed my wrist and he sleepily opened his hand and turned his face into his pillow. Gradually, I eased away from him and let the covers take my place. He barely stirred.

Time to shower and dress. I'd neglected writing up my report last night. Now that something more important was on my plate, I wanted to close off this current contract. It was time to move and find Julian's murderer. Spending time with Will was an added bonus.

Will laid still. His eyes stayed closed as he heard the shower start up. The sofa bed was still warm where Helly had lain next to him. He had woken in the predawn hours to find her spooned up against him.

He had grasped the arm she had wrapped around him and pulled her even closer so it rested across his chest. She had sleepily snuggled against him with her cheek against his back. A surge of satisfaction, and yes, happiness flowed through him with an intensity he'd never experienced before.

Will didn't regret for a second what had happened be-tween them. The attraction he had for Helly was unbelievably powerful. It was overwhelming at times. This time, he had let that attraction rule him.

His instincts made him want to be with her. He had the urge to protect her with every fiber of his being. Even though his rational brain told him she didn't need to be protected. It was an unusual feeling for him. He also figured that if he tried to do that, Helly would not be happy and that was putting it mildly.

Will had held himself in check over these feelings for years. It disturbed him that he had this attachment to Helly. He shouldn't allow himself to get too close to her or anyone. But when he was with her, he didn't care that he knew there was something "not right" about himself. It was the dark and violent feelings he kept locked down and hidden that got in the way. He knew he was He knew her shapeshifter nature made Helly keep standard humans at arm's length, even though she said she was interested in him, and she certainly showed it. Will was so tempted to see where this attachment went with her that it was almost unbearable. Shapeshifters usually were naturally suspicious of standard humans. That Helly expressed her desire for him, and it said a lot.

For Will, he found it exciting. Most people feared shapeshifters and their unpredictability. They could be violent and deadly. A pack in California had gone public a couple of years ago, shifters were not well understood.

Last year the Wild Rose Pack in Alberta had announced their existence. Their alpha had taken a different approach with his shapeshifters. While the California shifters stayed out of the public eye as much as possible, the Wild Rose Pack appeared in mainstream media a few times a month. They were trying to educate people and stem the distrust and fear toward shifters.

Both packs worked to discredit the myths that sur-rounded this diverse branch of the human evolutionary tree. They were trying to gain acceptance into normal human society. Will thought that was all a waste of time. Human beings were ignorant and xenophobic.

Screw them if they couldn't accept shapeshifters. It wasn't like they had a choice. This genie was out of the bottle for good.

Will scrubbed rough hands over his face and sat up. He couldn't shake the feeling that Helly belonged to him. He had felt it as soon as she had touched him and that was the scary part.

He couldn't belong to anyone. the weirdness inside his head, if he ever could. He'd been living with this thing that made him feel like he was "other"—a darkness in his soul, for as long as he could remember.

How could he have let Helly in under his guard? A relationship between them could never work. He knew SPS needed her talents and skilled leadership, but how could he work with her again when they had crossed this far over the line into uncharted territory? He would just have to live with it and the situation as it was.

It wasn't that they'd had sex. It was that all he wanted to do was be with her every minute. To touch her, inhale her scent, to talk to her and hear her voice and feel the warm touch of her hand. And yes, he wanted to make love with her, many, many times.

His body was reacting to the knowledge that Helly was wet and naked in that tiny bathroom. He knew if he tried the door, he would find it unlocked and she would welcome him into her shower.

Will also knew he had to put the brakes on that impulse. These things he wanted weren't a reality he could buy into, not if he and Helly were going to work together again. It didn't matter that she'd made it very plain what she wanted. He wasn't stupid.

But, he told himself that he had to be a professional in his relationship with her. There were some times when he would have to ask her to risk her life in any number of crazy dangerous situations.

How could he do that and have a personal relationship with her? They would start focusing on each other and not on the job. He would make a mistake, or she would, and someone would be dead.

No, it was better not to get involved. Okay he had slipped up, but it was time to rebuild those barriers.

Will intended to go with Helly to find Geoff Howard. He'd put arrangements in place and made preparations to take out this threat to the VIC shapeshifters. It would allow Helly closure with her brother's death.

The success of this personal mission would also put Helly in a more receptive mood to returning to SPS. At least he hoped so.

That should be his only goal, and it was time he made it his main focus.

He reached for his clothes and frowned at the strange tightness in his chest. He paused and breathed in. There was no constriction, and he had no idea what he had done to have caused it. It felt like a pulled muscle so he shrugged it off and dressed.

Will had coffee brewed and toast made when I came out of the bathroom. My eyes found his and we looked at each other for a moment. He pushed a full mug coffee across the breakfast bar toward me.

"Good morning," he murmured, and his expression gave nothing away. He wasn't going to let me know what he was thinking or feeling. He had the barriers up and locked. He still wasn't ready to let me in.

"Good morning." I smiled at him and yes, it was a bit smug. I tried to get a handle on my grin but it was "Did you get enough sleep?" So much for being cool and aloof, I was failing at this horribly.

His dark eyes were unreadable. "Yes, I did. I got all I needed." His eyes slid away from mine again. Will seemed farther away this morning than when we sat in the diner together and spoke for the first time in months.

Getting physical may have been a mistake but I couldn't bring myself to feel any regret.

"Good," I said as I sipped my coffee. I realized this was going to be much harder than I thought. "So, what's the plan? I assume I'll travel to the Island as soon as I opened the crunchy peanut butter and spread it thickly on my multigrain toast.

"Yes, we have a plane at Edmonton International, and I have everything setup for the operation." He sipped his own coffee and leaned forward to accept the butter knife and the peanut butter jar from me. "We'll land in Camp-bell River and drive into the interior of the Island today. Since the VIC compound is south of Schoen Lake Pro-vincial Park, we'll need a couple all-terrain vehicles to get us around in the bush. I doubt Howard is keeping to the roads."

"Who's picking up the tab on this? I have funds." I licked peanut butter off my index finger and was gratified to see Will's eyes flicker over the movement.

"The company is paying, this is an SPS issue," Will said and put his coffee mug down on the breakfast bar. "It falls into the 'Lethal Threat to the General Public' category. If Howard decides to use his escaped felons as a force against the public, it will be a blood bath. So far it's been contained to the remote part of Vancouver Island. We need to ensure the situation stays that way until we end it."

"All right, I'll pack and get my report finished. We can stop at my client's office on the way to the airport, and I'll drop it off. Give me twenty minutes." I gave him a nod and took my toast and coffee into my bedroom to sit at the desk and finish up the paperwork on the contract.

I also wanted to make sure the Edmonton Police got the info I had gathered on the Pendejos. email address to accomplish that and then packed up my laptop. I loaded my clothes and the rest of my gear into a duffle bag. I usually traveled light so it didn't take me the twenty minutes I had estimated.

We met in the small foyer. Each of us had a duffel bag that could have been procured from the same military supply company.

"Look at that, we have matching luggage," I said as I pulled on my boots.

"Funny," said Will. His voice was devoid of any of the warmth it held yesterday.

Great, we were back to one word answers.

Will led the way, and I dropped off the keys to the apartment at the office. I received a reimbursement for the three remaining days on my credit card, and we were on the road.

Next, we stopped briefly at my client's office. I made my report verbally and handed the building owner the full report on a generic memory stick. I got paid in cash, and we were off to the airport.

We cleared airport security and then loaded Will's truck into the back of the C-130 Hercules cargo plane. An hour later, it was wheels up and we were headed to the coast.

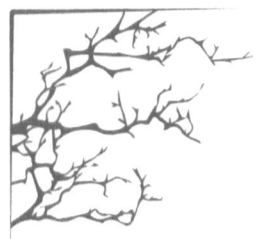

Chapter Five

The Lockheed aircraft had four turboprop engines. The aircraft was capable of taking advantage of short and rough runways. A couple of times in my career, this quick getaway on a short runway capability had come in handy. Today, at this large airport, it wasn't necessary.

The Herc was originally designed as a troop medivac plane and cargo transport aircraft. The C-130 class was a versatile beast with considerable room for whatever it was required to haul. It could, and was, used for everything from airborne assault to search and rescue as well as scientific research and patrolling. Some of which I had participated in, but today it would be used as heavy lift to drop us at the airport in Campbell River.

I was greeted by the crew whom I'd known for a few years. Sandy and John were the pilots and Amar was their navigator. All three were retired RCAF vets and They didn't know why Will was picking me up. Or why we were traveling to Campbell River, or what we were tasked with. That was the way they liked it.

After we shook hands and got the air briefing over with, Will and I made use of the Hercules limited amenities.

The cargo space was considerable. The inside of this older model heavy lift aircraft wasn't actually furnished for much more than hauling bulky payloads. It could more than handle our little bit of gear—Will's truck, a trailer with two all-terrain vehicles, and supplies we'd need, which included weapons and ammo.

All the items were tied down in the mid-section with the truck last in line near the tail of the fuselage. This tiny load didn't even scratch the surface of what this bird was capable of.

Will had backed the truck up the ramp, and I had helped the crew strap it down, while Amar handled the controls to close the massive hinged doors in the rear of the aircraft.

I wondered about the two ATVs. Was someone joining me? Could I hope I knew who that person was? Mostly, this was because I doubted Will was going to loan me his baby—his truck.

I figured Will was leveraging his position at SPS with the threat the escaped shapeshifters posed to cover the expense of this mission. I was also sure he had called in a few favors for this Op., including our crew who were currently up front in the cockpit.

Sandy, John, and Amar had ensured we had every-thing in hand out here in the cargo-slash-passenger area. After that, they had moved forward to get us in the air and left us alone. No one had mentioned my absence from SPS. Although I could see it was in their thoughts as we worked side-by-side stowing the gear and equipment.

It was funny how the smell of oiled metal, aircraft fuel, and old coffee made me feel right at home. This, along with the familiar faces, and the routine mission planning, made me appreciate how much I had missed my old job. And how much I had missed working with Will.

There were four seats in a group that faced each other behind the cockpit and galley bulkhead. There was also a battered metal table in the center that made up a planning area. All of the furniture was locked down and fastened to the metal floor of the aircraft.

The rest of the cargo area had little in the way of com-fort. The green nylon seats that ran down the length of the plane under the side windows could double as bunks as required...well, a single bunk anyway. Right now the seats were folded up to make room for crates.

These items had coded labels and nothing to do with my mission. Clearly, we were not the only task on the aircrew's schedule today.

Seated in the planning area, I looked over a map. the northern end of Vancouver Island. I compared the map with the satellite pictures Will gave me of the compound and the surrounding area.

I glanced in Will's direction. "You have to love Google Earth. Nobody has a secret encampment anymore, at least above ground."

the planet could get location image intel," he commented, not looking up. "But that all changed. Every-thing is wide open now that GPS technology is in the public domain." His dark eyes briefly met mine.

"I remember during the Afghan war when we were running a camp outside of Dubai in the United Arab Emirates," I said, trying to draw Will into conversation. "We were under orders not to disclose the location to anyone, under any circumstances. However, if you Googled the coordinates, you could find it."

"So, now people with bad agendas, or good, have to figure out more stealthy ways to hide their encampments. It's good for the people on our side that the bad guys aren't all that successful at hiding anymore." Will returned to his reading. He was catching up on some work of his own. His laptop was open and he had a legal pad full of notes next to him.

"How many people does Howard have with him?" I asked.

"Four at the last report, but it could be more. Our source is not right on location anymore. She did a recce day before yesterday but the resource isn't a shapeshifter, so she couldn't get too close."

A recce or reconnaissance was vital for the success of this venture. We needed to know where Howard was likely to be, what weapons he had access to, and if possible, any intel on his plans.

"Will we be making contact with the resource?"

"No, she was relocated to another tasking. She got the info as a favor for me." Will kept his head down as he typed.

I was tempted to ask who "she" was, but squashed the thread of jealously as it was unreasonable. "That will make it five-to-one odds. Not great, but not horrible," I said. I dug into my pile of information from the recce.

"Five to two, I'm coming with you."

Will looked over at me and our eyes locked. I could see the commitment in his expression. He wasn't letting me out of his sight, and that kind of gave me a nice warm feeling in the pit of my stomach.

There was lots I could say, lots I wanted to say, but I figured it was best to keep it simple. "I appreciate that, Will. Thanks." I wasn't completely surprised by this, but I was still touched by his gesture.

"You're part of my team, and this is personal. I've got your back." His dark eyes were serious and his expression was grave. "I know how this is going to go down."

"There is no way we can allow a shapeshifter to be put in the hands of the justice system," I agreed. is prepared to handle shapeshifters. People will die if they try to imprison one shifter wolf, let alone five."

"Have you got a plan yet?"

"Do we have silver frag rounds on board?"

"We do, and a few other toys," Will said with a con-firming nod.

"Then plan 'A' will be to bring the escapees back to the compound and the facility to be re-incarcerated. If that fails, well, you know what plan 'B' is." I shrugged.

"Yeah.".

He turned back to his laptop. I returned to reading the backgrounds of the escaped shapeshifters Geoff Howard had in his little gang.

Will and Helly both crashed for a few hours at separate ends of the aircraft. Will had taken a sleeping bag and bunked down in the back seat of his truck. He needed to put some space between them.

When he was close to Helly, there were other priorities on his mind beside the mission they planned to undertake.

staring up at the roof of his truck cab and massaged the muscles across his chest. The tightness hadn't eased, but he could ignore it. He had ignored worse in the field before. If it persisted, he'd get a medical when he got back to the SPS office. For now, he would just deal.

It was weird how aware he was of Helly and her movements. It was like they had this psychic link or something. He knew right now she was sleeping lightly, reclined in one of the briefing chairs.

He had this urge to go to her and curl his body around hers. Where the hell did that thought come from? Yes, he was attracted to her, but it was getting more powerful as time went on. He had to curtail it before he was too distracted to focus and someone got hurt.

Will was avoiding being near me as much as possible. It didn't matter. I knew where he was at all times. It was only my self-control that was keeping me away from him.

I was confident that, if I put my mind to it, I could convince Will we should take advantage of our down time. He was a guy after all, but we did lack a certain amount of privacy. So, the circumspect thing to do was what all of us did when we were stationary for a time and safe. We slept.

We were on final approach for Campbell River Airport in the late afternoon that same day as promised. It had been a smooth trip until we got to the Rockies. Turbulence was normal whenever there was a high pressure system coming through. It was my luck to leave Edmonton when the weather was starting to improve.

As the landing gear of the Hercules touched down, the sun was thinking about approaching the horizon and concluding the late fall day.

I looked out of my window at the gray landscape. It was too dim to make out much and the airport lights were on, due to the short day and approaching night.

The terminal building was small. I make out a couple of private jets amongst the smaller aircraft chalked and tied down on the runway apron.

As we came to an engine-whining halt, I unbuckled and stood, gathering my pack. I went to the passenger side of Will's truck to load it behind the seat. There was a rolled and tied sleeping bag in the back seat. I tossed my pack next to it.

I turned toward Will as I felt him move forward and head my way.

"Sandy and John will help us off load the gear and then they have to head back. They'll come back for us if we need them to," Will said from behind me.

"Okay," I acknowledged in a neutral tone as I closed the cab door. "I'll hitch up the trailer." I turned to look at Will. He looked tired. There was tension around his dark eyes.

"John's going to run the door and ramp." Will rubbed the center of his chest with the heel of his hand.

"Are you okay?" I asked, frowning.

"Yeah, I didn't sleep much," he said dismissively.

We all got busy and it didn't take us long to off load the truck, trailer, and gear.

"Are you folks going hunting?" One of the airport ground crew asked Will.

The fuel truck parked at a forty-five degree angle be-side the big Hercules. The driver got out and worked with Amar to hook up the nozzle to allow the aircraft to start fueling up.

The chatty kid held a metal clip board and started writing out an invoice. He was young, probably sixteen, with a ruddy complexion. His curly blond hair was only subdued by the peaked cap sporting the airport logo.

"We're headed up to the bison ranch, do you know it?" Will asked.

"Sure, I've been out there a couple times." The kid had a quick smile. "This is a pretty cool way to fly in." He was angling for information as he tried to figure out who we were and if there was a tip in it for him. I suppressed a smile.

"Yeah, the owner owed me a favor. Too bad I have to drive back home." Will grinned at him and extracted a black credit card from his wallet.

The fuel truck driver ambled over to give the kid the number of liters the Herc had sucked up.

"I'll get this processed, please come with me, Mr. Oaks."

Will strolled along beside the shorter young man to the fuel hut. Harry Oaks was one of Will's aliases, as Alice Munroe was one of mine.

Sandy touched my arm. "Helly."

I turned to her with a smile. "Thanks for the lift, Sandy."

"Anytime, you know that. Get your business settled and come back to us, we need you." Her eyes flickered over to where Will stood at the half door of the gas hut. "He's been a cranky bastard since you left."

"I second that," John said as he walked up from completing his pre-flight check. "Good people like you are hard to find."

"I'll think about it, for sure." I nodded goodbye. "Thanks again," I said as I shook everyone's hand, He had walked back down the ramp to say goodbye as well. The navigator waved at me as I walked over to the truck and climbed in. I had to get away from their kind eyes.

My own eyes clouded over a bit with unfamiliar moisture. The crew returned to their aircraft and disappeared as the back doors closed. SPS had been my pack for nine years, ever since I joined as a newly graduated second lieutenant at twenty-two years old. The agency bought out my contract. Since they were affiliated with the government and the military, it was a seamless transition. If there was one weakness shapeshifters had, it was the need to belong. We needed to be part to something bigger than us, and I was no different.

I cleared my throat and put those feelings away. I needed to focus on what was to come.

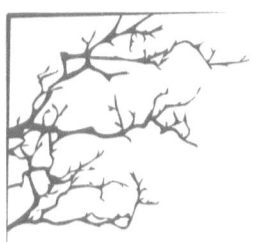

Chapter Six

Once we hit the highway, I figured I had put it off long enough and dug for my mobile phone.

"Are you calling your sister-in-law?" Will asked as he turned the truck on to provincial highway nineteen so we could head south.

Later we would head west on a set of gravel roads that would take us to the compound.

"Yes." I sighed. "It's long past time I spoke to her."

I scrolled through my contacts. and selected it. I would have to work on my tone. I had to be civil with Lasha, even though it would be I never liked her.

"What are you so pissed at her for?" Will was good at picking up my moods.

I paused, thinking about how much to tell Will. You know what, screw it, I thought. I was done keeping things inside. It was also true that, if I expected Will to open up to me, I had to open up to him.

to protect the people—shifters, betas, and everyone else weaker than themselves." I turned to him as I spoke. "This is even more important for the ruling alpha," I "Everyone under his or her protection is their responsibility. The alpha must ensure their charge's safety and survival."

"And Lasha failed to protect Julian?" Will asked.

I could see it was hard for him to get his head around that a male couldn't protect himself.

"Yes, it's abundantly clear to me she failed. of her screw ups is documented in detail in the re-ports you supplied me with. As a shifter, I know what she was on the hook for. She let Julian and her son down."

It was good that SPS had gotten their hands on the in-formation. I needed to know what the VIC Security team and George Mathieu knew. This data gave me a good pic-ture of the past events. It was also fortunate that shapeshifters were obsessed with communicating among the packs. SPS must have intercepted the reports well be-fore the information was delivered to the White Pine Pack. That was how SPS and, in turn, the government, kept tabs on the packs.

Some packs did supply some basic information to SPS. However, I was fairly sure they didn't know how detailed the agency's files were. This included the smaller clans which didn't rate pack status. Most small clans have never required intervention by SPS.

As a field operative, I knew the agency and the gov-ernment needed the information. But as a subject of that information, I felt uncomfortable. I had no control over the situation, but I did hope the data was used with due caution.

"How so?"

"Lasha failed on a number of levels. First—" I held up my index finger, "—she never challenged Julian on his self-obsession with his health. It was his weakness. A weakness that Howard and the Foggles exploited. —" I lifted my middle finger. "—she did not ensure that the people she trusted to keep her pack whole and healthy were not compromised. Namely, Doctor Charles Hector and his clinic staff. She blindly trusted the doctor. Even after evidence showed he might have been com-promised. That evidence should have caused her to re-think her strategy." I held up my ring finger to tick off the last point. "Lastly, the one person she could have trusted, the one person she should have kept in the loop on all levels of communication, she forced out. Whether that was a paranoid episode triggered by losing Julian or not, isn't clear. But Lasha should have trusted Jessica

Raiway, her—" I was going to say mage but changed it to "chief advisor."

No way was I going to explain Jessica Raiway's role with the pack to Will. had nothing with regard to our mages and their functions. It wasn't up to me to leak that info either. Some secrets were just too sensitive.

"Something hinky was going on. How would she know Jessica was her ally?" Will was playing devil's I arched one eyebrow at him. While I knew what he was doing, I didn't have to like it. I shook my head. I knew how alone you could feel when you were on your own. It couldn't have been easy for her. "She also didn't put up much of a fight to leave. The report Jessica filed with the White Pine Pack ques-tioned Lasha's decision to remove her from the pack. She asked about recourse, a way to get back in. The report was practically dripping with wounded feelings and con-fusion."

"Was there any recourse for her?" Will asked as he slowed to allow a semi-trailer to pass us.

"No, she couldn't get enough council votes."

Although there was no mention of her doubt about Dr. Hector either. Maybe the mage had missed it as well? I fiddled with my phone, I should get the call out of the way, but talking this out with Will was good too.

"Okay, I have a question," Will said, and I looked over at him. "Why does the Vancouver Island Clan report into Ontario? Why not the Wild Rose in Alberta? That hierar-chy doesn't make sense."

Will slowed the vehicle and signaled to pull into a Tim's drive thru. We order ludicrous-sized coffees, sandwiches, and of course, doughnuts. Nobody went to Tim's without getting a doughnut.

"It's the way it evolved mostly, I think," I answered as we waited for our order. "White Pine was the first pack to be established in Canada. Then Griffe Bleu in Quebec, which was disbanded due to issues with the alpha in charge. The result was members of Griffe

Bleu were Either by White Pine, Salt Wind Atlantic Clan in the Maritimes, or they went south to New Orleans."

We were inching our way through the drive thru line to the window to pay and receive our order.

"White Pine is the largest pack with Wild Rose as a close second. In addition, Jess Raiway was mentored by the White Pine pack when she was on her exchange there. Exchanges are popular with the packs because they add new blood into their lines. The exchange of members among packs also builds alliances. members, it allows them to achieve an education or training in a field their home pack might not offer."

"Okay, that makes sense. Let's go back to Julian for a moment. Wouldn't you say Julian bore some going on inside his own pack. He was an alpha as well." Will gave me a careful look, clearly to see if I was going to remain impartial. Julian was my brother, after all.

"Of course, but again, he was only an alpha in name. Lasha should have known what was going on. She was either incompetent or compliant and I know she wasn't compliant." I shut up when we got to the delivery win-dow and Will paid and accepted our order.

We parked in the lot to wolf down our sandwiches. There was no point in getting a ticket for distracted As well as all the proper stamps for wolves and white tail deer. If a conservation officer were to look at our cache of ammo, they would know we had more than what was reasonable, but we could pass a casual inspec-tion. At least for two people going out to hunt.

We also carried our Possession and Acquisition Li-censes or PAL, necessary for Canadian gun laws. These documents validated traveling with this selection of weapons. Some were currently rack mounted over the rear window. Not to mention the ammo in the cargo box of the truck...well, if it didn't suffer a close inspection.

Even so, we didn't want to have to explain anything to authorities if we got pulled over. Not that it was likely the police would want to search our vehicle. However, the possibility that we could be stopped still existed. If we were stopped, it was a quick phone call to Henry.

After a bio break, we headed back out onto the high-way again with Will continuing to drive. "You're avoid-ing calling your sister-in-law," he said, and the look in his eye told me he wasn't letting me get away with it.

I held my phone in my left hand and stared at the number. The cup holder was convenient to my right hand, and I placed my coffee cup into it. "What I can't forgive is putting the kid in danger. If Lasha wanted to clean house and install a new security head, she should have done it right after Julian's death. But she didn't. She waited almost a year before she called Iain Trennor back to the pack. Howard had been running security for some years by that time. He couldn't have taken it well when he was demoted," I said compressing my lips in thought. "Then there's her father, George Mathieu, he's partly to blame, too."

"How's that?" Will rested his elbow on the window sill and steered the truck with one hand as he sipped his coffee.

He seemed more relaxed now that we had eaten, but there was still some tension around his eyes and mouth. I didn't comment, if something was bothering him, and he wanted to talk about it, he would. Men like Will didn't require a lot of maintenance.

"Mathieu was the power that orchestrated Julian and Lasha elevation as ruling alphas. After he stepped down, he left to retire up north. He also shouldn't have sent Iain Trennor away for more than the usual maximum three-year exchange. Seven years was excessive. It was that absence which allowed Geoff Howard, barely a beta, to slide into the power vacuum." I fiddled with my phone settings. "It was also evident to me that Lasha and Julian weren't the best choices for ruling alphas. I knew this when I came to the Island for their wedding. If Lasha believed she was the most fit to rule, she would have never made her best resource and ally leave the pack. Pushing out Jess Raiway was a mistake."

I couldn't share the other reason—the mage was the only one who could question an alpha's decisions. If the mage could swing enough council votes, he or she could reverse an alpha's decision.

Lasha probably felt threatened. Maybe she was even questioning herself and her leadership.

Will knew about shapeshifters, most handlers and field operatives at SPS did. He didn't need to know about the magical side of shifters. We had a law that expressly for-bade divulging any information with regard to mages. The penalty was death.

First and foremost, we protected our mages. They were our blood line record keepers and holders of our lore and laws. Mages kept our history and, in a lot of cases, were our healers.

Usually, in a disagreement, a pack council would side with their mage if there was a dispute between mage and alpha. This was another reason I felt something wasn't right with the leadership of the VIC pack with Lasha in charge.

If there was a deadlock, the council could request a third party arbitrator from another pack. But that never happened. No alpha wanted another alpha to tell them what to do.

"If Jessica Raiway wasn't there at the time this all happened, how could she know what was going on?" Will pointed out. "Would the other wolves keep Lasha's secrets? Wouldn't they report things to Raiway? Share gossip, even in passing?" he asked, rubbing his forehead.

The sun was almost gone. I wondered if the headlights from the oncoming cars were affecting his vision. He seemed to be experiencing some discomfort.

"Do your people ever cross you?" I asked.

"No, not if they want to continue working at SPS. But I do encourage people to discuss any concerns they may have with me. Although ultimately, all decisions are mine, you know that."

"Exactly," I said. "You also won't rip somebody's throat out for crossing you." I watched Will rub his eyes again. "Do you want me to drive for a while?"

"No, I'm good." He shook his head. "So, you're say-ing it's the same type of command structure, except for the throat ripping out part?"

I nodded. "Pretty much."

"It's a fortunate thing Lasha finally recalled Trennor and Raiway, so they could figure out what was going on with Howard and the Foggles and then put an end to it."

"Yes. I also think that if Lasha hadn't stepped aside after that, Trennor would no doubt have challenged her."

Will glanced over at me with raised eyebrows. "So you're saying Mathieu, from the get-go, destabilized the VIC to hand off leadership to his baby girl?"

"It looks that way to me," I said.

"That's a bit cynical."

"If you think that's cynical, then how about Mathieu being involved in Howard's escape?" I suggested.

"That's not cynical, that's down right distrustful and possibly paranoid. The escape has to make him look bad. What would be Mathieu's motivation? What could he possibly gain helping Howard to escape?"

"Okay, try this on for size. Howard blamed Jessica Raiway and Iain Trennor for destroying his plans. He wanted to be ruling alpha alongside Lasha, with Julian gone. If Howard took them out, he could actually take the alpha spot and reinstate Lasha as alpha and his mate. Mathieu would support that."

"But Howard is responsible for killing your brother, Lasha's husband and mate." Will didn't sound convinced.

"Yeah, so what?" I questioned. "It wouldn't be the first time the conqueror took the widow as his mate. I'll have to share some shapeshifter history with you. You also have to understand how old Mathieu is."

"How old is he? How long do shapeshifters live?"

"Usually around two hundred and fifty years or so, unless you're a crappy fighter," I said. "And Mathieu is getting up there. Lasha is probably his last offspring. I found in reading his reports that some of his opinions are downright medieval. If he wanted to build a dynasty, he would want her back in the alpha spot."

"That still sounds pretty cold blooded. that Machiavellian?"

"Why not? Standard humans are all the time. What makes you think shapeshifters are any less so?"

"True," he said. "Call Lasha and, after that, you can drive for a while, if you wouldn't mind." He rubbed the center of his chest again and fished a tube of chewable antacid out of his jacket pocket. "You've given me a lot to think about," he said and popped two into his mouth.

I called Lasha. I spoke briefly to my nephew before he handed the phone to his mother. The conversation was short. I told her we were on the Island and were headed to the compound to assess the situation and meet up with her father. It was over quickly with hardly twenty words exchanged between us. I had kept my tone neutral. Score one for my self-control.

The conversation I had with my nephew was a bit more unsettling than I had bargained for. He sounded like a good kid, smart, and he knew who I was. I told him we would probably be meeting soon. I couldn't leave the Is-land now without at least seeing my nephew. He was all I had left familywise. Well, except for my Aunt Rita, but I hadn't seen or spoken to her in years.

That thought made me look over at Will. I wanted to increase my family by at least one.

We had stopped briefly and changed over. the last hundred kilometers to the compound.

Will was on his phone with George Mathieu. Pack leaders knew about SPS. At times, they had to ask for help dealing with incidents that went sideways and before news got out to the public.

SPS knew way more about the packs and their busi-ness than they let anyone know. I knew our boss, Dray-ton, didn't like the fact that some packs were not playing ball anymore, like the Wild Rose Pack.

The Alberta alpha had come out to the world in a press conference almost a year ago. I was told Drayton turned purple when he found out. I wished I'd been there to see it.

A hunter shot a wolf from the Wild Rose Pack last year. I could see why Mike Sydorenko had gone public. probably felt enough was enough.

SPS had wanted to cover up the shooting, like they had with my parents. had decided it was time to be honest with the general public. In so doing, maybe he hoped he could protect his people better. I wish someone had come up with that idea before my parents were killed.

With the California Pack—who were first—out, that made two so far. I was willing to bet in the next couple of years, more were going to announce their existence, then things would get real interesting.

"Howard attacked us last night. So far he's managed to kill one of my staff members and wounded three others," Mathieu was saying to Will. "The shifters following him are not very strong but three to one can do some damage."

"Are you dealing with it or do you require more help? We have more resources we can tap into if need be," Will said.

"We're dealing with the situation with our own people. When you get here, I'll run it all by you, and you can help us recapture the escapees." At least this former alpha was cooperating. That would make working with him and finding Howard much easier.

But that didn't mean I trusted George Mathieu.

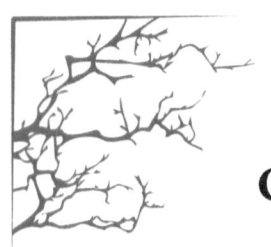

Chapter Seven

T hat the shapeshifters used as a sort of prison farm or rehab center.

The former alpha of the VIC pack was a bit over six feet and could look Will in the eye. His once-ebony hair was shot with heavy strands of silver and white. Even his bushy dark eyebrows sported a few white hairs. Although his face was lined, it was tanned and radiated a vitality that was not usually present in a man of his age. Even for a shapeshifter.

It was full dark by the time we arrived, but the place was brightly lit up with flood lights. There were wolves patrolling the outside perimeter. This was no doubt be-cause Geoff Howard and his band of merry nightmares had attacked the night before. Mathieu didn't want a re-peat, at least not without some warning.

The inmates still inside the compound numbered around twenty. He pointed out inmates who wore green coveralls, and the LDCs all wore jackets with gold slashes on the left sleeves.

Will thought the grizzly bear shapeshifters, LDCs, were more like guards and not so much inmate social workers, but what did he know?

"That's the female quarters and across the square are the male quarters," Mathieu said. for all but the most troublesome shapeshifters." He pointed out the different buildings to Will and me as they strolled through the compound. The buildings formed a square and left the center open, for a courtyard. "We have better secured facilities for shifters who are more dangerous, like Howard.

Most aren't as violent as him and don't require a more secure type of incarceration."

"Most of your inmates aren't murderers," Helly "No, they're not. Most have trouble fitting in with the standard human population. They are sent here to learn better control and atone for past transgressions," Mathieu explained.

Mathieu's statement actually exploded some of the He understood Helly and Zav were exceptional shapeshifters. They functioned in any type of environment SPS tossed them into. But he still held the opinion that shapeshifters weren't all that stable. He had expected this compound to be housing more hard-core killers than Geoff Howard.

"The wolves Howard escaped with are petty criminals. Charged with things like car theft, destruction of private property, and some are runaways. A few are guilty of as-sault against standard humans and other offences of that nature."

"What about assault against other shapeshifters?" Will asked.

"That's dealt with by their alphas," Helly answered. "The same as rogue shapeshifters. Usually, their alpha tracks them down and makes the offender accountable for whatever they've done." She didn't go into what that could mean.

Will supposed it depended on the alpha and their advisors' judgement. Helly read the full reports on what had happened in the VIC pack territory. She'd commented to Will she thought Howard had gotten off lightly.

"The majority of your inmates are juvenile delinquents and outside the judicial system. Who made the decision to bring Howard here?" Will frowned at Mathieu. He thought bringing a killer here had been a bad idea.

"The VIC pack council approached me, and I agreed to bring him here." Mathieu drew himself up to his full height as he explained. The old grizzly bear seemed an-noyed by Will's question.

"We felt it was best to remove him from the pack and incarcerate him. It is true that up until then, this facility had only housed lesser offenders. Howard is our first serious felon."

Will was tempted to ask what happened to other shapeshifter murderers. But really, it wasn't hard to figure out.

"How long did you plan to keep him locked up?" Helly asked.

Will moved to stand behind Helly's right shoulder, and he rested a hand on her back to show his support. This couldn't be easy for her. They were getting closer to her brother's killer.

The casual contact must have taken Helly a bit by sur-prise. She gave him a quick glance over her shoulder. He was glad his touch wasn't unwelcome. If anything, she leaned into the contact. What surprised Will was the fact that touching her eased the discomfort in his chest. Or maybe it merely distracted him. Either way, he let out a long slow breath in relief.

Helly must have sensed something was off. She glanced over her shoulder at him again, this time with a puzzled frown, before turning back to Mathieu.

"The hearing we gave him came down with a judgement of twenty years at the compound. After which, Howard will be sent back to his home pack in Washing-ton State." Mathieu explained. "His alpha in Portland can decide what to do with him after that."

"That's pretty lenient," The dissatisfaction in Helly's tone was evident. "He killed an alpha."

"No one from the VIC pack was ready to carry out the traditional sentence," Mathieu sounded disgusted.

"You mean Lasha wasn't strong enough to do it." Helly had tensed with the older shifter's words and Will realized she was struggling to keep her tone neutral, and she wasn't completely successful.

"The traditional sentence is death?" Will guessed. Since the shifters had brought it up, he figured it was okay to confirm his assumption.

"Yes," Helly said, confirming, as she faced the older man squarely. "What about you, Mathieu, he killed your daughter's mate, your son-in-law. He endangered your grandson by poisoning him. Didn't you feel the need to make him pay?"

Mathieu met Helly's glare but didn't react. He kept his tone and expression low-key. "It wasn't my place to carry out the traditional sentence," he said. He turned away from them as if that ended the subject.

Helly was vibrating under Will's hand. He moved it up to her shoulder and gave it a squeeze. This clearly wasn't over as far as Helly was concerned, but she let it go for now.

"Howard's quarters are in another building. I'll take you there so you can see what you will be dealing with for yourselves."

His tone made Will frown. There was obviously some-thing he wanted them to understand, and it wasn't good. Will figured a change in subject would be a good idea. And allow both shapeshifters to regain full control of their tempers. Defuse the tension. "You run this place as a bison farm, why?" he asked.

Their boots crunched on the gray crushed rock that covered the walkways around the yard.

"It gives the inmates something to do. It's therapeutic for some and also makes the compound self-sustaining. So we aren't a drain on the various packs that send us inmates. Not all packs are well off," Mathieu explained.

They had left the courtyard behind and rounded the corner of the male quarters, to a metal structure being worked on by a handful of compound personnel.

The inmates were assisting in the repairs to free up the compound staff to do patrols. They were still under the watchful eye of one LDC.

"This is the high-risk shifter quarters." The older male waved his hand at the small building. "The serious felons wear silver alloy shackles at all times. The shackles pre-vent them from shifting to an animal form, and they're easier for us to control." Mathieu stood to the side so they could watch the construction crew lower in a new plate of half-inch steel, using a crane. The crew was preparing to weld it in place to cover a hole in the metal wall.

"The silver also reduces the inmate's strength. And makes it much harder for them to overpower the staff or each other," Helly murmured to Will.

"I remember."

They both knew first hand exactly what silver did to a shapeshifter. Helly had once been shot with a silver alloy round when they were on a mission in the Ukraine.

They had been a forward recon team to gauge the depth of an incursion by a separatist group. , the separatists were not what they seemed. They were backed by some serious firepower from an unconfirmed source. The separatists had also known there would be shapeshifters in the forward team. investigation some time later.

The silver in the round had sucked Helly's energy level dangerously low. The poison also impeded her healing capabilities and had prevented her from shifting. Will was forced to drag Helly to safety and call for an air evac.

Merely thinking about that operation and almost losing Helly as she bled out made him clench his jaw. Nothing he had done had stemmed the flow of blood until the slug was removed. The memory of seeing her blood on his hands caused the pain in his chest to increase threefold, and he sucked in a deep breath. He was seriously messed up right now, and he had to get a handle on it or he'd put her in danger.

Will focused on Helly standing next to him and the fact that she was alive, whole, and healthy, although very pissed off at the moment. Heat radiated off her. He in-haled her scent and released it slowly. This slow breathing also helped him to get the discomfort under control. The pain was becoming increasingly annoying.

They stood silently for a moment, watching a woman clamp the steel in place. A male shifter stepped forward and began welding the metal edges together.

A pile of wood siding was stacked by the fence Will figured it was probably used to disguise the building's function from casual observers or visitors to the bison farm.

The crack and pop of the MIG welder filled the silence. The bitter acidic smell of wire melting to create the weld drifted on the light breeze. It made all three of them wrinkle their noses at the sharp scent.

"Are those plates silver and steel alloy?" Will asked.

"Yes, and we're doubling up on them. Howard tore through the original construction like it was paper." Mathieu turned to look at them. Will could see fear in the old man's eyes. "He shifted into his half form and tore off his shackles. He shouldn't have been able to do that." He blinked and the emotion was gone.

After that, Mathieu led them to a central dining area and left them. Will and Helly queued up in the line to be served the evening meal. There were some vegetables, but the meal consisted mostly of protein.

There were bison steaks which were grilled to various levels from blue—the rarest that served meat can legally be—to well-done. Whole roasted chickens cut in half were offered with a rich gold gravy, as well as thick slices of pink salmon, grilled with a lemon sauce.

The food was prepared simply, but well. The silver-ware station offered a selection of condiments and spices to liven up the fare.

Helly partook from the bowl of salad along with the stir-fried vegetables to accompany her steak. She did go back for salmon once she had finished her first plate.

Will indulged in a steak and surprised himself with a helping of chicken too. At a raised eyebrow from Helly at only meat and poultry on his tray, he added some of the vegetables as well.

He was feeling a bit better but couldn't explain why. But, if he brushed his arm against Helly's at the table, it eased the ache in his chest. He chalked it up to anxiety—no doubt from the flashback when Helly had been injured.

They ate by themselves. The other diners kept a wide berth for whatever reason. And beside a few words about the meal, both Will and Helly avoided speaking about anything, including the previous night.

Once they had eaten their fill, Will and Helly met with Mathieu in his office. They needed to plan their strategy for the next day, beyond tracking down Howard and his followers as soon as possible.

Finally, they agreed Will and Helly would go out as one team and head south. Mathieu and another shapeshifter named Victor would go out as the second team. They would take the northern trails. A third team would remain close to the compound in case Howard made an appearance back there again.

After that, Mathieu had a staff member take them to their rooms. They were shown a set of guest rooms across the hall from each other. They were told the accommodations were used for inmate families when they came to visit their delinquent offspring.

Their bags were each at the foot of a single bed in a separate room, brought in by another staff member.

The place was comfortable enough. Will shed his clothes and showered before climbing between the crisp cotton sheets. He turned out the light and lay alone in the single bed.

Even with his eyes closed, he could sense Helly's presence across the hall. He knew she was getting ready for bed as well. Will made himself relax so he could sleep. The whole situation couldn't weird him out any more than it already had. It had been a long day but still, it took a while for sleep to come.

Will half hoped Helly would join him in his bed. After an hour, he rolled over and sleep finally claimed him.

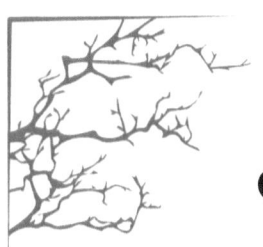

Chapter Eight

The logging road was rarely used. Ruts were over grown with moss, while saplings and ferns were trying to retake the flatter areas.

We were several kilometers past the fenced-off area where the bison were allowed to graze. Before we got here, Mathieu had the animals brought into the south paddock so the staff could keep watch over the snorting beasts. The thought was the lack of food would make the escaped shifters reckless and try for some fresh meat.

I guess it depended on how hungry they were. From what Mathieu and his second, Victor Shamir, had told us the majority of the inmates were from urban areas. They were the ones who had trouble fitting in and were the problem children. Rural shifters seemed to thrive better. I wondered if these city kids knew what to do with a live bison. I kind of doubted it.

It was to our benefit, though, if the escapees had little food. That would take some of the fight out of them.

After Will and I had met back in the office this Victor shared their latest intel on where they had tracked Howard and his band of misfits. We reviewed the maps and confirmed our plans for the day.

The sun was only now breaking the horizon. into the bush along one of two likely southern routes. Howard's scent was on both.

Mathieu suggested we take some of his people, but we declined, without explaining. With one shared look at each other, we agreed we were more comfortable working by ourselves—and more than capable of dragging Howard back to the compound.

If we brought him back. I was still on the fence about that.

Last night, we had bunked down in the guest quarters. My room was across the short hallway from Will's. of us had brought up the possibility of sharing a room, although I wouldn't have minded.

Will seemed more and more irritable as the day wore on and, by the time, we called it a night, he wasn't speak-ing much. I had no idea what was causing this mood, but I ignored him and went to bed. We both needed proper rest to deal with what was to come today.

We'd unloaded the ATVs off the truck trailer and loaded up the cargo boxes with ammo, equipment, and supplies, in case we ended up staying out in the bush overnight.

We added our chosen weapons to the scabbards on the right side of each of the all-terrain vehicles. Both of us favored a 410 short-barrel shotgun. It would ride within easy reach and was loaded with silver mixed shot.

In addition, I strapped my sidearm, a 9mm Kimber Pro Aegis, onto my right thigh. Its nylon harness would flex when I shifted.

Will favored an AF2011-A1 double barrel pistol that evolved from a Sig P10. He liked to carry a heavier .38 caliber weapon. And it was always good to have The trail looped past a stand of four-hundred-plus-year-old cedars. Four or five people would have to link arms to encircle an entire tree, Each cedar extended This made the trail we were taking dim, perpetual twilight. I was glad for my shapeshifter eyesight. It was easy to make out potential pitfalls or a possible ambush. I could make out the smell of crushed greenery and the sharp tang of broken spruce bows.

It was not a surprise to see Geoff Howard stood as he in the middle of the trail, alone. He was thinner than the picture from his file. His face was more angular, but it was him.

His eyes tracked me, and he ignored Will. Howard sounded his defiance with a long undulating growl. He was challenging me.

He wore only a pair of torn gray sweatpants. His hair was greased back, his feet were bare, and he was filthy and smeared with blood. He smelled terrible, rank.

No matter how long a shifter stayed in their animal form, they stayed as clean as possible. It was instinct for us. That is, if you are in you're right mind.

Howard watched us with narrowed eyes as we both came to a stop about fifty meters away. I could see the crazy from here.

After only a few days of living rough, Howard looked like he had reverted to a feral state. The kind we had to hunt and put down.

I killed the engine. A second later, Will did the same.

Not taking my eyes off my quarry, I slowly climbed off my quad and removed my helmet, placing it on the seat. The jacket was next, in case I needed to shift. , it wasn't if I shifted, but when.

Howard tracked my movements. He didn't seem in any hurry to fight me. I didn't know what he was waiting for, but I was ready.

I kept my eyes locked on him.

Will stayed seated while he removed his own helmet and dropped one hand into the scabbard at his right side. He drew his short-barrel shotgun and leveled it at How-ard then climbed off his quad.

The rogue shifter wolf sneered at us and sniffed the air. "It's a kitty cat!" He laughed. "Lasha sent a kitty cat and her gun-toting human for me."

I ignored his lame taunting. It was interesting to know Howard wasn't informed on the current state of the VIC hierarchy. Lasha had stepped down in favor of Iain Tren-nor and Jess Raiway, but he didn't seem to know that.

"Are you ready to go back to the compound?" I rested my hand on the butt of my Kimber. I didn't think there was any point in pretending we didn't have enough fire power. We had more than enough to take on five rogue shapeshifters.

"Um, let me think, do I want to spend twenty years in that hell hole? No!" He laughed at his own joke.

"Good," I said. I gave him a nasty smile as I drew my weapon.

Howard frowned at my reaction. Did he think I was going to plead with him to come back with us?

"I came to play." My smile got wider, I showed my teeth. "Murderer," I hissed at him, allowing my cat voice to dominate as I loosened my control on my shifter half.

I flicked the safety off and brought the weapon up in a one-handed grip. I gave him two heart beats to Of course, he wouldn't, but then I hadn't expected him to.

And true to form Howard broke into a run and leapt at me.

I squeezed the trigger and shot him.

The Kimber round blew the back out of his left The shot spun him around and he landed a few feet away from me. He got up, shook himself, and kept com-ing.

I put another round into his thigh, which made him stumble. I had hit the femur. He didn't get up right away.

The first shot was meant to get Howard's attention. The second was meant to stick, and put a small quantity of silver into his system to stop him from shifting. He would be easier to catch if he couldn't shift.

As he slowly straightened, Howard let out a shrill whistle.

Shifters dropped out of the trees on top of us, the four we were expecting.

Two bodies knocked into Will. He fired as he went down and put silver shot into a small female. She rolled away, screaming.

The male, who was in a sad half form—similar to a werewolf with mange—leaped and missed Will as he dropped to one knee.

They all looked weak, malnourished, and scrawny.

We hadn't scented them with the prevailing wind coming toward us. They must have been high up in the trees for me not to detect them.

I side-stepped a large male in human form as he swung at me. I punched him in the face with the back of my fist and heard his nose crunch, I'd broken it. He howled and turned away covering his face with dirty hands.

His reaction confirmed my suspicions, these shifters were not fighters.

It didn't matter that he would start to heal almost His eyes and face would be screwed up, with tears and blood obscuring his sight.

Will jumped to his feet and continued firing silver rounds into each of our assailants. He emptied the shot-gun and drew his pistol.

I put a round into a large female. She staggered but didn't go down. The pain seemed to make her more She advanced and knocked my gun hand aside. I kept the momentum going and spun, connecting with my side thrust kick to her mid-section. She flew back past Howard.

He didn't even seem to notice or care that his people were taking damage. He stood back watching us.

A male jumped on my back. I braced my legs to flip him off.

"Stay still," Will ordered and he fired. My Kevlar vest absorbed the blast from Will's pistol and the male fell off me.

Will fired four more times. I looked for Howard in the mess of bleeding and snarling shapeshifters.

He was gone.

It dawned on me that he had been waiting for them to drop on us, so he could high-tail it out of the clearing.

I grabbed my own shotgun from my scabbard. "Will," I called and he wordlessly gestured for me to toss it to him. He had no time to reload, these shifters couldn't change but they could still attack.

With light effort, I tossed my SBS to him and he plucked it out of the air at the same time he holstered his pistol. He brought up the barrel and chambered a shell all in one motion.

I dropped my Kimber back into its holster, shifted into my half form, and ignored the tearing of the sweatshirt. I had planned to shift when I dressed this morning so it was no loss.

My animal was a cougar. But make no mistake, being a female didn't mean I was small. For shifters it was all about the amount of magic we held that determined our size. I held a lot. Not enough to be a mage, but enough for my half form to reach seven and a half feet tall.

I stood on thicker, more heavily muscled legs to sup-port my larger upper body and longer reach. My face elongated in to a cat muzzle and fangs extended in a size to match that of a sabre tooth cat. My hands were larger and sported razor-sharp claws. My face said cat, so did the fur coating my body, but it was not a complete shift, no tail, and I was upright like a human.

It was time to end this party. I let out a long, low, rumbling snarl that echoed around the clearing. That got their attention and all the skanky shifters froze in place. Silence.

With that snarl, I announced I was superior to all of them. I dominated in rank, in size, and in the ability to take away their sorry excuses for lives.

The result was they either ran away or dropped to the ground and curled into a ball of submission, no doubt try-ing not to piss themselves. Most of them were successful.

I felt eyes on me. I turned.

Will was staring at me with a shocked expression.

Great.

He'd probably never actually seen a shifter take a half form before. I knew he had never seen me do it and we could look like a nightmare, half human/half animal with fangs and claws. I had always been careful not to let any-one see me change shape, in the field or out of it. The on-ly form he had seen me in was my full animal form. Never my half form.

Well, this could be a deal breaker, I guess. Screw it. I had to pursue Howard. I didn't have time for self-pity. If Will couldn't handle me as I was, oh well.

"Do you have this?" I asked. I could speak, it didn't matter what form I wore. Not all of us could. were running high right now, but I was in total con-trol of myself. "Will?"

"Yeah," he said hoarsely and seemed to come back to himself. "Yeah, do what you have to."

He pulled his eyes away from me. I could see he was struggling to put his game face back on. He cradled the shotgun and pulled out the silver alloy handcuffs from his quad's cargo box.

I didn't waste any more time and took off in the Will had only three to deal with, and I knew he could handle them.

With a lung full of scent, I gave chase. I didn't have time to worry about Will's reaction to my shift or my re-action to his shock. I had to focus on the task at hand.

Food must have been hard to come by for the past week. A shifter's metabolism ran at a higher rate. We burned through calories much faster than standard So, it was no surprise to find the other escaped male lying under some brush. He was trying to hide among the ferns only half a kilometer down the trail. I reached in to the brush and dragged him into the open.

"Don't be stupid." I growled as I slapped down his at-tempt to fight. "Do you want to die out here?"

His macerated form shuttered. "No!" he wailed. "I hate the forest. I want to go home." He smelled and sounded young. The back of his calf and his chest were bleeding.

"Can you shift?"

"No," he said miserably. "It hurts too much."

Good, it was safe to send him back to Will.

"Head back to the others in the clearing and call out before you try to enter or you'll get shot again." I hauled him to his feet and shoved him back the way we had come. He crashed and stumbled through the brush. It was obvious he was city bred by the noise he made.

I broke into a fast jog. Howard's stench was easy to follow. Another trail intersected with the current one, and I could tell a wolf had used it. But now, there were two scents. Howard and one other that was particularly rank. Foul, so bad that if I wasn't a seasoned professional, I'd be puking on the trail.

Instead, I ran on for a full kilometer and ended up on a logging road. I paused to listen. A truck motor was rapid-ly putting distance between me and it. I put on a burst of speed and reached the new road as the tailgate of a white Toyota half ton disappeared over a hill. At least I got a partial plate from the truck.

The vehicle had been parked on this side road for a while. It had leaked a considerable amount of I could track it, but it would take a while. I didn't want to leave Will with four wounded shapeshifters to herd back to the compound.

I also would be too far behind Howard and his I needed transportation.

Resigned, I turned and headed back down the original trail to the clearing where I had left Will with the rogue shapeshifters.

When I got back, I paused just outside the open area.

Will had cuffed all four of them. I had found and sent back to him.

Man, they stank.

I shifted back to my human form before calling out to Will. "I'm coming in."

He waved at me, and I walked to my quad to extract a fresh pair of yoga pants and shirt from my bag, which was strapped to the rack.

"I radioed the compound, they're sending transport." Will never took his eyes off our prisoners.

"It shouldn't take more than half an hour to get here. We aren't far from the compound."

"Howard got away," Will said.

It wasn't a question, but I treated it like one. "Yes, he had a truck stashed on a logging road. He and another male are heading south." I pulled on my boots and stood.

"While we're waiting, I think we should ask this bunch some questions."

"I agree." I walked over to the largest male and hauled him up to his feet. His lank brown hair dropped in to his face, and he flipped it back defiantly. Right now, he was taller than me in my human form, but that didn't matter.

I gave him my hard stare.

He tried to keep his eyes locked on mine, but he had obviously never held a dominant rank in his life. He couldn't do it. He dropped his eyes and his shoulders slumped.

"Well?" I asked. "Did you know Howard was going to use you as a diversion to get away? Or did he promise to take you all with him?"

"He said we would go with him when Mullin got here."

"Who's Mullin?"

"He's a friend of Geoff's. He was supposed to come up last night."

"How did Mullin find you?"

"I don't know. I never saw him. Geoff went off by himself last night, when he got back he said Mullin was here."

"Did Mullin bring the truck?"

The shifter shrugged, keeping his eyes on the ground. "I don't know," he said again.

"Where's Mullin from? What does he look like?" I asked, I was running out of questions and I wasn't happy with the answers I did get.

"I don't know. I never saw him, I never talked to him."

"What was the plan?"

"We were supposed to kill you then head to the truck. Mullin was supposed to get us out of the area."

"What's Mullin's full name?"

"I don't know, Geoff only told us his name was Mullin."

"Were you planning to cross the border? to leave the country?"

"I don't know, he never told us."

I nodded. "Drop to your knees," I said. I helped him lay back down with the others.

"Has anyone seen Mullin?" I raised my voice. "Does anyone know anything about him?" These questions were met with silence and head shaking.

"Does anyone know anything else? Anything you want to tell me?"

The miserable shifters shook their heads again and mumbled negative replies.

I checked their wounds to make sure none were in danger of bleeding out. Two, I made stay still while I used a pair of needle-nosed plyers to extract a slug. One from an upper thigh, the other from a chest wound. had taught me to always carry a pair. I stepped back from our captives and walked over to Will.

It was evident he had questions, but I shook my head and tapped my ear. "I don't want to talk about this until we're out of earshot. One of them may try to get infor-mation to Howard."

Will nodded in agreement and continued to pace the perimeter of the clearing. I kept one eye on him and one on our prisoners. He was agitated, and I didn't like it. He seemed in pain or something, but he had no obvious He didn't smell like blood either.

I watched him rub the back of his neck for the third time. If he had taken a wound, I had to know about it before we continued to track Geoff Howard and his accomplice, Mullin.

A short time later the transport truck arrived from the compound with two of the staff and Mathieu.

Being understaffed didn't seem to matter now. There was no more fight left in these pathetic shifters. The lack of food, shelter, and a cohesive plan had taken its toll on the group. The last of their loyalty was spent when they realized they had been used by Howard as a distraction. Plus having your ass full of silver shot didn't help either.

Howard may have briefly convinced them he was their alpha, but reality had finally set in. He didn't see to their needs. Howard didn't care for them while they were with him and, when they needed him most, he abandoned them.

We helped load the scraggily bunch up into the back of the truck.

"Howard must have sold them a sweet story about running away and setting up their own pack," Mathieu said as he helped the last one board the vehicle.

Then Will closed the tailgate. A staff member had started first aid on the shifters.

"Probably," I said noncommittally. But that's not what I was thinking. This whole exercise had been pointless. Mathieu walked away to speak to his driver.

I spoke quietly, for Will's ears alone. "The only reason Howard recruited these shifters and attacked the com-pound was to waste time. He was waiting until Mullin got here with the escape vehicle."

"Could be," Will said. He glanced at Mathieu then back at me. He acknowledged the fact that I didn't trust George Mathieu with a slight nod. My instincts told me there was something off about the old shifter.

As soon as the truck trundled down the logging road, I turned back to Will. His long body was leaning against his quad. His head was down and his was breathing was labored.

"What's wrong?"

Will lifted his head. His face was pale and he was sweating heavily.

"I don't know. I've never felt like this before." He shook his head. "I'm in pain, but I didn't take an injury." He winced as he rubbed his chest. "This tightness has grown over the past day or so. It seemed to ease a bit last night, but now it's back."

I walked over to him and ran my hands over his scalp. He started to breathe easier as soon as I touched him. He closed his eyes and leaned into me. Our bodies brushed up against each other.

"I can't find a head wound. Are you hit anywhere?" I wondered if he had taken a blow from one of the shapeshifters. Standard humans weren't as robust as a shapeshifter and it took a lot less to injure them than it did one of us.

"No, it's something inside me. My guts are in knots. I'm hot and my bones are aching." He opened his eyes and I looked into their depths.

His pupils were even, although dilated. Will brushed against me and placed his hands on my upper arms to hold me there. For Will to initiate this type of physical contact was out of character.

"Sounds like the flu," I said, frowning up at him.

"Maybe, if it were multiplied by a factor of three." He blinked as he seemed to realize he had hauled me up against him, and he dropped his hands to step away from me. "It doesn't matter. We have to get back to the truck. We're losing Howard."

"I can't take you with me if you're hurt or sick," I said, antsy to get going.

"There's no 'taking me with you,' I'm going and that's the end of it," Will snapped.

That tone made me raise my eyebrows at him. "Really, even if you're slowing me down?"

"You need someone to watch your back."

"I've done fine on my own up until now."

Will took a long breath. "I know, but you don't need to be on your own, not anymore."

They were nice words, but I didn't have time for this. I had an escaped felon to catch, two actually. "Can we get touchy-feely later? We need to get on the road."

That snide remark pulled a dry laugh out of Will, as I had intended. "Saddle up then, let's get back to the truck."

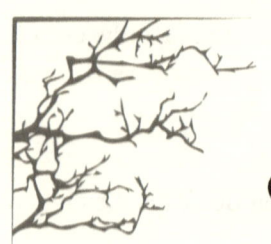

Chapter Nine

We both agreed that Howard would take the There was no way he could avoid the main highway for too long. He would need Highway 19 if he wanted to reach any of the ferries, whether at Campbell River, Nanaimo, or other points farther south.

There were cameras on the highway at various points to allow commuters to check road conditions and ferry availability. The CCTV also allowed law enforcement agencies to monitor the motorists. We could leverage the system via our office contact, Henry, to track Howard and his white Toyota.

Will put in a call and supplied the make, model, color, and partial plate I had given him. "Okay, Henry, let me know when they pop up. We plan to keep traveling south." Will thumbed off his phone and stared out the front windshield. He closed his eyes for a second to rub them wearily.

I was in the driver's seat of Will's truck, and we had about sixty kilometers to go before we hit the main artery. We would turn south to access the majority of the ferry routes.

We were still surrounded by huge cedar and pine trees as we sped along the twisting road back to Campbell It was deserted. We hadn't seen another vehicle for the past hour.

"It's unlikely Howard and Mullin will take a ferry to one of the smaller Gulf Islands," I said to Will. "We can probably skip the ferry at Campbell River. No doubt, he will be making for one that would get them either to the mainland and Vancouver or possibly one that would take them farther south, to Seattle." I glanced over at his silent form. "That could mean one of several terminals in Nanaimo, Sydney, or Victoria."

Will didn't answer as he leaned back against the head rest and his eyes slid closed. I knew he wasn't sleeping, I could sense it. What was more disconcerting was the fact that Will's scent had changed. I frowned, griping the steering wheel. He really had me worried.

We had a lot of time to fill between here and the first ferry terminal in Nanaimo, and I had some questions. It would be best to know what he was thinking.

"Did I freak you out earlier?" I asked bluntly. "When I shifted into my half form?"

"No." He stirred himself to answer. "I've seen that kind of thing before. I was working with Zav Koering in Columbia when it was still a hotspot. We were given a location where some political prisoners were being held by a rebel group. I saw him shift for the first time when we had to chase some cabal members through the jungle. Man, Zav was fast. He had those guys treed in seconds and all I had to do was round them up." He grinned at this thought. "It was freaky at first, but I got used to it," he commented with his head still back and eyes closed again. "Working with a shapeshifter is never dull."

I digested this and said, "So, why did you have that look on your face when you saw me shift?" I asked care-fully.

Will was quiet for a moment, thinking I guessed. "It was weird," he said in a pensive tone. "Watching you change or shift so easily was kind of awe inspiring. It startled me, and yet I was drawn to you. I—I felt like I should—" He broke off and, rolling his head on the seat back, looked over at me. "This is going to sound crazy."

"What?" I prompted.

"I felt like I should shift with you, that we're some-how connected. Crazy, right?" He looked at me, at bit apprehensively.

Whoa. What the hell? Why would he feel like that? "At least you didn't hurl." I had to say something. had kind of thrown me. "Some people do."

He quirked a dark eyebrow at me. "And what about the rest of the people?"

"They turn into groupies. I think you fall into the latter category."

"I'm not your groupie," he growled.

I gave him a teasing, knowing look. "That's not what your scent tells me."

"Funny."

We were once again back to one-word answers, not helpful.

I could feel him retreating from me. I thought over what he had said and came to a startling conclusion. There was only one answer. "Are you in pain?" I asked. "Right now?"

"Some," Will acknowledged, rubbing his forehead again.

I made my decision. I didn't know where my choice was going to take us. I didn't know if I would regret this later, but hell, I didn't have an alpha to answer to so what did I have to lose? I pulled the truck over on to the "What are you doing?" Will demanded, sitting up. "We aren't even on Highway Nineteen yet."

"We need to investigate something," I said and put the truck into park. "Might as well turn off the engine, this might take a few minutes."

I unbuckled my seat belt and leaned over to Will, I stepped over the console on the transmission hump and straddled Will's lap. Much to his surprise.

"What the hell are you doing?" grasped my upper arms. He pulled me against him to increase our body contact. I didn't think he even realized he had done it. The same as he probably didn't realize he was touching me every chance he got.

"You're not in pain when I touch you, are you?"

His eyes were dilated. The black pupils were taking over the whisky-brown irises. "How could I be, when all the blood is rushing to my core because you're pressing your sexy body against me?" Again with the levity. "What are you up to?"

"I'm letting you have your way with me," I said, way too flippant. I still gave him a smile as I grasped his face between my palms then planted a hot kiss on his mouth. The kiss wasn't necessary but I needed him thinking about something else. I needed him to relax so I could see if his body actually was more than it seemed.

Kissing Will was also a huge pleasure. I loved the taste of his mouth, the feel of his lips, and, most of all, his hands on my body.

"We don't have time for this," he said against my lips. His voice had grown husky. "But it feels so good when you touch me."

"We'll make time," I retorted and teased him with my tongue.

I was no mage, but I understood a few things that had been passed down to my generation. One of them was that we shapeshifters could touch each other's magic if we knew how to reach out. I knew how to reach out.

Cats were much more in touch with their bodies and reactions than most shifters. We were also big on touch-ing when we trusted, and I trusted Will a lot. If there was anyone I could share this information with, it was Will. I hoped he trusted me as much.

He pressed me tighter against him. His mouth moved over mine, taking control and exciting us both.

I pictured my magic flowing around us like smoke. I reached out, touching him, stroking his skin with magic just as my fingers were doing. I pictured it delving gently into him, penetrating I was looking for a spark of what I suspected lay hidden deep inside William Conall. I allowed it to sink deeper into his aura and phys-ical being. Then I found it. The spark was faded and very tiny, but it was there. I gently encircled it with my magic. I touched it, igniting it with my own flame.

Will groaned with pleasure as he broke the kiss and gasped as I stroked it again and again. He spread his thighs and I slid deeper into his lap, I could feel him react through the soft material of my yoga pants. It was intense and was definitely going to lead to more.

Will's phone rang. The insistent ring made us break apart. I quickly disengaged, releasing the flicker of his magic, as I released him.

As he reached for his phone, I grabbed the door handle and opened the door to drop to the ground. I had to get myself under control. This wouldn't help us catch Julian's killer. I had to get a grip.

Will grabbed his phone from the dash console. "Will Conall," he answered it tersely. He listened a moment, and said, "Thanks, Henry."

Will climbed out of the truck and stood in front of me. Our eyes locked. There was so much to say and so much that neither of us wanted to voice.

I had my arms folded over my midsection as I debated how much I was willing to explain to Will. I actually should have someone more qualified, but there was just me right now.

"Has someone spotted Howard?" This was a good time to change the subject.

"Yeah, a camera outside Parksville picked them up. They're traveling south. You were right to give Campbell River a miss." His eyes drilled into me, and he stepped into my personal space.

I let him.

"Are we going to discuss what just happened?"

"Are you ready for the shock of your life?" I asked, tipping my head to the side as I took in his puzzled "Hit me."

"You're in pain again right now, aren't you?"

"Yes." He nodded and frowned as he recognized the truth, but he didn't break eye contact. more acutely on me.

"Take my hand." I offered him my right hand and he took it immediately. "The pain is gone now, right?"

"Yes, why is that? What do you know?"

"You're a shapeshifter, Will," I said simply. There was no point in being dramatic about it.

He was still for a second, and then he erupted. "What the hell are you saying?" His eyes turned thunderous, but he still clasped my hand in both of his. He was absently rubbing my palm with his thumb. He so knew how to touch me, even if he wasn't conscious of it.

"You are a shapeshifter and your parents were shapeshifters too," I told him emphatically.

Will stared at me, completely nonplussed. I could see he wanted to deny it, but he could feel the truth of it in his heart.

"You can feel it." I nodded at him and he returned the gesture.

His free hand was resting on his breast bone. "How did I not know? Why is this just surfacing now?" he said incredulously.

"I don't know how a shifter can live for over thirty years of his life and not know what he is," I said with a shrug. "We need to talk to someone about this when we get the chance."

"Who do you talk to, an alpha? Would Mathieu know about this type of thing?"

"Maybe, but I'd rather talk to someone with a wider experience in shapeshifter things like this. I think she can explain it to us. But there are a couple other things you need to know." This was the part where I figured he'd really freak out.

"Please continue, I doubt my life could get any more complicated." He said this last with mixed sarcasm and exasperation.

"I wouldn't bet on that. The next thing you need to know is that you and I are sharing a mate-bond."

"What?" He nearly shouted the word.

"Don't get excited, we aren't engaged," I said dryly. I hoped it wasn't abject horror I was seeing in his I left out that there had to be more between us than sex to generate a mate-bond. I would repel from that cliff when I was forced to. "You have to understand that shifters are more emotional than standard humans. We feel things deeper, I think." I shook my head. "The point is that our connection may have triggered your dormant shifter side. It's possible your parents didn't know they were shifters either. Possibly, they decided not to acknowledge that side of themselves and didn't tell you."

"How could they tell me? All I know about my parents are their names." His exasperation was growing. "I went into the foster care system at eighteen months old."

His eyes were boring into me, and, for a fraction of a second, I saw a golden sheen roll over his eyes. Oh, my.

"You feel a connection to me as well?" he demanded.

"Yes, I do." There was no point telling him I had felt that connection for a long time, at least not yet. "You need to calm down, Will. Breathe with me."

I leaned into him, placing my hands on his chest to in-crease the contact and took a deep, slow inhalation. He did the same and his warm breath fanned my cheek. I loved his scent. I wanted to rub up against him like the cat that I was.

We each took a couple of breaths and released them slowly. Our eyes were locked on each other and the sheen over Will's eyes receded. Then it was gone.

"Meditating helps?" he guessed and sounded a bit calmer.

"Yes, especially for non-shifting shapeshifters. They have the same volatile emotions, but can't trigger a change to expend them." I paused. He was listening in-tently so I decided to continue. I might as well lay it all out on the table now, so to speak. "Not all people who carry the shifter genes can change shape. It depends on one other important factor, and you may want to sit down for this part."

I met his gaze steadily and gave his rough hand a squeeze by way of reassurance. For an answer, Will hauled me against him. His hands were on my back, and I slid mine around his waist, again increasing our physical contact. Giving and getting reassurance.

"When have you known me to take difficult news he murmured, watching me closely.

I could see that already his shifters side was becoming more dominant. "This isn't so much bad news, as it is hard-to-believe news." I looked up into his dark-colored eyes. I was working my hands up and down his broad back now, massaging it to drain some of the tension out of him. "This is something no standard human knows. We take an oath, and swear upon our own lives, not to divulge it to standard humans," I cautioned him.

"All right what's the big secret?" He gave me his sexy half smile. He clearly wasn't taking me seriously.

"I'm going to explain how we actually can shift, what makes it possible." I took a second to center myself. This was a big deal. I had never told anyone about this before. I looked up at him and took the plunge. "Shifting your form depends on how much magic there is residing within you." I waited for his reaction and I wasn't disappointed.

"Seriously, magic?" His tone was skeptical. "Helly, you're screwing with me, right?"

"No, I'm not, and, yes, seriously, we use magic." I was as sincere as I could be.

"Magic is real? You have magic?"

"Yes, I do and so do you." I tapped his hard chest with my fingertips. "Magic is the term we use for the energy that allows us to change shape."

"How much magic do I have?" He still didn't seem to be taking the situation or me completely seriously. He needed to be shown before he would fully believe me. Unfortunately for him, I was prepared to do that.

"Let's find out, shall we?" I reached out again with my magic and delved into the pool that resided inside Will. I wasn't as gentle this time as I stroked it, and Will gasped, mostly with pleasure.

"Holy shit!" he expelled through his teeth.

"Yes, powerful, isn't it?" I couldn't help but grin at the reaction I had triggered. "You seem to have a fair amount of magic, and it's growing. I don't think your parents could have been non-shifters, you have too much magic for that." His magic reserve was growing, true, but something was holding it in check—like a dam holding back water.

"What happens now?" Will was gasping with the force of his reaction.

"Nothing," I said, shaking my head. "We have to get back on the road and deal with Howard. After that, we can take you to a mage. You're going to need to learn how to shift or you could cause yourself some serious damage," I said adamantly.

"That sounds practical. Is there anything else I need to know?" He looked down at me a bit apprehensively.

I was tempted to tell him the rest, but maybe it was better to wait until my other suspicions were confirmed by a mage.

"There's one last thing to confirm. Can I look at your chest?" I asked as I slid my hands down his body and up under the hem of his shirt.

Will raised his eyebrows at this request. "If you think you need to."

He dropped his hands and let me unbutton his flannel shirt. I spread the material wide and ran my hands over the smooth skin underneath. It was feathered with a mat of darker hair. It spread over his pectoral muscles and down his sculpted abdomen. Tapered and disappeared under the waistband of his jeans. I had to reset my focus and look for what I was really after.

"It's hard to contain yourself, isn't it?" Will grinned at me. I knew he was using humor to cover his emotional state.

I smiled back. He had to learn not to bare his teeth like that. "All your scars are gone," I said and grinned at his shocked reaction. His magic was already changing him.

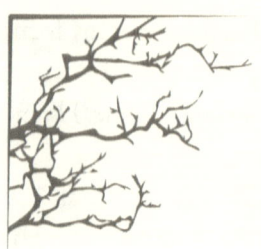

Chapter Ten

Will was behind the wheel again as the truck He was listening to the conversation between Helly and Iain Trennor. The possibility that Howard and Mullin may be heading their way. She was concerned that Howard was making for a Seattle ferry. And he might take it into his head to stop by his old stomping grounds on the way.

Will could hear both sides of the conversation and that didn't surprise him. He had always had sensitive hearing. Now, he understood why that was so.

A shapeshifter, huh, who knew? Will found it hard to get his head around it. It was unbelievable was what it was.

He had never known his father. His mother had passed away from cancer when Will was no more than a baby. Maybe if his mother had known she was a shapeshifter, she could have tapped into her "magical side." Maybe she would have survived the cancer. Then he wouldn't have been raised in several foster homes. Not a great But it wasn't productive to go down that thread of thought, so he killed it.

Although some the foster parents he had encountered were okay, others had been complete bastards. Even so, they had never been his people and didn't care what When he'd turned eighteen and aged out of the system, he joined the military.

The CF was the first family he had ever known. Will had taken his first level of basic training at Canadian Forces Base Shilo in Manitoba. It was there he felt like he belonged somewhere for the first time in his life.

He remembered Master Corporal Lukas. He was trying to bring the green recruits of his troop together and make them think as a unit. People thought of "me" first, naturally, and it took time, effort, and iron persuasion to change their thinking and get them to think of each other as brothers and sisters.

After a couple weeks of banging his head against a brick wall with Will's group, Master Corporal Lukas came into their common room. He looked at each of them in turn, and then took off his beret and said, "I'm not your master corporal right now. I'm one of you and that means that I'll watch your back and you'll watch mine. It doesn't matter if we're cleaning the barracks or running live-fire team exercises. We watch each other's backs and we help each other. It's what we do and who we are in the Princess Patricia Canadian Light Infantry. Being a CAF member sets us apart from other militaries. It's a responsibility, a challenge, and an honor."

Will remembered how each member's posture and Some hadn't gotten it and were dropped, but the ones who did formed a core team and a tight unit.

Master Corporal Lukas's words had stuck with Will. Especially after he had moved up the ranks and rolled out with several different deployments all over the world.

Will glanced over at Helly. She had been part of his family at SPS. Now he knew why he had always felt a special connection to her. His subconscious must have been aware of their similarities as shapeshifters. Okay, he could accept that he was a shapeshifter, that wasn't so hard, but this magic thing. It was so freaking out there.

Magic, it sounded so ridiculous, and implausible. He tentatively lifted his hand away from Helly's where it rested on his thigh.

He rubbed the spot on his chest where Helly had touched him earlier. It had felt like she had drilled right into his heart but, after that, the release had been incredi-ble. It was like he had been crammed into a packing crate and had been constrained by it all his life. She had re-leased him.

Will looked over at Helly again with no small wonder. She discussed with Trennor the precautions the pack had to take in case Howard should show up.

"Shifters need to patrol in teams of two. One in their animal form, and one in human form for easier She didn't look at Will, but she gave his thigh a squeeze. "How many of you can pull off a half form?"

"Two, maybe three," Will heard Trennor reply.

By Helly's compressed lips, he could tell she wasn't happy about Trennor's answer.

Will let the words wash over him as he moved his hand to touch his sternum and concentrated on the feeling of magic inside him. He could feel a warm It seemed to surround his heart.

The feeling was so foreign, and when the pain started to escalate again, he moved his hand from his chest and placed it on Helly's. Instantly, the pain diminished and the discomfort dropped to a more tolerable level.

She had...for lack of better words...unlocked his When he wasn't touching her, the discomfort went up. The reason was supposed to be because of this mate-bond thing she said they had between them.

Will allowed himself to relax and try to sense the bond. It took him a second to identify it, but it was there. He could feel her almost as an extension of himself.

Helly slipped her fingers around his hand as she talked to Trennor, and the pain receded even more.

He wondered if the pain would completely go away if he was making love to her. Now that was a pleasant idea. However, this wasn't a good time for those thoughts. They both needed to focus on the threat Howard Will let out a slow breath and focused more intently on the highway.

He wondered what type of animal he was. A wolf would be okay, but Helly was a cougar. He had found her shifting to be amazing. She was remarkable in so many different ways. Even after all this time, he was learning things about the woman.

He wanted to raise her hand and put it against his lips to kiss it. But first he needed to find Howard and deal with that asshole. Then he could concentrate on what be-ing a shapeshifter meant. What did it mean to his He wanted—

Wait a minute, this mate-bond thing. Did she know she was going to trigger it when he had sex with her? Did he even care?

Will glanced over at her. No, Helly had been as sur-prised as he was to discover his shifter side. He'd bet on it. He'd always known there was something different about him. He was well adapted to the work he had taken on for the military and later SPS. Nothing much had bothered him. He knew he was messed up, but maybe it was his shifter side that handled the adversity of each situation. Who knew?

He frowned. He had a lot to think about.

Helly ended her call with Trennor and looked over at him. "You heard all that." It was a statement.

"Yeah, this shifter thing is going to take some getting used to, but I always had great hearing." with another thought. "And sight."

She nodded. "There are many, many benefits."

Somehow, she made that sound sexy. He had to ignore it for now. "I have a couple questions, if you don't mind."

"Shoot," she said.

"Do you know what type of animal I can shift into?"

"I'm not a hundred percent certain, no. Maybe once you shift, if you can shift, your scent will become more distinct."

"But you can guess." He surmised.

Helly glanced up at him with somber blue eyes. "I think you're a feline of some kind."

"There's more than one kind of cat shapeshifter?"

"Yep, several."

"This just keeps getting more complicated. you give me triggers more questions."

"Like what?" she said pleasantly.

Will flipped an agitated hand. "What makes you think I'm a cat?"

"Instinct, mostly." She frowned and inhaled. "But, partly, you smell good—familiar..." She waved her own free hand, as if searching for the right words. "You smell like you're mine, is how it feels."

Some of the tension eased out of Will at her words. "I know what you mean."

They both looked straight ahead. Neither of them knew what to do with this information.

Helly moistened her lips. "I should call Henry for an update," she said into the awkward silence.

I ended my call and looked over at Will. Neither of us wanted to prod at the revelation we had shared. There were too many unknown factors right now. It was best to ignore it and deal with what was in front of us.

the Toyota, on any manifest yet, the partial plate isn't much of a help either."

"They could have obtained a different vehicle or walked on to a ferry," Will suggested.

"It's possible, I guess, but I don't think so. I think they're headed to the pack's farm. If they were hell bent on getting off the Island and running, they would have done it a couple days ago."

"True, Howard could have stolen a vehicle from the compound. Do you think he wanted to make sure we were chasing him? Maybe he wants an audience."

"Yep, that follows. He wants to punish and humiliate his pack. We get to witness it."

"It's one possibility." Will pointed down the highway. "Look there."

"That's the truck."

The white Toyota was on the south-bound shoulder of the road, its right-side tires sunk into the soft ground next to the ditch.

Will slowed the truck and looked at me. "Are you ready for an ambush? This would be a good place for it."

We were surrounded by trees on both sides. Only the briefest glimpses of water were visible along the coast as we travelled south, and traffic had been light.

I pulled my Kimber out of the shoulder harness under my jacket. I had switched to this harness before we left the first ambush area. I checked my mag. "I'm as ready as I'll ever be," I said, slipping the pistol back into its holster. I reached behind my head, took down one of the shotguns from the rack, and checked it, too. I would hand it to Will when he was ready.

He pulled over some twenty meters behind the Toyota. At least we were on a deserted stretch of highway, and I didn't hear any approaching traffic at the moment.

We got out, and I handed Will the short-barrel shot-gun. He chambered a round, and we slowly approached the smaller truck. We had our weapons drawn and walked almost soundlessly. Only a shifter would have heard us.

The truck seemed abandoned, and then the wind shift-ed.

I tightened my jaw. I looked over at Will briefly and he nodded. We both smelled the blood.

"There's no one here," Will said as we got closer to the vehicle.

"The blood is at least a couple hours old," I noted. "So is Howard's scent."

Will raised his eyebrows at me. "You can tell how old the blood is?"

"Yes, give or take a few minutes. I can tell whose scent was here, too, and how long ago."

"That is freaky shit," he murmured, shaking his head.

"I was trained to know these things." I shrugged. "You have a lot to learn."

"Apparently," he agreed, looking into the cab of the truck. "Clear. There's blood in the cab. Is that Howard's scent?"

"Yep." There was nothing in the box so I looked under the truck. Nothing.

I opened the passenger side. "I smell Howard and something unbelievably rank, that must be Mullin. The blood is Howard's, though, but this is mine." I picked up a slug off the floor of the cab and held it between my forefinger and thumb so Will could see it.

Will frowned. "What the hell?"

"He must have dug it out of his leg so he could heal and shift if he needed to."

Will cursed in disgust. I holstered my pistol and fished out an evidence bag from my jacket pocket. "What? I've done it." I dropped the silver alloy slug into the plastic bag and tucked it into my pocket. I wiped the bit of sticky blood off my fingers and down the seam of my jeans.

"You've dug slugs out of your own body?" Will asked in disbelief.

"Yes, sometimes it's necessary. Like if you're under threat. Or you need to shift to either cover up that you're a shapeshifter or so you can change form and escape."

"When did this happen? Where was I?" I had to be careful here. "It happened when I was in North Africa last year. It was no big deal." My nose twitched. I turned and looked down into the steep ditch.

"Hugh never said anything about you getting shot. There was nothing about it in any of your reports."

"I asked him not to say anything. I dug it out, shifted, and it was healed in a day." I had found another scent and source of blood smell. "Look down there."

Will joined me and followed my gaze. He handed me his shotgun and walked sideways down the wall of the ditch. He sank into the soft earth up to his ankles as he approached the body of a male.

"This is an innocent bystander," Will said, dropping to his haunches. He didn't touch the dead man sprawled at the bottom of the ditch except to look for his ID.

"No wallet," he said.

"It was probably stolen for his credit cards."

The victim was approximately between seventy and eighty years of age. His clothes were torn. His face and the tufts of white hair on his head were smeared with blood. I could see slashes over his torso and legs, where his clothing was torn. The victim's body had been badly savaged.

"It looks like a wild animal attacked him."

"Or a crazy shifter wolf," I supplied.

"The poor guy smells like Howard and something else."

Will was starting to trust his senses more, and, in my opinion, that was a good thing.

"That would be Mullin. This man probably stopped for some reason, and they stole his car after they killed him."

"I'll call Henry and get a clean-up crew out here." Will pulled out his phone and snapped some pictures of the victim's face and his right hand, the left arm was gone. "Henry should be able to get prints from the photo. SPS can match the face to his license and hopefully to a vehicle registration. We should cover him up."

I walked back to Will's truck and racked the shotgun in the cab again. Then I went to the back of the truck and opened a cargo box to fish out a six-foot tarp.

I tossed the tarp down to Will. "There's still no way to confirm where Howard has gone."

Then he climbed out of the ditch and called SPS again. "Henry, have you got my GPS coordinates? Good, we have a homicide at this location. We need a crew."

I shook my head, looking down at the poor guy who had lost his life. All because two low-life parasites like Howard and Mullin needed to change vehicles. Bastards.

"Are we going to give the authorities info on Howard and Mullin?" I asked Will in a low voice.

Will shook his head at me as he spoke to Henry. "I'm sending you pictures of the victim. We need to know what he was driving."

This poor unfortunate man had probably stopped to help supposedly stranded travelers. It would have been easy for Howard to overpower the old man. They could have just stolen his vehicle. They didn't have to kill him. The victim's missing arm was even more disturbing.

I didn't want to think about the missing limb right now so I put this sadness in the same place I stored my hate and anger for Howard. He would pay for this too, I resolved as I stalked back to the truck, climbed into the driver's side, and waited for Will.

As the minutes ticked by, a few cars and semi-trailers passed our location in both directions. Silently, we leaned on Will truck as we waited for the team Henry had called to get to us.

The team was preceded by an RCMP cruiser which parked behind our truck. Will walked over and spoke with the officer. A white panel van tagged with the BC Coroners Service logo parked on the side of the road, The SPS crew had arrived.

I could see in the rear-view mirror that Will and the cop knew it too. Will nodded at the officer and walked back to the truck.

"Is the cop part of the team?" I asked as Will climbed in to the truck.

"Yes. Officer Stephen is part of our team."

I nodded and put the truck into gear. We drove past the abandoned vehicle and the three-person crew that emerged from the van.

We traveled in silence for a time.

"Henry is monitoring all the ferries. We don't have anything on Mullin, but the vehicle Insurance Corporation of BC's database has Howard on file. We have his photo ID," Will said, breaking the quiet. "With this new body, I'd say it is more likely they'll try to leave the island sooner rather than later."

It was getting on to early afternoon. "There are accessible cameras at each terminal. Henry should be able to spot him and give us a heads up. So, I guess we head to Nanaimo and the middle ground be-tween the ferry terminals."

"Sounds good," Will said, glancing over at me. what he saw in my expression. Whatever it was, he didn't comment on it. "We should probably grab some food."

"Probably," I agreed.

We drove the rest of the way in silence. I put my foot down with some vague hope that we would catch up to our escaped felons before they reached the ferry. But without knowing what type of vehicle to look for, it was a complete waste of fuel. Although it did make me feel better to have a solid goal.

As we got closer to Nanaimo, the landscape stretched out and the trees thinned. We had a wider horizon and a panoramic view of the coast.

Pale blue water sparkled under the November sun and made me flip down the visor to block some of the glare. It didn't matter to me how pretty the landscape was or how warm the temperature. All I wanted to do was find Howard and Mullin and put a stop to this horrific journey.

"That's the last ferry tonight," I said as we watched the Queen of Owen Sound depart. The massive white vessel carried hundreds of people and vehicles. It was bound for North Vancouver's Horseshoe Bay Terminal. It slowly and gently powered away from the ferry dock for the hour and a half trip across the Strait of Georgia.

The immense parking lot had been used to marshal hundreds of waiting vehicles. Now it was deserted. The workers in their orange traffic vests were closing the ter-minal down for the night.

description board any of the ferries up or down the coast. Or the navy blue Crown Victoria they stole," Will said as he dropped his phone back into his pocket. Henry had texted Will the plate and description of the stolen car about an hour earlier.

I zipped my jacket closed against the evening chill. "So, he's either much better at covering his tracks than I'm willing to give him credit for or leaving the island isn't his intention, at least not yet."

"You still think he's going back to the farm, to go after Raiway and Trennor?" Will was not convinced.

"Or Lasha. He still thinks she is the ruling alpha. He has a score to settle with all of them. What other motive could he have? I mean besides being a wacko?" I turned around and began walking to the truck. We had left it parked on the other side of the lot where the work crew kept their vehicles.

"I was afraid you were going to say that." Will sighed with resignation, falling into step next to me.

"It looks like you'll get to meet what's left of my "Should I bring gifts? Do they like steaks?"

"Don't be a smartass. By the way, you're insulting yourself along with me and every other shapeshifter." I knew he was using bad humor again to cover his disquiet.

"Mm, true."

"They're just people," I said as Will unlocked the truck and we climbed in.

"Sure, they are." He sounded derisive. "And so am I."

"Okay, a special type of people," I amended. "Yes, you have lots to learn, and they can help you with some of it. The VIC pack also has a mage."

"Are you kidding me?" Will asked a bit desperately. I noticed his white knuckled grip on the steering wheel. "You're pulling my leg, right?" He turned onto the Old Island Highway and stopped at the traffic light.

"Nope," I said as I met his eyes. "I told you we had to get you to a mage to check you out and teach you to shift. Jessica Raiway is their mage, and I'm sure she has lots of experience with stuff like this."

"Sure, why not?" Will sounded exasperated and re-signed. "Is it like going to see the wizard of Oz?" he asked flippantly.

I ignored his tone and put my left hand on his right thigh. He automatically covered it with his larger, warmer one. I was glad. Touch was important to our species, and it seemed to settle him down.

"Will, this morning you knew there were shapeshifters in the world, but you weren't one of them, you were a standard human. Now you know you're a shapeshifter. Your world view has to be affected by all this. Do you want to talk about it?"

He had to be feeling a bit overwhelmed.

Will compressed his lips. "Not right now. Let's just get there," he said. "I get that there's a lot I'm going to have to learn and, yeah, it's all a bit hard to take. At least some of it," he acknowledged. "But if Jessica Raiway can take away this nagging pain, I'm all for that. It's starting to piss me off because it's distracting me from the job at hand."

"All right, let me know when you want to discuss any of it." I settled back into my seat and dug out my phone. "I better call ahead and let Trennor know we're on our way."

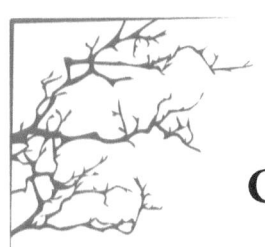

Chapter Eleven

We were met about two kilometers away from the farm. "Would this be part of the welcoming committee?"

Will and I were both looking at the large brown timber wolf with eyes that reflected the headlights' glow in an eerie way. The shifter ran along the left-hand side of Herd Road. The wolf was larger than average, even for a shapeshifter. I detected a trace of scent, a female.

"I would assume so." I watched her turn her head to-ward us, and her eyes glowed yellow. She ran across a field, taking a short cut to the farm no doubt.

The farm sign came up. -cut inset lettering and brightly painted. It proclaimed that this was the VI Valley Farm Group. It gave the farm store hours of operation with an arrow pointing the way.

We turned left onto the approach and passed between a set of square stone pillars that held the metal gate which was currently open for us. As we cleared the entrance, the wrought iron barrier closed automatically. We rattled across the cattle grate and passed a small wooden The gate and guard post hadn't been there the last time I was here, although that was some years ago. Things weren't all sunshine and roses for the VIC pack if they needed guard shacks.

We continued left. Right took you to the farm store, which was closed for the season.

Ahead we could see the large gray-stone main house. It was well lit up. The yard lights were blazing as well. It was nice that we were expected.

As we rolled up into the gravel parking lot I could see three people waiting. They stepped down from the porch and walked down the wide path to meet us. None of them were Lasha, my sister-in-law.

"Why do I get the feeling they are not real happy to see us?" Will said, turning off the ignition and releasing his seat belt.

"You can't blame them." I shrugged. "I've only been here once so most of them don't know me, and none of them have ever met you. This also isn't the happiest of occasions either."

"I suppose." He shut off the headlights while he watched me unbuckle my harness and stash my Kimber under the seat. "What are you doing?"

"It's impolite to bring firearms with silver into a I zipped up my jacket again. "Some shifters don't want to have anything to do with guns. For others, it's the silver and what it does to us." I smoothed the loose strand of hair back into my braid. I should have taken more trouble with my appearance, but I'd had more important things to worry about.

"How do you want to play this?" Will was watching the two men and one woman stroll toward the parking lot.

"Let me get out and introduce myself. If there's no trouble, join me." I reached for the door handle.

"To hell with that," Will said harshly. "We go He had cut his eyes to me, and I knew there was no way he'd let me do this alone.

He wasn't treating me like a professional. He was get-ting protective, like I was actually his mate. I had to cut him some slack, the mate-bond thing was driving him, and I was sure he didn't realize that.

"All right," I said. My logical side was a bit annoyed by this behavior. However my animal side, my cat, loved it. I was so messed up. The mate-bond was affecting me more than I thought.

We got out of the truck as the three shifters came to a halt in front it.

I looked at the tall, dark haired male, a wolf. "Are you Iain Trennor, alpha of the Vancouver Island Clan?"

"Yes, I am. You must be Heloise Cooper, Lasha's His green eyes were wel-coming.

"Please call me Helly," I said as Will came around the front of the truck and stood beside me. Close, beside me, I could feel the heat radiating off of him.

Will's stance inside my personal space caused Iain Trennor's black eyebrows to rise up a fraction. He knew Will was telegraphing he was my mate, but at least he refrained from commenting.

"This is my associate, Will Conall," I interjected before Will could speak.

Iain slowly offered his right hand to me. "Pleased to meet you, Helly." We shook hands.

"Alpha," I said, briefly dropping my eyes to acknowledge his rank and the fact this was his territory.

Trennor turned and acknowledged Will. "Mr. Conall."

Will, for his part, stared the alpha in the eye for a So I grabbed his right wrist and held it up at the same level as Trennor's. hand, Will. We are in his territory," I said pointedly.

Will blinked and seemed to come back to himself. "Nice to meet you, Alpha," he bit out and frowned, "We're here to help any way we can," he said a touch smoother.

He glanced at me and I deliberately dropped my eyes. Will copied me a fraction of a second later.

"Will is a bit new to the shifter culture," I said, looking back at the VIC alpha now that all the required forms had been met.

"I see," was all Trennor said to the information. He never broke Will's gaze as he gestured for his cohorts to come forward. Trennor's nose twitched, but again he didn't comment. I got the feeling he was amused by Will. Trennor introduced his people. "Lottie Fistbinder, head of pack security and Russell Bradley, her deputy."

Lottie stepped forward, and I remembered meeting her briefly at Julian's wedding. She had to be in her late twenties now. She was taller and more muscular than I remembered. Her long ebony hair was bound in a braid like mine, and her chocolate brown eyes missed nothing. Lottie had some First Nation blood in her background and a very firm handshake. I could feel rough calluses, no doubt from constantly running as a wolf. To the body, it was protection from the environment, not an injury. I suspected this was who had met us on the road earlier.

Russell Bradley was younger than Lottie with buzzed blond hair and alert amber eyes. He also had pale fair skin to Lottie's dusky brown. He was as tall as his boss, although leaner than her, and he vibrated with energy. He was getting to sit at the big people's table, and he was excited about it.

The situation with Howard could not be in any way typical or routine for these people. I hoped Lottie could keep the kid in line so he wouldn't get hurt. We weren't playing here. We were dealing with a couple of murder-ers.

After the handshakes, Trennor directed us forward, "Let's get out of the cold, shall we?" He led the way to the house.

I was relieved the hard part was over. I touched Will's wrist to get his attention as we walked side by side. "You probably aren't aware of it but you're broadcasting With flashing neon lights and a full marching band. This is Iain Trennor's territory, we don't want any trouble," I whispered and looked at Will meaningfully. It could always be tricky getting two alphas to meet Will nodded. "I get it. I need to watch myself closer." He took a cleansing breath and, with it, released some of the tension in his shoulders.

"You can dial it back up later." I gave him a wink. "It's kind of sexy."

Will rolled his eyes at me, but smiled back.

We followed Trennor up the steps with his security people bringing up the rear.

As we entered through the large double doors, I glanced around the foyer. I remembered most of it—the dark walnut wood floors and the oak paneling along the walls—from my first visit years ago.

The staircase, with its worn painted treads was the same, too. It wound its way up to a landing and on to the upper floors. A wolf resting on its haunches, with its head lifted like it was howling at the moon adorned the newel post. That was new.

The welcoming warmth of the house was enhanced with the fragrance of food cooking. I was immediately hungry. The prefab food we had picked up at the ferry terminal paled in comparison. With all the activity today, I had burned through those calories some time ago.

Iain Trennor brought us to a conference room. There was the wonderful smell of fresh hot coffee and ginger snap cookies.

"Help yourselves to refreshments. will join us shortly."

I poured a large mug and snagged a cookie before I dropped into a chair at the table and shed my coat. I had polished off my cookie before Lottie took a seat across from me with her own mug.

"I remember meeting you at Lasha and Julian's wed-ding," I said and sipped the excellent brew. I didn't know what was better, the heat or the flavor.

"Yeah, I was one of the servers at the reception. I re-member you as taller."

"I remember you as shorter," I replied, and we both smiled.

The door opened and a young female about five foot three entered. She had long auburn hair cascading down her back that reached her waist. Her bright hazel eyes passed over us and, even though she was hugely "Jess, this is Julian's sister, Helly Cooper."

I rose to shake the smaller woman's hand. Even if I hadn't known Jessica Raiway was a mage, I would have as soon as I touched her. There was significant power in this woman who was Trennor's wife, mate, and mother of his child.

"Alpha, Mage. Pleased to meet you," I said with a dip of my head to show I respected her positions, both of them.

"And you're Helly. May I call you Helly?" She had a soft smile but there was strength in her hazel eyes and in her handshake. My nose told me she was a wolf like most of the VIC pack.

I smiled back. "Of course."

She turned and looked at Will and he stepped forward.

I saw her nose twitch and the warm smile slid off her face. The female alpha's eyes opened wide as she stared at Will.

"Jess, this is Will Conall, Helly's associate," Iain He frowned, no doubt picking up his mate's dis-tress. He glanced at me and then Will, trying to determine the cause.

Will sensed something was wrong, by the way his eyes darted to me, then back to our hosts, but he held out his hand anyway. "Alpha." He glanced at me for a second time and continued, "Mage." And he dropped his eyes for a moment as I had.

Jessica Trennor stared hard at Will and, though she lifted her hand, she didn't touch Will's out stretched one right away. Her breath seemed to be coming a bit faster than normal and her eyes locked intently on Will.

Iain tensed and Lottie stood up. Everyone could feel the tension ratchet up, including me and I had no idea what had triggered it. What was it about Will the mage didn't like?

"Jess?" Iain asked uncertainly. His eyes narrowed. "What is it?"

She patted the arm that encircled her in a reassuring gesture. She never took her eyes off Will. "Are you named for your father?" she asked as she slowly took his extended hand.

"Yes, I guess so." Will raised his eyes to meet Jessica's gaze. He was a bit uncertain of the question. "If I ever meet him, I'll ask him." He always got a bit flippant when he was asked a personal question, especially by strangers.

Jess took in a long slow breath and released it, along with some of the tautness in her body. She locked eyes with Will. "My father's name is William Conall."

This was the second time in one day I had seen Will nonplussed and completely knocked off balance.

"What?" Will and Iain said at the same time.

Correction, both men were knocked off balance.

"And my nose tells me," Jess said. She gently stepped out of Trennor's embrace and advanced on Will. "You smell like family." She walked right up to him and placed her hand over his heart. She crinkled her nose and smiled. "And you're a cat." She was pleased by this knowledge. "I always thought we had some cat in our lineage."

"I think he's a cougar," I put in and Jess glanced my way. "Like me."

"You're not sure?" she asked, frowning and looking alternately at first me, and then Will.

"I didn't even know before today that I was a shapeshifter," Will said a bit desperately. He stepped back from her touch slowly. Maybe not to cause insult or maybe he thought she might pounce on him. His body language said Will was not comfortable with any of this.

I stepped closer to him and slid my arm through his. I didn't care about being too forward with him. His need for comfort touched me, and I knew I had to reassure him. Will in answer, folded his hand over mine.

"You think he's your brother?" Iain came up behind Jess and encircled her waist again. Staking his claim no doubt and demonstrating his protection.

"I know he's my brother. Well, more like my half-brother." Jess leaned back against Iain and tossed a smile over her shoulder at her protective mate. She seemed un-concerned now that she had figured it all out.

"Did you know your mother?" Will asked her I could hear a faint hope in his tone.

Jess's smile turned sad. "Yes, but she died when I was twelve. She was a non-shifter."

"Did you know our father?"

"No, sorry, I've never met him either. I guess we have that in common." Her eyes softened, taking in Will's dis-appointment.

He nodded, and I could see he was frustrated by her answer. Had he been hoping Jess's mother could tell him about his father?

"Well that's pretty cool!" Lottie said as she pulled out a chair for Jess. "Who knew you had a brother Jess?"

"Is it pretty cool you have a sister?" Jess asked Will.

"Uh, yeah," he said a bit hesitantly but recovered quickly. "It's going to take a little getting used to, though." He lowered himself into a chair next to the one I had taken.

"Don't take too long, you're going to be an uncle soon," Trennor remarked as he helped his wife into the chair Lottie had pulled out for her.

"I'll want to get your family tree details," Jess told Will. "Maybe we can figure out how we can have the same father and not know each other existed."

"I'd also like to find out how I can be a shapeshifter without knowing it," Will said.

Iain frowned at Will. "Come again?"

"All I know was I was experiencing some discomfort and Helly figured it out. She helped unlock that side of me," he said as the rest of us moved to take our places at the conference table.

"Part of that side of you," I interjected.

"Interesting," Jess said. "I can help you the rest of the way," she told him then turned and gave me a speculative look. "You and I are going to need to have a chat, too." She made the promise with a brief nod at me.

We were getting way off track. "I hate to break up this family reunion, but we have more pressing business to discuss. What are we going to do about Howard and Mullin?"

Lottie placed a mug of herbal tea in front of Jess and the alpha scowled at it, making Lottie snicker. "Have a cookie. It will make the tea go down easier." The last of the tension in the room dissipated.

Jess sighed and took a cookie off the plate. "I will be so glad to have caffeine in my diet again."

More people filed into the conference room and My sister-in-law looked much different than the last time I had seen her, of course. Her hair was still long and black but now with silver strands running through it. She had it gathered off her face in a tight pony tail, not one wisp was free.

She was much thinner than I remembered. Her cheek bones and chin were sharp. That was not something you saw much in shapeshifters. We liked our food. Her blue eyes drifted over me, then she looked away. Overall, she seemed fragile and brittle, not even a shadow of the alpha she had been.

," Iain said, and everyone took a seat.

I remembered these people from my first time here and, of course, from the files SPS had supplied.

Lasha regarded me warily across the table. We hadn't even shaken hands.

"Hello, Lasha," I said. I kept my tone neutral. I didn't bare my teeth at her or anything.

It helped that Will placed his hand on my thigh briefly and gave it a consoling squeeze. He knew I was angry with her. His touch underlined to me that I had to play it cool. I reminded myself I also had to keep my emotions on an even keel so I wouldn't upset Will's tenuous She had asked for my help, and I would give it, no matter what I thought of her.

"I'll go first," Iain offered, which surprised me.

Will and I were the visitors here and should be As an alpha, he didn't seem concerned with how he looked to us. But then, he was probably pretty confident in his place in the pecking order, which was at the top.

Iain outlined the precautions the pack had taken to He and Lottie had setup regular pa-trols. He'd communicated the threat Howard represented to all their people. "Lasha is probably under the greatest threat from Geoff. We've asked her to move back into a guest suite on farm property with Dylan, for the time Iain glanced at Lasha, and she nodded at this but didn't say anything. Clearly, she was comfortable with her new submissive role under Iain and Jess. "Lastly, no one goes out alone." Iain gave Jess a particularly hard look when he said this.

However, she ignored him completely and sipped her tea. "Patrols are a minimum of two people, one in animal form and one in human form at all times. This is to give them two ways to communicate back to the office here at the house," she added as she put down her mug

"How are they communicating?" Will asked.

"Radio," she said and gestured at the charging station to one side of the room. "Or mobile phone and, of course, a good howl in the valley travels a long way." She gave Will an amused look. He obviously wasn't expecting the latter part of her statement.

Will followed this up with what little information we had on Mullin and Howard. He included the homicide we had discovered on the highway outside of Nanaimo. "We don't have any intel on a ferry they could have taken. It's possible for them to have taken a smaller craft off the Is-land and headed to the States. US Customs is mostly concerned with drugs and contraband. Even so, all boat traffic that crosses the border is tracked by radar. Especially at night. Boats are expected to report in, or else Customs sends someone out to investigate the craft—if that's how Howard and Mullin left the Island. But there's been no report from US Customs or Border Services," Will explained.

"It's not likely Geoff Howard would have taken a small boat," Ben Case said. He used his left thumb to push his cap up to scratch a patch of gray hair. Ben was not as old as Guy, but I could sense he had spent a fair amount of time on this earth. Merely looking into his eyes told me that.

"Can you please elaborate?" I asked.

"Wolves don't like to cross the water in boats. Geoff Howard and this Mullin, I assume he is a wolf as well, wouldn't have used a small boat. They could handle go-ing across to the mainland on a larger vessel like a ferry. They wouldn't feel enclosed or trapped, but something smaller is out of the question."

"They would freak out." Lottie translated. "Something about crossing water in a boat is unsettling for some I got the feeling Lottie didn't include herself in that group.

Will nodded. "Good to know."

"Did you get a scent on this Mullin?" Iain asked me.

I frowned, remembering the stink. "Yes, but not a clear picture. It was a rank smell and not something I would have expected from a shifter wolf."

Jess was watching me closely. "What do you mean?"

I shrugged. "It didn't smell like wolf to me. It smelled like something bad, evil."

"It," Jess repeated as she studied me. She leaned back in her seat and pressed a hand to the small of her back.

Iain touched her arm. "What is it Jess?"

"I think I need to make some calls. My Spidey sense is tingling."
She slid her chair back so she could get up from the table and left,
closing the door behind her.

Lottie looked between her alpha and us. "So, what do we do now,
other than wait?"

"Not much." I shrugged. "Our office will let us know if they dig
up any more information that could be useful."

"Let's go back a bit." Guy crinkled his eyes and fur-rowed his
lined brow at Will and me. "What was the plate on the Toyota? Was
it a British Columbia plate?"

I nodded. "Yes, it was."

"And yet we don't know anything about this Mullin shapeshifter.
The VIC is comprised of members at the compound and the pack
members here. We can account for everyone." Guy tapped the table
with a thick "This Mullin is not one of ours."

"We don't know where he comes from," Will supplied. "I asked
the office to see if there was a Mullin in the Seattle pack, and they say
no."

"How about the Wild Rose Pack, could this Mullin come from
there?" Trudy asked.

"Negative, all the members with the surname Mullin or close to
it, were accounted for. According to our office," Will replied.

"This is troubling." Trudy's dark eyes met her husband's briefly
before looking at Iain. "Are there more shifters out there we don't
know about? Could Geoff have recruited more than Mullin?" Now
that her fears were voiced, Trudy folded her hands across her ample
lap. She sat back waiting for us to decide upon our next move.

"*Lottie, this is Katherine,*" a voice crackled over the radio receiver
on a table at the far end of the conference room.

Lottie got up and walked over to the radio receiver. She picked
up the mic. "I'm here Katherine."

"Our perimeter has been breached. We found a navy blue Crown Victoria parked half a kilometer from the north barn, Geoff was here and he left a message."

"We're on our way," Lottie said. She looked at Iain and he nodded.

Will and I stood. I wanted Will armed before we got close to Howard again so it made sense for us to take Will's truck.

"Russell, you stay with Jess and keep her safe," Iain ordered the younger wolf. "Remind her to activate the wards once we're gone."

"Will do." Russell nodded and then left the room. No doubt to track down his alpha. He was young but he obviously took his responsibilities seriously, and I liked him for it.

"Secure the house, Ben. Guy, Trudy, can you please contact the other patrols?"

"Yes, Alpha," Guy assured him, standing. "We've got this."

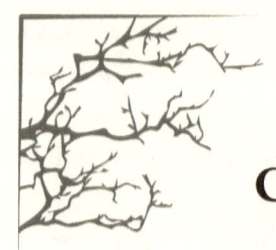

Chapter Twelve

Lasha hadn't suggested she would come with us, but then she did have a kid, so I cut her some slack on that one. But I knew I wouldn't have been able to sit around and wait for other people to take care of my problems.

We rolled up behind Iain's truck. Lottie and he had led the way, the half kilometer to the north barn. It appeared to be used to house farm equipment. I was glad there were no dead animals to worry about.

"I wonder what Howard's eating," I said as I shed my coat.

"I don't want to think about it," Will said as he took his 410 shotgun down from the rack. He removed the trigger guard and checked the weapon.

There was something to be said about a titanium pocket shotgun, especially when you used a 410 slug. That was a big piece of lead. It could take down a shifter wolf with no problem at all, particularly if you pumped several shells into the shifter.

"You saw the homicide victim was missing some parts," Will said. He strapped on his double barrel pistol. He was done playing and so was I.

"God, I hope there are no more bodies," I said.

"Henry would have called us if there were more re-ported."

We got out of the truck.

He frowned as he looked at me. "Are you planning on shifting?"

"If I have to, yeah." I was still wearing loose clothing from earlier in the day. It made shifting easier.

We moved up to where Iain and Lottie were talking to a younger female. She had blue-black hair and walnut-colored eyes, which made her Chinese heritage evident. Iain made quick introductions and let Katherine Choy continue her report.

"Silas found Geoff's scent," Katherine said to her al-pha. "He's doing a wider sweep right now and should be back in a minute. Here's the message we found." She turned on a flashlight and shone it over the side of the barn. In five-foot letters the message read: Come out and play Lasha and no one else will get hurt.

We walked closer and could see the message was burnt into the wooden siding of the building. It stank of the rank smell I thought of as "Mullin," and I could make out Howard's scent as well.

"That's it, that's Mullin's scent," I said.

"It's like nothing I've ever encountered before," Iain said solemnly. "I don't think it's a wolf."

A howl split through the air.

"Silas!" Katherine turned sharply toward the eerie call.

In seconds, Helly had shredded her clothes and shifted into her cougar form. Will felt the bond between them tighten. The link pulled hard on him as Helly shifted.

The urge to follow her was overwhelming, but he clamped down on it and resisted. He had no idea how he should attempt a shift on his own. Now was not the time to try it, not for his first time. Besides, he felt more comfortable with the shotgun.

Within a similar time frame, Iain had shifted to his wolf. He hadn't bothered to remove his sweats either, and his clothes shredded as he shifted. Instantaneously, an enormous gray and black wolf stood in front of Will. Then with the alpha in the lead, he and

Helly dashed off with a preternatural speed into the night toward the howl-ing.

It was not a pleasant sound. It was full of pain and fear. There was no way Will could follow on foot.

"Son of a bitch," Will bit off. He grabbed up Helly's weapon and strode back to his truck.

"No, come with me. I know the roads," Lottie said. She was already in the pack's truck with the engine running.

Will jumped into the passenger side and they were off. A second later, a sound in the truck box made Will snap his head around and bring up his weapon. It was the girl, Katherine. She rode low, hunched down in the box of the truck, and relayed information back to the house over her hand held radio.

Lottie's smirked at Will. "You're kinda jumpy, aren't you?"

"Funny."

"I try to be." Lottie sped up until she was only a few meters behind the wolf and cougar.

The predators ate up the road with lunges and long strides.

emotions startlingly stronger now. He was getting flashes of images.

"God, I hope so. I want to smear that little shit all over the scenery." Lottie took a hard left and trees whipped by. They had left the farm proper and were heading across a field.

"I think you'll have to take a number, Helly's got dibs."

"Heh, yeah, I guess she does. I'll take whatever's left." She stood on the brakes as the shifters cut to the side of the road and leaped a gate.

"Katherine!" Lottie shouted and the younger woman was over the side of the truck in a heartbeat. She hauled on the gate to swing it open for the half-ton.

They were through and Katherine stayed to close the gate. Lottie floored the truck's accelerator and the vehicle shot forward.

Will took a firm hold on his weapon and kept the He leaned for-ward, as the pickup raced through the night, trying to see beyond the truck's headlights.

Willows and brush scraped the sides of the truck. The bushes bounced off the mirrors as they moved along what was no better than an animal trail.

"There they are." Will pointed to the lighter flash of Helly's tawny coat in the fan of the headlights.

Lottie stood on the brakes again this time to stop and put the truck in park. There was a body on the trail. The wolf and the cougar paused beside it and looked back at them.

Lottie and Will got out and ran up to the nude male laying on his stomach in a dark puddle Will knew was blood.

"Silas." Lottie's voice quivered a bit. She leaned in past Iain's wolf and placed her fingers on a vein in his neck. "He's alive. Thank you, God," Lottie whispered and turned the young man over exposing the extent of his injuries.

Lottie sucked in air at what she saw, but didn't comment. Instead, she pulled off her sweatshirt to wrap it around Silas's midsection. The male was slashed from a hundred different cuts over his body. The worst was definitely his midsection. Will was sure he saw a bit of the kid's intestines drooping out of the gash before Lottie tied her shirt around the young male.

Iain and Helly were nosing around on either side of the path, now trying to regain the scent trail.

"He's gone," Will He felt Helly's anger and frustration.

He dropped to his knee to lay down his weapon and stripped off his coat. "Put this around the kid. He's going to bleed out if we don't get him to a hospital."

"We need to get him home." Lottie nodded her thanks at Will and wrapped up Howard's latest victim.

Iain shifted and walked over to Silas. "Get him to Jess. She'll take care of him."

"That's my plan." Lottie scooped up Silas like he weighed nothing.

"Silas?" Katherine's voice trembled as she came running over.

"Keep it together, Katherine, he needs you now," Iain said sharply.

Katherine swallowed and nodded then ran back to open the passenger side of the truck and slid in.

Lottie laid Silas across her lap. "Keep pressure here," Lottie said as she released him and closed the truck door. "Are you going to track him?" she asked as she moved around to the driver's side.

"Yes, maybe we can catch them," Iain's voice growled. There was a lot of anger being held in check right now.

Helly turned electric eyes on them and gold rolled over their depths. She let out a snarl and vanished into the bush. She had their scent.

Will was torn. He wanted to follow her but he knew he didn't have the speed to keep up, and he also didn't know the area.

Iain saw his dilemma. "You can't follow in that form. Go back with Lottie and tell Jess everything. She may be able to do something to tell us where they are headed. Geoff might have triggered one of her wards. You and Lottie can meet up with us."

"Where?" Lottie asked.

"Head toward Maple Bay road, I have a feeling he's running that way. Tell Russell to stay sharp. We don't know where Mullin is." Iain shifted back into his wolf and was gone.

Will cursed as Iain disappeared. He wanted to stay with Helly but he had to trust Trennor. It seemed Helly did.

Will turned and climbed up into the box of the half ton as Lottie threw the truck into reverse. They retraced their route. This time

Will took a turn opening the gate. They sped past the barn and were back at the house in minutes.

Jess was waiting on the front porch when they came to a gravel-flying stop in the parking lot.

Will opened the passenger door, picked Silas up from the front seat, and carried him into the house. Jess directed him down the hall to a room with a gurney, Lottie walked along with him. She kept her sweatshirt pressed tight against Silas's gaping wounds. Katherine trailed behind them, gingerly carrying Will's shotgun.

Will laid the young male on the gurney. Jess drew a sheet over his lower half. The sheet was instantly stained with his blood.

"Okay, let me see," Jess directed Will and grabbed his wrist in a surprisingly strong grip to urge him out of her way. She removed the coat and shirt and exposed the gaping slashes across Silas's body.

He had been right. Some of the boy's internal organs were slashed and exposed. Gut wounds were always the worst for pain and infection.

"We have to get him to a hospital. He needs surgery." Will tried to get them to see reason.

"I need you to step back and give me room," Jess said as she elbowed Will back out of the way and placed her bare hands on the boy's chest.

Will stumbled back, shocked at her attitude. The kid was going to die if they didn't do something soon.

"Just watch," Lottie said quietly as she plucked a scrub top from a shelf and pulled it on over her sports bra.

"Silas Xavier Johnson, you need to heal." Jess's voice vibrated with power, and her hands began to glow a pale blue. "Begin."

The kid's eyes fluttered, and Will could see the Slowly at first, the exposed intestines started to knit together. As the blue glow pulsed, the mending sped up.

Once the tissue was whole again, Jess slid it back into the open cavity. The skin that was in tatters began to realign and close over the wound as well. The mage then placed her hands over the area and, with eyes closed, she chanted quietly. Will couldn't make out the words.

The other gaping slashes over Silas's body closed too. After a moment, Jess stopped chanting and took a cleansing breath. "Sleep now, Silas." She straightened and turned.

"In a minute," she shushed him. "Katherine?" She looked back at the doorway where the younger female was hovering and shifting from foot to foot. Jess gestured for her to come forward.

"Yes, Alpha?" She maneuvered between Will and Lot-tie to reach Silas's bedside. As she passed Will, she held out his weapon, and he took his shotgun from her.

"Sit with Silas, please."

All that remained of the young man's wounds were some pink scars. Jess pulled a clean, starched sheet over her patient and reached for Katherine's hand. She wrapped Katherine's hand around Silas's limp one. "He's going to be fine, but when he wakes up, tell him he has to shift at least once to ensure there is no infection. I'll ask Trudy to bring you both some broth."

Katherine nodded, but her eyes never left Silas's face.

Jess ushered Lottie and Will out of the room. She closed the door behind them. "Let's go to my office. I want to know what happened and what you saw." Jess directed them down the hallway.

Will trailed behind the females. "Are we going to dis-cuss what just happened in there?" He jerked his thumb over his shoulder, gesturing to the room they had exited.

"What do you want to discuss?" Jess flicked on a light and held the door for the other two, closing it after they entered.

"How did you do that? What did you do?" Will was flummoxed by the events of the last few minutes.

"Hellooo, Mage here." Jess drew out the words almost singing them. "You've got a lot to learn."

"So people keep telling me," Will said with a bit of ill temper.

"Are there silver rounds in that weapon?" Jess waved at them to sit down, but Will was antsy to get going. He stood inside the door.

"Yes, inside the four-ten shells." Will realized he just broken protocol and was preparing himself to defend dragging the shotgun along with him into the house.

"Good," Jess nodded. "Geoff needs to be stopped, and we have to use whatever it takes."

Will blinked at his half-sister. He just might like this woman.

Lottie began to give Jess the run down, when there was a knock on the office door.

"Yes?" Jess answered.

The door opened and Lasha stood outside with a tiny, much older woman. She was dressed in a uniform gray from her hair down, to her cotton shirt and cardigan, trou-sers, and sensible shoes. A wooden crucifix on a black cord hung around her neck.

"Come in, Sister Ben, Lasha. You'll both want to hear this."

Jess quickly introduced Sister Benjimina and Will to each other. Will automatically pulled out a chair for the older woman. She perched on the edge of the seat and gave him a glowing smile. "Thank you."

Lasha went over to lean against the wall across from Jess.

Jess nodded at Lottie. "Geoff left a message for La-sha," the mage prompted.

Lottie glanced over at the former alpha before turning back to Jess. "The message said to send Lasha out to him and no one else would get hurt."

Jess bit her bottom lip in thought. "That's it?"

"Yes." Lottie shifted restlessly, too. "Iain said to meet him on Maple Bay Road. He thinks Geoff is heading that way."

"He also said to ask if you knew if Mullin or Howard had triggered any of your wards. Whatever that means," Will put in.

"No, I don't have any wards on the farm perimeter. There's too much traffic for them to be practical. I did ward the house but I haven't activated them yet. Is there anything else you can tell us?"

"The scent that is supposed to be Mullin." Lottie paused for a second to swallow. The information clearly bothered her. "Iain isn't sure it's even a shapeshifter."

"Did he say what he thought it was?" Sister Ben asked.

"No. But it is pungent."

"It smells wrong, evil. Like nothing I've ever encountered before," Will said from his position by the door, and four pairs of female eyes pinned him. He shrugged. "That's the vibe I get."

Sister Ben stood. "I'll need to see this message and check out Mullin's scent."

Jess stood as well and moved to the door. "I'll get Russell to take us over to the north barn."

"No, you won't, Alpha, you need to stay here." Lottie shook her head at the smaller woman. "Will and I can take Sister Ben out to the barn. stay here and watch your back. You know Iain will have my head if anything happens to you, we can't risk you."

As if hearing his name, Russell appeared in the door-way of Jess's office. "Guy suggests you activate the wards now, Alpha." Russell paused as he took in the rest of the room.

"That's an excellent idea, Jessica." Sister Ben gestured at Will. "Shall we go?"

Jess compressed her lips in resignation. "Fine, go, I'll set the wards." She waved them out of her office.

Will could see Jess was being managed by those closest to her. While she wasn't happy about it, he was glad that she wasn't arguing. He didn't want to see anything bad happen to this feisty woman. It didn't matter that he couldn't quite think of her as his sister yet.

Lottie led the way past Russell and down the hallway back to the main entrance with Sister Ben in the middle, and Will bringing up the rear.

A nun, they had a nun on their team, and nobody thought that was odd. Will merely shook his head and followed. It was an understatement to say he was bewildered about all that was going on.

The three of them passed a closet next to the front doors. Lottie paused to open it and tossed Will a rough jacket. She offered one to the senior in the group but Sis-ter Ben declined.

"I have my sweater, that's all I need. I create my own heat."

"You can do that with magic?" Lottie asked, donning a coat herself. They exited and quickly walked down the porch steps and to the truck.

"No child, with menopause."

Lottie snorted.

Will rolled his eyes.

Sister Ben waited for Will to open the passenger door of the truck. He offered his hand to help her step up on the running board and into the cab.

"Magic?" Will's eyebrows raised in surprise as he figured out the subtext of Lottie's words. "You're a mage too, like Jess?" He'd seen it all now, a magic nun.

"Yes, I am," Sister Ben said in a matter-of-fact tone. She settled in between Lottie and Will. "Are you all right, my son?" she asked, as the nun studied Will.

"I'm fine." Will exhaled and rubbed his eyes. "Could this day get any weirder?" He muttered to himself.

"Oh, probably," Sister Ben said with a nod. She frowned slightly at Will as Lottie started the truck. "Are you in pain, my son?" She grasped his arm in a surprisingly firm grip.

"Yes, Sister, I think it's something to do with the At least that's what I'm told."

"Ah," the nun said and closed her eyes briefly, still gripping Will's left arm.

There was a flash of warmth. Immediately he felt an easing of pressure in his chest and head as the pain And the weapon's barrel settled against the truck floor boards.

Will relaxed his shoulders. "Thank you, Sister."

It had to be the farther Helly traveled from him, the more discomfort he was experiencing. He didn't know what the nun had done, but he was grateful for the "Not at all," she said as she patted his arm.

They bumped along the gravel road the short distance back to the north barn. When they got there, Lottie parked. Sister Ben got out with Will's help and walked up to the barn.

She read the message burnt into the wood. Next, she briskly walked around the area, inhaling deeply and ex-haling.

It had only taken a few minutes, but the added delay, on top of the time they had spent in the infirmary, was making Will more restless. He was anxious to follow Helly.

Will knew his worry was unreasonable. Helly was more than capable of looking after herself and he sensed Iain Trennor would be good in a fight. But it didn't mat-ter. Will had an overpowering need to find her.

His link with her didn't broadcast any trouble. Still, he felt her elevated stress level and he needed to be there with her.

"Well?" Will asked. He couldn't help the impatient tone in his voice. "Do you see anything we missed?"

"Yes, a bit, but you wouldn't have seen it anyway. You would need Sight."

"Sight? What's that?" Will suspected it was something else he'd have to learn about.

"It's a mage thing," Lottie said. "They see deeper than us regular shapeshifters." Her hand gesture included Will.

He was taken off guard by Lottie casually including him in the group of regular shifters like her. It felt odd, but good.

"Okay then. But other than the fact that Howard wants to lure Lasha Cooper out so he can use her for a distraction. Which, I assume, is so he can get at Jess. What else do you see?"

It was Sister Ben's turn to raise her eyebrows at him in surprise. "Very good, William," she said and smiled at him.

"Hey, I'm not just a pretty face and this is not my first rodeo." He cocked one eyebrow at her use of his given name. When the nun said it, he felt like she had told him to sit up straight and eat his broccoli.

"You are right, I'm afraid. That's no doubt what Geoff Howard has planned." Sister Ben walked back to them. "This Mullin is another matter entirely."

"So, you don't think he's a shapeshifter either?" Lottie folded her arms across her chest. Will identified Lottie's action as the defensive move that it was. Lottie was un-comfortable.

"No, I don't think Mullin is even human," Sister Ben said as they bumped along. "Or even corporal."

"What do you mean?" Lottie asked as they climbed back into the farm truck for the return trip back to the house. "You think Mullin is Geoff's imaginary friend?"

"No." The older lady gave Lottie a grave look. "I think Mullin is an evil entity and has latched on to Geoff. I think it's driving him."

"Oh, yeah, now it's getting weirder." Lottie didn't look happy.

"You are saying Howard is possessed?" Will asked carefully as he tried to suppress his derision.

"Partly, but not against his will, I'm sure. You have to invite evil in. It may be more like once Mullin got a foot hold in Geoff Howard, it infected him. Like some para-sites take over their host. We should see if we can't catch up to the others."

They pulled up into farm yard.

"I'll take my truck and head toward Helly and Iain," Will informed Lottie as he got out and made for his vehicle. It took him only seconds to unhitch the trailer.

"I'll come with you," Sister Ben said abruptly, striding around to the passenger side of Will's Dodge. This time, she didn't wait for assistance to climb into the cab. It was a struggle for the tiny older woman, but she made it.

Lottie's jaw flexed. "Okay, I'll follow you. I assume you can sense Helly's location?"

"Yes, through that link thing we share," Will said. He shook his head at the strangeness of that statement. "Can you radio the house and let them know what we found?"

"I'm on it," Lottie called over the noise of the truck engines.

Instead of following the original path across the field, Will drove on past the house and down the driveway to reach the main road.

He glanced briefly over at the little nun next to him. She had her seat belt on and was watching the dark scenery pass by the windshield with a slight smile on her weathered features.

"Are you enjoying this?" he asked as he slowed for a turn and took Lakes Road east.

"Enjoy isn't actually the right word. Interested is more like it. It's nice to get out in the evening once in a while."

"Are you a shapeshifter, Sister?" Will asked as he turned the truck south-west.

"Why do you ask?"

"I'm confused as to how you are connected to the pack. They already have a mage, but they also have you. I wondered if you have a vested interest with the pack, like being a shapeshifter."

"I see," Sister Ben said.

Will glanced her way and he knew she was studying him. He got the feeling she was deciding how much to tell him.

"I'm a shapeshifter but I was raised old school. Back then, you chose your animal or chose your mage magic. There were, and still are relatively few mages. Anyone with magical potential is guided toward that calling. I wasn't typical mage material. I had another, higher calling."

"To become a nun?"

"To become a Sister of Charity," she corrected with a soft smile. "I'm originally from Alberta and the Wild Rose Pack. I was sent here to rest after helping to That was some time ago. I came in contact with the shapeshifters here, as well as some other local practitioners of magic." She paused and her brow puckered in a frown. "I realized there was a need for both callings, and I could help more people by using both. Now I work at keeping each in balance." She gave him the most angelic smile he had ever seen.

Will shook his head in wonderment. The magic thing was beyond incredible. But he'd seen it work. He felt it. But this was no time for that now. He turned his concentration to the pull of the binding he shared with Helly. She was frustrated right now, and her temper was rising. Not a good thing. Magic is a tool, nothing more, just leave it at that, he told himself.

They came to an intersection, and Will turned left onto Stanhope Road. It felt like the right direction. He was sure he would be able to find Helly at the end of this road. Right now, he wanted to find something that felt familiar. He needed an anchor. The farther they traveled down the road, the more certain he was Helly was his anchor.

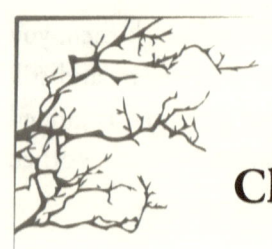

Chapter Thirteen

It was a dark evening. There was no moon which was a good thing. It would make it that much harder to see a wolf and a cougar circling the small lake. The water bordered a field that smelled like sheep and geese.

I was hungry, but I wasn't interested. That would be stealing. I also preferred my mutton and fowl cooked. , I'd had to hunt down my food in my cougar shape. However, I avoided doing that for the most part.

Without going into much detail, suffice it to say that the after taste, when I shifted back to human, wasn't my favorite thing.

We had covered a lot of ground, but we had lost I knew he was here somewhere, watching us and laughing. I could feel him, the bastard.

Once more I circled back, along the edge of the lake. I had taken the north side and Iain had taken the south to see if we could find Howard's scent again. It had led us this far but then disappeared. Something which should have been impossible.

I wanted to let a cougar scream go in frustration though I held it in. There were too many houses around us and people would hear. If residents suspected a cougar was in the neighborhood, the news would bring out the conservation officers. I had no time or patience for that right now.

Also, I could feel Will getting closer to our location. I also sensed his exasperation at something or someone close to him. I didn't think it was aimed at me.

Because of everything he'd been through today, I felt a bit guilty for abandoning him with people he didn't know in a situation completely out of his depth. But I knew Will could handle it. He was tough and flexible.

Thinking about him as I picked my way through the willows by the lake ignited a warm feeling inside me. As I moved closer to the road with no noise other than my own breathing, I felt the same answering warmth in Will.

I twitched my whiskers and raised my head. I scented Iain. He was coming along the opposite shore, and we'd meet up again shortly.

Headlights and heard the familiar rumble of the hemi engine grabbed my attention. I sprinted along the ditch and knew the wolf followed me.

"Thanks." I shivered as Will draped his borrowed coat around my shoulders. It smelled like Ben Case the farm's general manager.

"So, no sign of Howard?" Will asked. He stood so that he shielded me from the road.

Will kept his hands on my shoulders. When I looked up into his eyes, I saw how much he wanted to bundle me up and stuff me into the truck.

He had a leash on that impulse, which I was thankful for. I was sure he knew what would happen if he pulled any high-handed crap on me.

"No, we lost the scent at the lake. He's here some-where but we couldn't find him." I glanced behind me. Iain was still in his gray and black wolf form, and he paced in the ditch. "We should get back."

The farm truck with Lottie driving rolled up behind Will's. Iain padded over to it. He paused and stared at Lottie.

"Don't look at me. I didn't make the rules," Lottie ad-dressed Iain. "Either shift to human to ride inside or stay wolf and ride in the back, you're covered in mud."

He narrowed his eyes at her. Lottie shrugged, and Iain heaved a mighty sigh. .

"What?" I asked as I climbed into the driver's side and stepped over the console. I was leaving muddy footprints but there was no help for that.

Will sighed in exasperation. "We appear to have lost the nun."

"Say again?" I said a bit startled. That wasn't some-thing I would have never expected Will to say.

"Sister Ben was right there, a second ago." He pointed to the passenger seat I now occupied.

I caught movement in front of the truck hood. There was someone standing on the downward slope that led to the water. "Is that her?" I pointed at the tiny lady all dressed in gray. She was standing with her head tipped upward, sniffing the air like a shapeshifter.

Okay, then.

"Yep, that's her," Will confirmed. "Sister, are you finding something?" he called down to her.

She turned around, waved at us, and started walking back up the slope.

I frowned. "How'd I miss her? She slipped past me."

"She's a mage like Jess. It's probably part of the job description."

"I see," I said, looking across at Will. "This sounds like an interesting story."

Will gave me a pained look. "I'll tell you later," he promised.

When Sister Ben reached us, Will opened the door to the back seat and helped the wee lady clamber in. I could see he was impatient to get going. He was thinking about giving her a boost with his hand to her butt, when I shook my head at him.

"I think you go to hell for touching a nun's butt, Will." I had my eyes opened wide, and I was biting my lip to keep from laughing.

"Yes, you will," Sister Ben agreed as she got herself in and settled in the back seat.

"Funny." Will gave me a grimace. He closed the doors and and got behind the steering wheel.

He introduced us, and Sister Ben was kind enough to fill me in on her "evil possession" theory as we drove back to the farm.

"What, are you planning, an exorcism?" I was only half joking.

"No that wouldn't work, even if we could," Sister Ben shook her gray head at me. "I believe Geoff Howard more than welcomed this particular evil into his life. I sense no pain or regret. There is no suffering or anguish. He hasn't paid the price yet and he might not until the entity Mullin consumes him."

Will turned the truck once again up onto the farm driveway and the automatic gate closed behind us. "I still have trouble believing Mullin isn't a person."

"It's possible, no one has seen him. None of Howard's rag tag little band from the compound could give us a I dug my phone out of the cup holder and dialed the former alpha.

"What did you mean by paying the price?" Will asked the nun while I listened to the ringing on the other end.

"Everything has a price or a cost. If you ask for some-thing, you have to expect to settle up at some point. Evil is the worst for that. I fear Geoff has lost his soul or will soon, to pay the price."

"Will that kill him?" He parked the truck back in our original spot.

"Sometimes yes, sometimes no." The older woman shrugged. "It depends on which evil he asked for help. It also depends on the agenda of the entity. It could make him stronger."

"So, like what? A demon, the devil, or something else?" Will couldn't help but sound skeptical.

"Yes, or something that has nothing to do with the theological side. There are other evils, primitive ones, that are very ancient and just as nasty."

"You were right," Will said to her as he released his seat belt and got out to open her door again. "It got weirder."

We trooped up the steps to the front door and were met by Lottie. She and Iain had made it back a few minutes before us. They must have opened the gate and deactivated the wards to let us in.

"Do you want to grab your bags and I'll show you where you'll be staying?" Lottie asked

She and I waited for Will as he returned to the truck for our duffels. I was only dressed in his coat. So unless I wanted to provide some entertainment for these virtual strangers and a nun, I left the bags to Will.

We followed Lottie up the curving wooden staircase to the third floor. "Get cleaned up and meet us down in the kitchen for supper. We can share our information and ideas then. I'll want you to meet the other patrols too. In case you need to work with them."

She left us by the open door of a large high ceiling bedroom with a king-sized bed. The room was done in blues and pale greens with a white ceiling making the room feel open and airy. There were two cedar doors that opened off the bedroom. A medium sized bathroom and the other I assumed was a closet.

"Dibs on the shower," I said, not waiting for Will to answer. I was coated with mud, and I smelled like swamp. I figured he wouldn't argue the point.

Fifteen minutes later, I stepped into fresh underwear and felt much more alert. Eating would go a long way to recharging my batteries. I could smell roast chicken. I pulled on clean jeans and a black and white plaid flannel shirt. By this time my mouth was watering with the scent of food from the kitchen.

I finished dressing and pulled my wet hair up into a clip. Food was more important to me right now than my appearance.

"Are you showering?" I asked Will as I dropped my duffle by the closet door in the bedroom.

He was lying on the big bed with his boots off. He had his eyes closed. "No. I'm good for now. I'll shower He opened his whisky eyes and viewed me through black lashes.

I immediately thought about the last time I had seen him come out of the shower and what had happened after that. My skin grew warm and my body reacted.

Will studied me from the nest of pillows behind his head. "Is sharing a room going to be a problem?"

I knew what he was asking me. "Oh, I don't foresee any problems." I sauntered forward and gave him a slow suggestive smile.

"Good." He returned my smile in kind and for a few moments we let the heat we shared simmer to the surface. Our eyes were making promises I hoped we could keep. I was glad we were beyond the barriers he had erected A lot had happened to Will in the past twenty-four hours, and I knew he needed me to be his anchor.

I slid my hand into his, and he automatically grasped it so I could haul him off the bed.

Will was on his feet with one lithe movement. He pulled me against him, and his mouth came down hot and firm onto mine. This pulled a groan from me.

I pressed up against him and deepened our kiss. Will circled my waist with his hands and he nestled me closer against his hard body.

Both our heart beats accelerated, and I knew we had to stop before someone came looking for us. I broke the kiss and licked his bottom lip before looking up at his hooded eyes. "You have to feed me first though."

He gave an exaggerated sigh, and we dropped our hands reluctantly. Hopefully, things would quiet down tonight and I could honor my unvoiced promise.

We entered the kitchen a few minutes later. There was no dining room in the house as I remembered it. All meals were taken communally in the big kitchen at long tables where everyone could be together. Shapeshifters were big on sharing things as a group, and chief among those things was food.

Jess, Iain, and Lottie were already seated and sipping some iced drinks. Will sat down beside Jess on her right while I sat down on her left. It seemed this was how she wanted it. She smiled at each of us and offered to pour us some of the fruity punch from the pitcher in front of her.

"It's all fruit juice," she said as she filled my glass, let-ting a circle of orange drop in with some ice. "It's my sneaky way of getting everyone to consume more fruit."

"I like it," I said after a sip of the tangy beverage and nodded at her cleverness.

She noted Will's puzzlement. "Shifters love meat and have to be reminded to eat their fruits and vegetables, sometimes forcefully to stay healthy. In that way, we are actually not that different than standard humans."

Will glanced over at Iain across from him. "I don't know. There are some things only bacon can fix."

Iain saluted Will with his glass tumbler of juice. "That's exactly what I've been saying."

Jess opened her mouth, but Will cut her off. "Please don't say I have a lot to learn." He gave Jess a pleading look as he lifted his glass and sampled the drink. "This is good," he said and she gave him a pleased smile and let the bacon remark go.

Sister Ben entered the kitchen and sat down beside Lottie, across from me. That filled the sixth place setting so I assumed we were all here. There was still room at the long table but there were only place settings for us. It was late for dinner, past eight o'clock. Everyone else must have been fed already.

"Shall we?" Sister held out her hands and we all did the same to join them. She said Grace for us.

Immediately after, Trudy and a teenage girl that shared Trudy's dark eyes brought in platters of food. There was roast chicken and stuffing, bowls of turnip, carrots, and mashed potatoes. A pair of gravy boats were placed at either ends of the table. There were three kinds of pickles and warm fresh bread with butter. No way was anyone leaving this table hungry.

To close the meal was a bowl of romaine lettuce salad with beets and feta cheese. Salad at the end of the meal was something shifters did to cleanse their palates.

We ate uninterrupted for a few minutes, but there was so much information to share we needed to get started.

"How is the young kid who was wounded?" I asked Jess. I couldn't help but notice that Jess ate her food in the same way that Will did. One type at a time. Well if we needed further proof these two were related, this "Silas is okay," Jess said, spooning her second helping of mashed potatoes onto her plate. "He was cut up pretty bad, but everything healed all right for the first stage. I had him shift to ensure any infection was killed off. He's sleeping off the shifts in a guest room."

"Did he tell you anything about what happened?" Will passed Jess the gravy and she ladled it over her potatoes.

"He told me Geoff had struck out at him from of the fence line. That's where he got the slash across the gut. Geoff went to work on opening as much skin as he could. He sliced the kid to ribbons. Silas said he was powerless to stop it from happening."

I paused to look at Jess. "Did he say why he couldn't fight back?"

She kept her eyes on her food as she spoke. "He said Geoff grabbed him and held him off the ground. He said Geoff was huge and too strong. There was nothing Silas could do. He thinks Geoff had been merely toying with him. The bastard laughed as he slashed Silas again and again. He kept telling him to call for help. He told him 'call your alpha, get her to come and save you' then he'd laugh." Jess swallowed and placed her cutlery on the side of her plate. Her appetite seemed to have disappeared.

"Was Howard alone?" I asked and glanced at Sister Ben. We were both wondering about her evil entity theo-ry.

"Silas said as much." Jess nodded and picked up her glass for a sip. I got the feeling she wished there was something stronger in the punch.

Jess put her hand on her distended stomach and straightened her shoulders. "If there was a second person, Silas didn't see him. Although he did say there was more than Geoff's scent around him. He wondered if someone was in the shadows out of sight."

"I think it's an entity of some sort. It smelled wrong, tainted and evil." than the rest of us, however, she didn't shift or use magic as far as I knew. "Trust me when I say I know what evil smells like." Sister wiped her mouth with her napkin and put it beside her plate.

I felt now was a good time to share what I had gotten from the compound staff.

"I have some information about Mullin." I glanced first at Jess then over at her mate. At Iain's raised eye-brow, I continued. "I called the compound to find out if Mullin had been spotted by any of the staff."

"Was there anything new from the recaptured shift-ers?" Will asked.

I shook my head. "There was nothing. No one had seen anyone with Howard. Nor was there anything on their surveillance camera footage." I left out that I avoid-ed talking to George Mathieu. I didn't trust what his an-swers would be. I had spoken to Victor.

Sister Ben nodded, like she had been expecting this. "It's as I told you, Alpha," Sister said to Iain.

"It still doesn't prove Mullin isn't a person." another chicken wing off the platter. He placed his fork on the side of his plate as he picked it up with his fingers. "I have to admit I've seen some things today that wouldn't rule it out. I still have a problem with thinking a malevolent spirit is possessing Howard." He sank straight white teeth into the poultry.

"Some things you have to take on faith." Sister fixed Will with a look. "However, this time we don't have to. I've called a...for lack of a better word...an ally in our field." She met Jess's wide eyes and gave a slight nod.

"No," Jess groaned. "Please tell me we don't have to go there." She dropped her chin to her chest in a slouch of defeat.

"Yes, we have to go there," Sister said emphatically.

Iain frowned at his wife. "Where are you going?"

"To Miss Agnes." Jess sighed and raised her head to look at her husband. "She's a witch."

"Agnes Esme is a senior witch who knows all the types of resident evil in this part of the country. She also knows how to fight it, defeat it, or contain it. 'How to Contend with Evil' was her master's thesis." The nun nodded at Jess.

Will snorted in disbelief and dropped the chicken bone to his plate. "Are you kidding me? There are witches? Witches with master's degrees?"

Jess gave him a sharp look. , why can't there be witches?"

"All right then, I'll play along. What's the difference between witches and mages?" Will shot back at his half-sister.

I let a smile curve my lips as I met first Iain's and then Lottie's eyes with amusement. We knew how this was going to play out. Even if Jess and Will didn't appreciate the fact that they were sparking off each other, just like siblings.

"Mage's are more science based while witches are more earth based, to put it simply. with the big picture, while witches concentrate on the personal and immediate," Jess explained sounding completely reasonable. "The down side is a lot of them are...crazy."

"Crazy, how?" Will's tone implied he thought Jess had a boarding pass on the crazy train, too. He was agitating Jess now. It must be something brothers are born with. Julian used to do the same to me, and I felt a twinge of loss

Jess must have sensed her brother's goal, which was to annoy her, as she narrowed her eyes at him.

"They talk to inanimate objects and expect them to follow their orders." Sister Ben supplied as she wiped her mouth with her napkin.

"What she said." Jess jerked her thumb at the Sister. "They're also bossy and controlling."

Lottie and Iain shared a knowing look then turned their eyes down, finding their empty plates fascinating. Jess for her part, pretended not to see this shared amuse-ment.

"She's not crazy. Maybe a bit eccentric, but we still need Agnes Esme's help," Sister Ben said, giving first Jess and Will a stern look. "I called her and we're to go over first thing in the morning and talk to her about Mullin. I have a feeling he, or 'it,' is a local entity and, if so, Agnes will know what to do about it."

"Why can't we go tonight?" Will asked.

"There's no moon, so she won't be home. Don't ask." Sister said, forestalling further questions.

"All right, so we go visit Agnes Esme tomorrow morning." Iain handed his empty plate to the teenager and accepted a mug of coffee in return. "Thanks, Courtney."

"Sorry, love." Jess turned an apologetic smile on Iain. "Ladies only, at least until the start of the new moon. Helly, Sister, and I will go over."

Before Iain could speak, Lottie beat him to it.

"I'll drive you," Lottie offered, and Iain gave her a small nod of thanks. It was easy to see Iain didn't want his pregnant wife to be under protected.

Absently, I became aware that a boy around eleven or twelve was sitting quietly next to me. He had been stealthy and had slid in while the table was being cleared and then coffee and teapots had been set out.

I looked down at him, and bright blue eyes the same shade as Julian's looked back at me under a shock of jet black hair.

"Hi, Dylan," I said.

"Hi," the boy answered quietly. His posture was not great, he had his shoulders rolled in, and he slouched forward. I didn't know if this was from nervousness of me or if this was his regular bearing. nervousness, if anything he was excited.

"I'm your Aunt Helly," I said with an encouraging smile.

"Yeah, I know." If anything, his eyes got bigger, and he grinned at me.

"Did you want some supper?"

"No thanks, I ate with my mom."

"I'm willing to bet Dylan is here for some of Trudy's blackberry crumble," Iain said and gave the kid a raised eyebrow.

Iain's gesture made the kid sit up and straighten his shoulders, "Yes, please."

"Sounds intriguing," I said, and a dish of the dessert topped with a scoop of vanilla ice cream was placed in front of me. The ice cream was melting over the warm berries and filling. The scent of cinnamon and brown sugar made me pick up my spoon. I was lost in my own little world for a few minutes as I devoured the dessert.

Iain was discussing his concerns about wards on the north part of the farm with Sister Ben and Jess. Will and I sat absorbing it all when the side door opened and two new faces came in. Both young females were around twenty. They had jet back hair and walnut-colored eyes. They had the same dusky brown skin tone as Lottie and the same heart shaped face.

"Annie, Bonnie, come and meet our guests," Iain called them over as he stood.

"Hello," each girl said as they pushed their pink hood-ies down and shook hands with me and Will. They moved and spoke almost completely in sync. Identical twins, I thought.

"These are my sisters, also Fistbinders. They're taking the next four-hour shift on the south side," Lottie said as she got up and went over to a side table to pick up a metal clipboard.

She beckoned the girls, and they went over to the lunch counter. One added some food items and a thermos to a shoulder bag while the other disappeared into a side door.

Ben Case entered and Iain got up to speak with the farm manager. I heard the older man mention something about what to do with the car Geoff Howard had Dylan touched my arm gently. "Can I talk to you, He looked at me with serious eyes.

"Okay, sure, but I should help clean up first."

"I've got this. You go talk to the kid." Will gave me a raised eyebrow look. He was obviously curious to know what was going on, but he would wait to find out.

"Thanks. Thank you for supper, Trudy. and your crumble is amazing," I said as I got to my feet.

Trudy looked pleased "It's a pleasure to feed healthy appetites, unlike some." She gave her server Courtney a dirty look.

"I'm not changing my mind, I'm staying a vegetarian." Courtney picked up the dessert dishes and put them on a tray for removal.

"It's unnatural for a shapeshifter to be a vegetarian," Trudy said. She gathered dirty dishes and stacked them on a tray.

"Oh, Grandma." Courtney sighed as she continued to gather dishes. This sounded like an old argument.

Will stood and took the tray from Trudy. "Where do you want these?" he asked.

"This way please." Trudy led the way into the back of the kitchen and the dishwashing area.

The scraping of chairs announced others following to assist with the dishes. But when Will turned, only Jess was behind him.

"Hey, Trudy, we'll take care of the dishes. You outdid yourself. Let us finish up." Jess smiled at the older wom-an.

"Thank you, Alpha. I'll go make sure Guy is awake for his shift." She gave them a curious glance before she left through the kitchen side door.

Most of the prep and cooking dishes were already washed. dishwashers, and wiping down the counters left to do.

Will sensed Jess wanted some time alone with him so he waited as she chose her moment. He didn't have to wait long.

Jess glanced up at him a bit uncertainly. "I asked the others to give us some time to talk."

"Sure, I'd like to talk to you, too." Will gestured for them to take a seat at the small kitchen table that probably doubled as a food prep area.

Jess gave him a nod and sank into a wooden chair. She rested her elbows on the stainless steel table top. Will sat opposite to her and waited.

"This has to be weird for you. I know it is for me," she confessed.

"It is strange. I'm still finding it hard to believe we're related. But again, this whole day has been one He couldn't help but shake his head as he spoke. The day had been filled to the brim with strange.

Jess gave him a sheepish smile. "If you can give me your background, I can do some digging. This is driving me crazy that I didn't know about you."

"How could you have known? How could I have known? It's not like our father hung around." He rubbed the back of his neck. Thinking about his father unearthed feelings he would rather keep buried. Although, this was an opportunity to get some information, so he should take advantage of it. "Did your mother talk about William Co-nall?"

"Rarely." Jess shook her head. "I would ask for stories about him and my mother. How they met, where he was now. She always deflected." She raised her eyes to meet his. "I did piece together one bit of information. My mother was from Bonneville, about an hour or so south of Cold Lake. She was fostered with a couple that ran a farm, both non-shifters. She met my father when he was assigned to help take off the crop one fall. He was there only a few weeks and that was the last she saw of him."

Will could see the lack of information bothered her. "I know what it's like not knowing where you come from or who your people are," he said.

She gave him a sad smile. "Were you in foster care?"

"Yeah, I was under the care of standard humans. I thought I was a standard human, too." Will flipped his palm in a "whatever" gesture. "So, your mother was an orphan?"

"Yes, she never knew her parents. She tested high for mage abilities but she was never trained. She told me she agreed to move here to the VIC pack if they would accept me. She was expecting me before she came here. Apparently, George Mathieu agreed to her coming to the pack if, in exchange, I would be trained as their mage.

It worked out for me." Her smile deepened, and Will could see she was truly happy, especially when she placed a hand on her unborn child. She glowed.

"All I can tell you was my mother's name was Sara Smith, and we lived in Vancouver. name on my birth certificate. I don't know why. When I was not quite two years, old she passed away from some type of cancer. system because there were no other relatives to take me. I wasn't treated badly." This wasn't completely true, but he wasn't prepared to go into detail. "I just didn't belong to anyone," Will said in a matter-of-fact way, like it didn't still hurt. "I made the best of it and when I graduated high school, I enrolled in the military and that's when my life took a turn for the better." He allowed a grin to escape. "I was an army cadet at twelve and the day I joined that organization, I knew what I wanted to do."

"You wanted to serve our country?"

"Well, that altruistic goal came later. At twelve, I was attracted by the fact that the rules were the same for It didn't matter what your background was, where you went to school, or who your parents were. I knew I fit in."

"I'm glad."

"I also met Helly. That made it all worthwhile." Will paused, and then decided to go for it. If he couldn't ask Jess, who could he ask? "All my life I felt like there was something wrong with me. That there was a part of me I had to hide. Why didn't I know I was a shapeshifter? How could I not feel it?"

"I don't know." Jess placed her hands over his. "But we'll find out, and I will help you be the shapeshifter you were born to be."

Chapter Fourteen

Dylan beckoned me out into the foyer and down a hallway. by us and went to sit beside her sister.

"Trudy's right," Dylan said as we walked sided by side.

"Oh? How so?"

"Courtney faints all the time. She thinks she can get by on celery or something." Dylan shook his head in much the same way Trudy did. I bit back a smile.

Dylan led us in to the library. He turned on the lights as we entered the room. It smelled of old books, paper, and leather bindings. The shelves ran from floor to ceiling with one of those sliding ladders you see in the movies. I loved this room right off.

There were four rectangular tables, each with four chairs neatly tucked underneath.

"We do our homework here. It has the strongest Wi-Fi," Dylan explained and pulled out a chair at one of the four tables. He stood by it so I figured it was for me to take a seat. He must have seen some other male do this. It wasn't typical of any eleven-year-old.

"Thank you." I sat down and looked at Dylan as he took the seat across from me.

He gave me back a stern regard, like he was deciding something about me. "So, you're my dad's sister?" he asked, sounding uncertain.

It wasn't a question but I treated it like one anyway. I didn't have a lot of experience with kids so I would have to wing this.

"Yep," I said. "You're my nephew, my only living immediate family."

He frowned at this. "What about my mom?"

"She's not my blood, you are."

"Are you a wolf? You don't smell like a wolf."

"No, I'm a cougar." In a later stage of my life, that statement would have a double meaning, but not right now. I bit back the joke. I doubt the kid would get it.

He studied me for a bit longer.

Let's get this going, kid. "I heard you had some What was small talk with an eleven-year-old? I had no idea. when I was his age.

"Yeah, my science teacher drugged me. He wanted to change my blood." Dylan shrugged. "All shapeshifter's blood I guess. He was a real nut bar."

"What happened?"

"Jess and Iain took care of him. Sister Ben helped. They made him forget everything about us. He barely remembers my name now."

In actuality, I knew it was Sister Ben who had done the real work. But I was willing to bet Jess had learned how to perform that particular magic trick.

Trick was probably the wrong word but since I didn't know how mages referred to their services, it was good enough for me.

"That's good. Are you okay? Is your blood okay now?"

"Yeah," Dylan said as he pushed dark hair out of his eyes. "Jerry Greenwood checked it. He's a lab tech guy. Jerry's a lynx."

I wasn't sure what I was supposed to do with this in-formation. "You let me know if you think Foggle might give you trouble again, or anyone else," I said instead. I gave him a serious look so the kid would know I was "Okay, thanks," Dylan said. He seemed heartened about my offer to help him. "I need to ask you a "Shoot."

"Can you do a half form?"

"Yes."

"How big are you in your half form?"

"Around seven feet tall."

"Can you teach me? I want to learn to do my half form." His eyes were full of desperation.

"Why do you want to know how to shift to a half form?" I was stalling. How should I handle this? What would Lasha want me to say to him?

"I need to know so that if anybody ever tries to hurt me again, I'll be able to fight back." He closed his hands into fists.

"I'm sure your alphas and your mom will keep you safe." I tried to think of a logical recourse here.

Dylan shook his head solemnly at me. "No, she can't. She was the alpha when Jess got kidnapped by Mr. Fog-gle, but she fought back. Iain had to rescue her cause this was before she knew she could shift into a wolf."

I nodded. "I think I remember something about that."

"She should learn how to do her half form, too, then she can protect herself." He frowned as he thought this through. "Probably she'll have to wait till after she has the baby. But Iain can teach her."

I put my palms flat on the table. "Doesn't your mom have a half form?" I asked.

"No. Only Iain and Lottie, maybe Ben and Guy can manage a half form, but they're old, I bet they don't fight anymore."

I knew there were only two able shifters in this pack from my earlier conversation with Iain. That wasn't a lot of fighters for a pack of this size.

"Can I tell you something?"

I nodded. "Sure."

"I'm scared all the time and now that Geoff's back, he's gonna kill me, I know it." Now there were tears shimmering in those sky-blue eyes.

I went still. "Tell me about Geoff hurting you."

"He was in on the blood changing thing with Mr. Fog-gle. He had to get some of my blood so he stuck me with a needle. He thought I was out, unconscious, but it woke me up, and I started to scream, but he put his hand over my mouth. He told me if I told anyone, he'd kill me. and my arm was all bruised." Dylan swallowed and gold rolled over his eyes. I could see he couldn't talk, his throat had closed up, and he was frightened.

"Breathe Dylan," I murmured and took long slow breaths myself. The kid matched me and minute or so later, he seemed to have his control back. "Go on."

"I told Iain and Jess after Grampa took Geoff up north. But Geoff must have found out 'cause he's back to kill me."

I got up and pulled Dylan to his feet and into a hug. It was a sign of his distress that he let me. I leaned back and looked into his fearful eyes.

"Geoff isn't here to kill you," I said steadily. "He's here to cause trouble and make the pack make mistakes so that the public finds out. After that, he'll try and run away. That's how these things usually go." Not that I would explain how this thing would end for Howard.

"How do you know?" he asked weakly.

"It's what I do. I find people like Geoff and make sure they are punished."

"For your work?"

"Yes, Will and I help people." I kept it vague. I didn't know what Lasha had told him. I also didn't want to give him information that someone could squeeze out of him at some future date.

"Will you teach me?" The kid sounded so desperate.

"Yes," I said as I released the kid. "I'm going to help you. I'll teach you the art of half form, but it depends on how much magic you have. It also depends on what your belt level is in defense class. What do you take here, Kung Fu or karate?"

"Karate and I'm a green belt in Chito Ryu style and orange in Shotokan." His eyes were pleading with me.

"I'll make you a deal then."

"Okay?"

"My friend Will has recently found out he's a shapeshifter so he doesn't know how to shift very well. Will you help him practice once Jess gets him figured out?"

"Yes, I will! Anything you want!"

"Careful, you might regret saying that. cranky sometimes." I laughed and stepped back.

"I don't care, as long as I learn." Dylan was ecstatic. "You'll teach me to fight in half form too?" he asked.

My instincts told me someone was in the hallway out-side beyond the door. It had to be a pack member, and I could probably guess who it was, even before her scent drifted into the room.

"Before I promise that, you have to talk to your mom and your alphas. They have to agree."

"I will, and she will let me. So will Iain and Jess."

"I hope so."

"Dylan." We both turned to the door. Lasha stood barely inside the room. "It's time you went to your room to finish your homework. So you can get to bed at a de-cent hour."

Lasha kept her expression neutral as Dylan walked over to his mother. I assumed she'd heard our She must have been standing outside the open door for a while. She placed her hand on his shoulder and smiled at her son. Dylan was only a head shorter than his mother. He was going to be a tall man someday.

Lasha looked over at me but all she said was, "Good-night, Helly." Dylan echoed his mother and they headed up stairs.

I didn't know how Lasha felt about me teaching Dylan to develop his half form. She was good at hiding her thoughts and feelings. I hoped she would let me help the kid. He seemed to have some trauma left over from his incident last year. It wasn't like he would be allowed to talk to a therapist about it but I wondered what Jess had to say about Dylan.

I walked out of the library and paused when I heard my name. I looked down the hallway. Jess had her head stuck out of a doorway and she beckoned me.

Changing course, I turned and joined her in a room that was their infirmary. "You're the pack's medical re-source?" Jess was cleaning the room. She had latex gloves on and had just finished wiping down the immediate area. The room smelled of disinfectant. Even though shapeshifters can beat most infections, there are still some things we can't.

"Yes, for now. At least until the clinic is finished. It will be nice to have a proper facility to look after our people." She threw the bloodied sheets into a laundry bag. "We're building the facility across the road about half a kilometer from the farm."

"Sounds like a good idea," I said for something to say.

"I'm a registered nurse and I would prefer a separate facility for dealing with illness and broken bones. It will be nice to have a doctor again, too. We do have a lab tech in the pack as well, but the more help we can get the bet-ter."

"Jerry Greenwood?"

"Yes, how did you know?" Jess pulled off the latex gloves and trashed them.

"Dylan mentioned him. The kid wants me to teach him the art of half form." I watched Jess's expression. "He'll be coming to you and Iain to ask permission after he gets approval from his mother."

"Ah." Jess nodded. "That's probably a good thing. He needs to work through his fears. In fact, we could stand to have a few more people around here capable of the art of half form."

"He thinks you'll have to wait till the baby is born." I widened my eyes innocently at her.

"Perceptive kid," Jess said as she grinned. "Yes, I'd like to know how to pull off a half form. And yes, I'll wait till after the baby is born." She patted her tummy.

"How are you at delivering babies?" I looked down at Jess's well advanced pregnancy.

"There we have it covered. We have several midwives. Mine is Joan Rippley and she is only down the road from us."

"Where are you going to get a doctor? Especially one that knows about shapeshifters or maybe is a shapeshift-er?"

"I don't know yet, but I'm working on it. That's not what I wanted to talk to you about."

I leaned against the counter and folded my arms under my breasts. "Oh?"

"Will said you helped unlock him. Correct me if I'm wrong, but you're not a mage, are you?" Jess tied up the garbage and went to the sink beside me to wash her hands.

I shook my head. "No, I'm merely a shifter. I also don't think I unlocked Will. I merely made him realize what he is."

Jess looked at me with one raised eyebrow. "Were you ever tested for mage abilities?"

I blinked at that. "No, why? Do you think I should have been?"

"Yes, I do. Unlocking a shifter's ability is not some-thing just any shifter can do." She pushed loose strands of auburn hair off her face and tucked them into a barrette at the side of her head. "I couldn't do it for myself. I had to have Sister Ben unlock me."

"I'm not a mage. I admit I can do a few things other shifters can't, but I have no idea how to tap into creation energy." I decided now was as good a time as any to broach a related subject. "Could you do it now, if you had to? Unlock a shifter?"

"Probably," Jess shrugged.

"Good, because Will has no clue how to shift, and I think he needs to be guided through it a few times before he tries it on his own. He is kind of old to be shifting for the first time."

"Absolutely," Jess said and tipped her head at me. "I also wonder if there is something about him and me, maybe from our father that suppresses our animal side."

"Good question. Stress should have triggered Will's animal side a long time ago." I bit my lip and looked at Jess.

She gave me a steady stare. She knew I had more to say, and she was right.

"I think something is holding him back and I don't know what it is. I think you and maybe Sister Ben should have a look at him and at his magical reserve," I said.

Jess frowned at the concern in my tone.

"Yes, all right."

I relaxed my shoulders and uncrossed my arms to put a hand on Jess's shoulder. "I don't know what it is that's damming up his shifter magic but it's starting to fail. I think he's pushing through it, but he should have some instruction before he attempts to shift."

Jess nodded, "That's a good idea. Well, let's get this current disaster resolved then we can deal with Will's issues."

"Thanks." I smiled. I was surprised at how much of a relief it was to tell this woman my fears about Will. Clearly, I needed to be in a pack of some kind again. It was good to have someone to confide in. "Do you want me to help you with the trash and the laundry bag?"

"No, no. I have help coming, but thanks. I wanted to stay busy while Iain is out on patrol. I can't sleep when he isn't with me. I think Will is planning on going out, too, and I'm guessing you will want to accompany him."

"Yes, I do." I released Jess's shoulder and headed back down the hallway to the kitchen.

Iain was dressed for outdoors and a huge sable brown wolf sat at his feet. Her tongue lulled between brilliant white teeth, and she seemed to give me a grin.

"Going out?" I asked Iain.

"Yes, Lottie and I are taking a patrol shift on the north side. I want to walk the area Geoff penetrated and see where he came in." The alpha zipped up his coat. It was patterned with trees and leaves like a lot of hunting gear people wore now.

"You're also hoping he tries to come in again," I guessed as I tucked my hand in the top of my jean pock-ets and cocked one hip.

"You could be right." Iain gave me a smile that showed a lot of teeth. It wasn't a nice smile.

"Can we take a shift?" It didn't feel right sitting around while others were defending us or tracking the threat.

Iain tipped his chin at the stairs. "Will already

I looked over my shoulder to see Will coming down with my coat and boots. ," he said, handing me my gear. "Iain gave us a map of the area."

"That sounds good to me." I pulled on my hiking boots, quickly tied them, and put on my coat.

"Take this to ward off the cold." Trudy handed me a shoulder bag that smelled like coffee and a tempting snack or two. "I can't imagine Geoff coming back here tonight. He must be spent." Trudy looked over at her al-pha. "But if he does, I hope he doesn't leave. Katherine told me what he did to Silas."

"We'll take care of it." Iain gave the older lady a firm nod.

We stopped by Will's truck and retrieved our arms and ammo.

"Do you have a problem with us keeping these Will asked Iain.

Iain's nose twitched. "Silver, good. problem with you keeping your weapons handy, and thanks for this. I know you have a personal stake, Helly, but this is our mess to clean up. Howard last year. I see that now." Iain turned away and headed north with Lottie trotting at his side.

"Not everyone can make that type of judgement and carry it out." Will slid his box of ammo into his coat pocket as he watched the alpha and the wolf disappear into the shadows.

"I think Iain could if he had to, but I don't want him to have to." I looked up at Will. "I want these people to be happy and not carry any of the ill effects of dealing with Howard."

"Exactly," Will agreed.

We followed the trail we were shown and walked We came across the current patrol team. We were met by a black and white wolf with Arctic blue eyes. He looked more like a husky than a wolf. He inhaled our scent. Turned, and trotted down the trail until we reached a man with ginger hair and amused green eyes.

"Jerry Greenwood." He introduced himself. "You must be Will Conall, Jess's brother." Jerry grinned at him as they shook hands.

"So I'm told," Will said. I got the feeling he didn't "Helly Cooper," I said as I shook the other man's hand. "Dylan told me a bit about you," I said.

"Any of it good?"

"Oh yes," I smiled.

"Did he tell you my secret identity is head of "No," I said. Jerry was a bit of a character.

"This magnificent beast is my husband Clarence Strong." He waved a hand at the wolf. The wolf huffed out a sigh.

Will and I acknowledged Clarence with a nod. He waved a black paw at us.

"Oh, yes, you're Julian's sister." Jerry brightened as he placed my relationship to the pack.

"Yes, I am." I couldn't help but smile at Jerry. There was something about his personality that made you "You don't look anything like him. You don't smell like him either."

"That's probably because I'm not a wolf." I could sense Will was getting impatient.

"Do you have anything to report?" Will asked. "Have you seen anything out of the ordinary?"

"No. It's been quiet since early evening. I understand Silas was attacked."

"Yes, we chased Howard to the small lake south of here, but we lost his trail," I said.

"It's called Quamichan Lake," Jerry supplied then frowned. "Why would he go there? Unless he plans on hiding in the Garry Oaks Preserve maybe. It's not open to the public." He shook his head and handed his radio to Will. "Are you ready, Clarence?" Jerry asked the wolf."

Clarence yipped a reply, turned, and trotted back down the trail.

"Have fun kids." Jerry waved at us as he followed Clarence.

It didn't make sense for me to shift for the patrol. I can't howl if I see anything, and anyway, we had weapon which had silver laced rounds. They were all we needed.

The crisp, clear November night smelled of wood smoke as it drifted over the area. About a billion stars were out and, while there was still no moon, we had no problem seeing the landscape around us.

The rolling forested hills dropped down into the flat bottomed valley. The neighboring farms and acreages spread out before us. , Jerry Greenwood had called it.

The lake was in the shadow of a mountain that loomed like a wall over the whole valley. I could see the lights of a suburb resting on the north face. I doubted Howard and Mullin were hiding on a mountain that contained so many people. I had a feeling they hadn't gone far, though, and we would be encountering them again fairly soon.

We covered our assigned area and met back at a large rock to share our picnic lunch.

"We never ate this good in the field." Will sank his teeth into a thick chicken sandwich.

I made agreeing sounds as I munched my own We were sipping coffee and nibbling the best Nanaimo bars I had ever tasted when Will asked about Dylan.

"He wants me to teach him the art of half form," I said. "He's scared, poor kid, and who can blame him? A lot of crap has happened to him in the past couple years. It would make anyone worry about their safety and that of their pack." I licked chocolate and custard residue from my fingers.

"I bet," Will said. "Are you going to teach him?"

"Yes. After he gets permission, I need to figure out how to schedule it in if I'm going back to work with you." From the wide grin Will gave me, I knew that agreeing to return to SPS with him was welcome news.

We patrolled the perimeter of our assigned area for the full four hour shift. It was just as well we had taken on the task. There was no way I could have gone to bed knowing the rest of the pack were taking turns guarding us. I knew Will felt the same.

While the shapeshifters had stayed in pairs, Will and I had broken up to cover more ground. We each had more than enough experience. And we were confident we knew how to handle anything that came out of the shadows.

I had a feeling Trudy was right though, and we had seen all we were going to see of Howard for the time It had been a long day for all of us.

By the time we were relieved by Ben Case and a glossy black male wolf named Isaac, we were ready to call it a night.

We handed off our radio and followed the track back to the house.

All was quiet when we walked up the porch steps. There was a faint green and gold glow that seemed to ra-diate from the actual stones of the building. I guessed this was Jess's ward. I glanced at Will to see if he had any reaction.

"Do you see anything different? Do you feel any-thing?" I paused with my hand on the black iron handle of the front door.

Will stopped as well and breathed in then shook his head. "I feel something in the air, like it's electronically charged or something, but that's it. What do you feel?"

"Jess has activated the ward on the house. Let's see if we can pass through it."

I pushed the latch and the door swung open for us. So far so good. I stepped through and Will followed me with no adverse effects other than every hair on my body standing on end.

I shivered.

"I guess it's okay." Will closed the door and we turned to meet the barrel of a shotgun.

"Hello there." Guy Tremblay dropped the barrel to the floor and let the gun slide down to the crook of his arm. His dark brown eyes were hooded by his wrinkled, time-worn features. But there was definite mischief in their depths. "I'm only making sure you're pack. How did it go, see anything?"

"Not a thing," Will said evenly. He narrowed his eyes at the older man.

"Well, that's good and bad, I guess. Here let me take that from you."

I handed him the thermos and bag Trudy had given us earlier. "I'll rinse this out, you kids get some rest. will be a busy day again." The older man shuffled off toward the kitchen.

Will grinned. "Old bugger."

I shook my head and we headed up stairs.

We stowed our weapons on a spare blanket on top of the dresser. This made them easy to grab if necessary.

"I'm first in the shower." Will suddenly seemed in a hurry to get clean.

I smiled as I stripped down to my underwear. Grabbed my toiletry bag, and headed in to the bathroom as the shower started.

Will's large frame moved behind the shower curtain. Even though it was after one o'clock in the morning, knowing Will was naked only a few feet away, warmed me. I felt invigorated and motivated.

With a small smile, I completed my ablutions and left the bathroom, stripped completely, and climbed into the huge bed. I relaxed between clean cotton sheets that were faintly scented with lavender. My time at SPS ensured that I never lost my appreciation for clean, dry sheets and hot running water.

The door opened, and I waited, lying on my side away from the center of the bed. The bed dipped, and I felt the mattress take Will's weight. He slid in next to me, and I could feel the heat radiating off his body. I waited a bit more to see if he would take the initiative.

I was gathering myself to turnover when I felt his touch on my shoulder. His fingers glided down my bare back, over my hip to my thigh, and back up again. He moved slowly and his touch pulled a sigh of pleasure out of me.

With a smile of anticipation, I rolled over and looked up at him. We could see each other's need so clearly. The walls were all down between us in the dark. I hoped they would stay that way but there were no guarantees, since there were no promises between us. For now, I didn't care.

Will leaned down and his firm warm lips met mine. If he had planned to go slow, as soon as our lips met, that plan was shot.

I arched against him and my naked breasts came into contact with his chest. I opened my mouth and accepted his tongue and its exploration greedily. That pulled a groan out of him. His hands tightened on me. We grasped each other and came together like we hadn't seen each other in weeks.

Will was on top, resting his weight on his elbows and knees, probably from habit. I bit his bottom lip and pulled him down fully on top of me so I could feel the heat and the evidence of his need. "Shifter girl, remember. I'm much sturdier than you're used to, don't hold back," I whispered against his mouth.

"I wasn't sure." He nipped my neck with his teeth. "Tell me what you want."

"I think you know what I want." I breathed in sharply as he touched me intimately. "Oh, yes, you do."

He chuckled deeply and there was no more time for words, only actions and ecstasy.

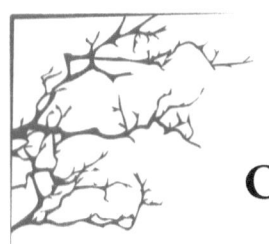

Chapter Fifteen

Breakfast started early at the farm, and I was all right with that. than ever to get our relationship solidified. Waking up with my head on his chest and his arms around me was a new bliss. I should have been in a more sedate mood, but I hated sitting around.

If it were up to me, I would have already spoken to this Agnes Esme and been back on Howard's trail. But I wasn't in charge, so I had to move at the same pace as the pack's pregnant alpha and an elderly nun.

Will had gone off with Iain already. The males had decided to back track to Quamichan Lake to see if they could pick up the trail again. In the morning light, they could maybe see something that would show them where Howard had gone.

None of us said it, but we all knew it was necessary for the alphas to do something. He, along with Jess, had to look confident and be seen controlling the situation, to ensure the pack would remain calm and trust their leaders.

Earlier, I had checked in with Henry and there was still nothing new on Howard's movements. He had to be in this region and it was only a matter of time before he'd try to get at Lasha again. Or maybe at Jess, who I knew Iain felt was Howard's real target, although I wasn't completely convinced of that myself.

I told Henry about the Crown Vic that was found on the property that belonged to Howard's roadside victim. SPS was sending a flatbed for it.

Lottie and I were waiting, beside a gray Honda four-door sedan, for Jess and Sister Ben. It was after breakfast and I was antsy to get going, but pregnant bladders must be seen to.

The head of pack security was going to play chauffeur and body guard for Jess to keep Iain appeased. about Jess and the baby, and rightly so, with Howard and Mullin on the loose.

"Finally," Lottie said under her breath. members of our quartet materialized. She opened the front passenger door and I opened the rear and got in. I left the front seat for the alpha.

Jess surprised me by climbing in the back and leaving the front for Sister Ben. Age before authority, I guessed. However, Sister Ben was no doubt the more senior mage.

"Mm, what's that smell?" I asked, buckling in.

"I have a basket of muffins as a bribe for Agnes Esme." Sister Ben balanced it on her lap as she got settled in the front. "Agnes and I go back a long way, and we haven't always been the best of friends. Well, all right. To be honest, we have never actually been friends, but we usually have the same goals. Although, at times, our methods have put us on different paths."

"I hope there won't be any fireworks." Jess sighed as she straightened her green cotton maternity dress around her. I didn't know what that meant, but it couldn't be good.

"I can't promise," Sister Ben replied. be best if I spoke to her first and if everything appears safe, you three join me." She clasped her wooden crucifix between wrinkled worn hands, stroking it absently.

We drove down Herd Road, and Jess pointed out the packs clinic construction site. The building looked Continuing on, we drove a few more kilometers through the village of Maple Bay and looped around on to the road with the same name.

At the stop sign, I looked left and took in the sun dap-pled waters of the bay. The shape of Mount Maxwell loomed across the mouth of Maple Bay and was reflected in the calm water. It was a shame we couldn't take some time to enjoy any of the area. Hopefully, that would change when this crisis was resolved.

Minutes later, Lottie was pulling into the long gravel driveway of a white clapboard house. The slate roof was covered with brilliant green moss. A massive Garry oak tree stood sentinel out front.

As trees went, Garry oaks were not the stateliest or most attractive of trees. And yet, their twisted shapes and claw-looking branches had a certain attitude. The air about them captured the imagination. If I was a witch, I would have these oaks surrounding my house, too. They definitely created the right atmosphere.

In addition to the trees, another interesting feature caught my eye. The amount and variety of gnomes the yard contained. There had to be over a hundred of them in and amongst the flowers and shrubs.

"That's a lot of gnomes." I said weakly. I was trying not to laugh at the multi-colored plaster figures. There were gardening gnomes, sleeping gnomes, wood cutting, and dancing gnomes. One was reading, another flower arranging, two were kissing. And several gnomes were playing football. There appeared to be a lot more of the football gnomes. All dressed in green and white, each one had a unique number on their jersey.

"Yeah," Lottie agreed, putting the car into park. "It's freaky as hell."

"Hang on to these for the moment please." Sister Ben handed Lottie her muffin basket. "I might need both hands free."

Jess and I exchanged a wide-eyed look.

We got out and stood back by the vehicle to allow "Why do you think Miss Agnes has so many football gnomes?" Jess commented.

Lottie shrugged. "Maybe she likes to run plays in the front yard?"

"Is it me, or do the eyes follow you?" of the wee garden ornaments was creepy.

"Freaky," Lottie agreed.

Sister Ben hadn't quite made it across the yard when a tall raw-boned woman appeared. in black with steel gray hair pulled back into a tight bun. She seemed to have materialized out of no-where. She stopped to stand beside the oak tree.

For her part, Sister Ben didn't appear startled by the taller woman. She turned toward her. "Agnes."

"Benjimina," Miss Agnes said, acknowledging her nemesis across the open space.

They glared at each other with a steely regard. . The tension between the witch and the mage was palatable. I held my breath. If both magic users let loose, it could be Armageddon.

After a moment, something must have changed. Agnes sniffed disdainfully, "I've got a fresh pot of tea on the table." At no time did she break eye contact.

"Loose or bags?" Benjimina countered.

"Loose, of course, what do you take me for?" Agnes snapped back.

"I've got fresh blackberry muffins." After a second, she added, "With bran."

That fact seemed to be important as Agnes nodded with satisfaction. "Bring them over, and I'll slice a lemon for the tea."

Sister Ben nodded and waved at us to come over as Agnes disappeared behind the huge oak tree.

"Well, that wasn't what I was expecting," I said as I raised my eyebrows at Jess and Lottie.

"Me neither," said Lottie.

"Very anticlimactic," agreed Jess. "Shall we, ladies?" She waved us forward.

We trailed after Sister Ben and saw there was a gate to the back garden behind the oak. In the garden, there was a hexagonal cedar table. It was laid out with a table cloth embroidered with orange roses. A tea party outside, in November. We were lucky the weather was playing along.

A silver tea service and five China cups, again, with orange roses and matching linen napkins, was laid out. It appeared that Miss Agnes had pulled out all the stops for this visit by her adversary.

Jess and I shared a look, although neither of us said anything.

I got the feeling Agnes and Sister Ben were actually not really at odds with each other as much as Sister Ben had claimed. Or maybe the years had mellowed them.

Sister Ben introduced each of us to Agnes Esme. As the witch shook our hands, she told us to call her Miss Agnes.

Lottie passed Miss Agnes the basket. She opened it with a pleased sigh then placed it on the tablecloth. the basket to her liking, she added a set of silver tongs for serving.

We seated ourselves at Agnes's invitation, and she poured the tea. "So." Agnes raised her eye brows and looked expectantly at Sister Ben.

"We need to ask you about the containment." Sister Ben sipped her tea.

"What about it?"

"Is Immundus still bound?"

"Oh, yes. He's still trussed up tight as a mummy."

Jess frowned at Sister Ben. "Who's Immundus?"

"He's a demon," Agnes answered before Sister Ben could put down her cup to speak.

My jaw dropped and Lottie's cup clattered to her "A what?" I said.

Sister Ben sighed and held up a hand to us, fore-stalling any further comments. "Let's leave the questions until the end, please." She turned back to Miss Agnes. "I didn't want to have to drag the pack into this if I didn't have to."

"Well, from what I hear, it's long past time to explain things to them." Agnes looked down her long nose at the other senior.

"Just what are you implying?" The nun demanded.

"I'm not implying anything. I'm saying you need to tell the pack or at least their alphas about the risks." nodded at Jess. "They need to know exactly what they have been exposed to all these years. won't benefit anyone or anything. At least not now."

Sister Ben breathed in through her nose and narrowed her eyes at the other woman. "Agnes, stop beating around the bush, what's changed?"

"I think something got out," Miss Agnes mumbled into her tea cup.

Sister Ben sat back and covered her eyes with "What do you mean by something got out?" Sister Ben asked in a patient tone one reserved for difficult children as she dropped her hands.

"The gnomes tell me something has escaped and it's been burning my oak trees. The incidents occurred Only once every couple of months or so. I think as the entity grew in strength, it increased the burnings up to one tree at least once a week for the past six months." She finally met Sister Ben's gaze. "I don't know what it is, but it's making headway in trying to re-lease Immundus."

"Burning the trees destroys the bindings." Sister Ben rubbed her forehead in frustration.

"Yes, thank you, Benny, I had figured that part out," Agnes agreed dryly. "Have you been to the Butter Church?"

"Not lately, why?"

"There's been significant damage. Someone is knock-ing down the walls. I think they hope to remove that The nun frowned. "The Butter Church, the Garry Oaks Preserve, what about the Cross?"

"Last time I was up on Mount Tzouhalem, the Cross was fine. It's been replaced with a metal one and the Cross has been blessed. It's right on the main hiking trail so there is lots of traffic. But it wouldn't hurt for you to have a go at it, too," Miss Agnes advised.

"That leaves Mount Maxwell, Paddy's Mill Stone, the sentinel at Octopus Point, and Saint Anne's church."

"Shyla keeps an eye on the Stone and the Point. Eve-rything is as it should be at those two locations. So that leads me to believe it can't go either through or over the water. Maxwell should be fine as well."

"Who's Shyla?" I asked Jess quietly.

"Shyla McTavish, she's a selkie, a sea lion shapeshifter. She's one of ours," Jess replied just as quietly.

"What about Saint Anne's? That's my parish." Lottie asked, ignoring the "let the adults talk" look the older women gave her.

"Saint Anne's is fine, too, there's been no trouble there, yet." Agnes passed around the muffin basket along with butter and jam.

"Saint Anne's is the most powerful anchor. It would be the last to be affected." Sister Ben sat back again, sucking air through her teeth as she thought.

I decided I was done waiting for them to explain to us in their own time. "Would the name Mullin mean any-thing to you?" I asked Agnes Esme.

"Yes." She cut her gaze in my direction and I was lieutenants, a helper of sorts," she clarified for us.

"He or it," I said.

Agnes gestured for me to go on. "What do you know?"

"Mullin is with Geoff Howard. Howard escaped from the compound up north a couple days ago. He killed one person there and wounded several others. He killed an-other person on the way down here and mauled one of the pack's wolves once he did get here."

"He's now demanding the pack to let him have Lasha Cooper, and no one else will get hurt." Jess added.

Miss Agnes nodded. "Mullin would use the pain and deaths to increase its power."

I drew out my phone and flipped through the pictures until I found the one I wanted. "This is the holding cell where Howard was kept." I showed Jess again. She and Lottie had seen it at the initial meeting, but I knew my manners.

I turned it to face Sister Ben and Agnes Esme. Sister Ben leaned forward. pocket and perched them on her nose. She didn't touch the phone but leaned in close to view the image.

"He broke through this double reinforced metal. It's a silver and steel alloy and he was also wearing silver George Mathieu told us he tore them off and broke out of his cell. Both are things that he shouldn't have been able to accomplish, at least not with the level of silver involved." I put the phone down on the table and leaned forward. "Would this Mullin be able to help Howard with any of this?"

"Yes, most likely." Agnes tucked her glasses away. "That building is touching the ground, which means a circle could have been used. It would be nothing for Geoff Howard to perform a summonsing to call Mullin if he knew how."

"How else can Mullin help Geoff?" Jess asked.

"It depends if Mullin has actually become part of Geoff Howard or not." to her cup and poured more tea in before topping off our cups.

Sister Ben compressed her lips. "I would expect Mullin has immersed himself in Geoff Howard."

"Mullin found a willing host in Howard," I surmised.

"Oh, yes, I'm sure he has," Miss Agnes agreed. -lieve Geoff Howard has been a growing canker for some time. Especially concerning that business with the Foggles and Julian Cooper's death."

I involuntarily clenched my jaw at the mention of Jul-ian. Put it away, Helly, I told myself.

"We think the scent which was Geoff's, has been As a result, the places where we know he has been smell pretty rank." Jess absently put a protective hand on her child.

"Like fetid meat?" Agnes suggested.

"Yes, that would be about right," I said with Jess and the other shifters nodding in agreement.

"Then he's the one that burned my Garry Oaks. Mullin has also been attacking the Butter Church."

"What is a butter church?" I asked.

"It's a stone church on an escarpment across the road from Mount Tzouhalem. Before Saint Anne's was built, the Butter Church was the first Catholic parish in the val-ley. The farm that the church owned produced butter to sell. The funds raised were for the construction of the first church. Hence the name, Butter Church," Sister Ben explained. "It is also an anchor to hold the bindings on Immundus."

"The same as the Cross on Mount Tzouhalem. And Paddy's Mill Stone, the Garry Oaks Preserve, the rock cairn on Mount Maxwell, the sentinel at Octopus Point, and Saint Anne's." Miss Agnes listed all the sites.

Jess frowned and glanced between Sister Ben and Miss Agnes. "Okay, so who is this Immundus?"

The older women looked at each other, and I got the feeling they were wondering how much to tell us.

"Just give us the highlights, ladies," I said and "Immundus is the name for a demon that belongs to the Evil One." By her tone it was easy to figure out who that was.

means unclean in Latin. In the under-world, he is the entity that controls sorcery," Miss Agnes supplied while sipping her tea and watching me to gauge my reaction.

"What about here on earth?" I asked.

"Well, here too, if he ever got loose. The portal be-tween the underworld and our world is bound shut. We made it so a long time ago. One of my duties is to keep an eye on the bindings to ensure he doesn't get the chance to cross over," Miss Agnes explained to us.

"When were you planning on telling the rest of us there was a problem?" Sister Ben frowned disapprovingly at the witch. "Have you spoken with Amelia?"

Miss Agnes had the grace to look uncomfortable. "I was going to contact you, but you called me first." She fiddled with her teaspoon. This was an obvious lie. We all could smell it. It was virtually impossible to lie to a shapeshifter. We were like walking lie detectors.

"Did you think you could handle it on your own?" Ben asked critically.

"I hoped I could. I didn't bargain on there being a shapeshifter involved. With Geoff Howard giving Mullin a corporal existence, this is going to be much more Miss Agnes straightened her spine. "It also depends on the state of the existing seal."

"Yes, of course, though we might need to consult Amelia. We will certainly need the pack's help. We'll have to go to the cave and see if we can lure Mullin out before any further damage is done and Immundus gets a toehold. It may be possible to force his underling out and slam the door shut."

"Amelia's in no shape to go up to the cave," Miss "Amelia who?" Lottie asked suspiciously.

Miss Agnes rolled her eyes at Lottie. "Amelia Fistbinder, of course."

"My granny? You have my granny involved in this craziness of demons and bindings?" Lottie was getting louder.

"We didn't involve Amelia. She called us, many years ago. Of course, a First Nations shaman would know about the portal between worlds. She didn't know how to stop Immundus from coming through. Nor did she know how to kick him out once he did.

That's where we came in. Agnes had the power to kick him out. I had the power to build the bindings to close the portal and keep him on the other side," Sister Ben explained.

"It takes a mixture of faith and belief systems to build successful seals and bindings." Agnes spread her hands like she was taking in the whole world.

"Can we see the trees Howard burned? Maybe there's something here to help us track him or find him," I asked, replacing my empty cup in its saucer.

"Certainly," Agnes said as she stood. "Come this way."

We followed the witch to a blackberry bush along the fence at the back of the property. As Agnes neared the bush, it dissolved and became a cedar gate with black iron fittings.

Jess, Lottie, and I gave each other sideways looks but we didn't say anything.

The gate swung open at Agnes's lightest touch and we walked single-file into a field. The land was thickly clustered with Garry oaks.

I remembered what Will had said yesterday by the lake about things getting weirder. Now I knew how he felt.

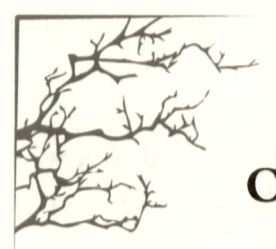

Chapter Sixteen

The trees were bent and twisted this way and that in impossible poses that didn't seem natural. The tree trunks sported Spanish moss and a couple other types of moss that varied in shades of green.

The smell of smoke and burned grass was in the air as we crunched our way through the dry scrub. We stopped at an immense, old tree located in the middle of a burned-out circle. It was charred black. No leaves were left on any of the stark branches. No moss on the trunk or any greenery left in the roughly fourteen-foot circle that sur-rounded the tree.

Agnes walked up to the tree and rested a gentle hand on its trunk. "This one has taken some serious damage, but I think it's coming back."

"The bindings still look good," Sister Ben commented. As she examined the ground from various angles, I guessed she was looking at something the rest of us couldn't see.

Well, Lottie and I anyway, Jess seemed to follow where Sister Ben was looking. I thought it odd I could see Jess's wards but not these bindings. Maybe there was some difference between witch magic and mage magic. Not that it was important right now. Then I narrowed my eyes as I felt something.

"Is that Quamichan Lake?" I asked, looking at a slice of blue water sparkling in the distance.

"Yes, it is," Agnes confirmed.

I could feel a power, a presence under my feet. I looked down at my boots and saw I was standing on ground that had a light-green, lime-colored glow.

"Jess, do you see that?" I waved my hand at the vast mat that glowed around our feet.

"Yes, I do, it's part of the Garry Oak Preserve ward system. I believe it's to keep malice out." She looked at Agnes.

The old woman nodded and tucked her hands into her sweater pockets with evident satisfaction. "What else do you see?" Agnes had a teacher's tone in her voice.

Jess paused to look at the ward for a bit. Something is interfering with the ward." She walked slowly over to another tree, this one in worse shape. It was barely more than a stump of wood left in the ground and probably damaged beyond redemption. "These bindings are ragged around this tree, they appear to have dissolved."

"Exactly." Agnes stabbed a finger at Jess. "That's what's happening to the bindings. Someone is trying to raise power. To do that, they are sacrificing my trees by burning them. Converting the energy as a force to dis-solve the next binding. It's a destructive circle."

"With the restraints removed, the next step is to release the evil in the mountain." Jess looked over her shoulder at the mountain. "Immundus."

"Yes." Agnes strolled forward and Sister Ben "What do you feel?" Both older women were looking at Jess intently.

Jess turned toward the mountain and stared skyward. "I can feel something bad. It's on the mountain."

"Do you feel anything else?" Miss Agnes asked. She joined Jess and stood by the scared oak tree.

Jess's attention transferred to the oak. "I—I feel—like I can help," Jess said in a dreamy tone as if she were She slowly raised her left hand and placed it on the trunk of the abused and burned tree.

Lottie sucked in a breath as a shoot appeared on the upper canopy of the burned branches. Jess chanted under her breath and an unseasonal bud appeared on the shoot.

Lottie stepped forward and placed her larger hands on Jess's small shoulders. "Alpha, Mage, I don't think this is a good idea." Jess didn't budge but continued to feed power into the damaged tree. "Think about your baby," Lottie whispered into her ear.

Jess stiffened and came back to herself, dropping her hand to her belly. "Yes, you're right." She turned and blinked at us.

"She's fine." Agnes peered at Jess. "No harm done." The witch patted Lottie's arm. She then turned to Jess. "It's nice to know you can tap the energy required to help me fix this mess. However, it would be best to let nature handle it on her own for now."

"You have to understand this evil has been sleeping for over a century or more." Sister Ben moved in front of us to get our attention. "You can't kill something like this, no one is powerful enough. You can only bind the portal closed and keep watch. It's our duty to keep it bound and ensure the Island and its inhabitants remain safe."

"This is a lot bigger than finding a killer." I shook my head and turned at the sound of footsteps.

"You've got that right," Will called. The rest of the women spun to see Iain and Will striding through the trees to join us in the burned clearing.

"We've found some more of Howard's handiwork by the copse of trees near the lake," Will reported. was locked down. It was the look I saw when we encountered bad things in the field. I hated that emotionless look in his eyes. This was bad.

"There's another burned out area down by the lake." Iain's eyes flashed with anger but no color rolled over his eyes. "This one is bigger and someone or something has slaughtered several animals. They attempted to destroy the remains with a fire but the evidence is still visible."

"There was also another message." Will came to stand next to me. He was inside my personal space and I could feel the heat radiating off his body. His hand went to my waist and, when I glanced up, I could see he was veteran, so it must be something personal.

He needed my touch right now so I leaned against him.

"What did the message say?" Jess asked as she slid her arm around her husband's waist and he did the same.

"Pretty much the same thing as the first one." eyes skirted meeting hers. "Except this one gave us a deadline and a location."

"I hate this." Will growled and I didn't even think he was aware he had done it. "We've been two steps behind that son of a bitch the whole time. First a shifter at the compound, the roadside victim, and then that kid Silas. "

I stood away from Will. "No, actually. The first victim was my brother. After that, my nephew, then Jess. He or 'it' has hurt many people and killed three. There could be more we don't even know about yet." I could feel myself slide into that cold place I had to go when final solutions must be dealt out.

"If we don't deal with him soon, there will be more casualties," Lottie agreed grimly.

"This has to end now," Iain said, acknowledging the inevitable.

As if in answer to the combined anger from all of us, the earth rumbled and shuddered. A loud crack split the air. It went on for about three seconds and more than a bit unnerving.

The movement was not enough to knock us down or even make us stumble. It was enough to let us know this entity, this evil, was aware of us. Or maybe it was the earth itself wanting to expel it. Either way, it was an "I'd say we just experienced a tremor, but it didn't feel like a regular one." Miss Agnes shivered. "That felt like a warning."

"This area is one of the few places in the world where all three types of tectonic plate movements take place." Sister Ben gathered us in by eye. "This results in signifi-cant earthquake activity all the time, almost weekly. While we experience them frequently, they aren't notably strong. There's nothing to worry about," she said in a calming tone.

We stared deadpan at the nun for a moment.

"All right," she admitted waggling her head in acknowledgement. "That one didn't feel like a regular quake to me either."

"It could also mean Mullin is trying to open the The two older women shared a concerned look.

As one, our eyes turned to the mountain. It shadowed the oaks we stood among. the midday sun and cast a sullen, brooding mood over the mountain and the valley.

"Those are the blackest clouds I've ever seen," Lottie commented. "I'd say we're in the path of a thunderstorm, but those are not common for the Island and especially not in November."

Iain stared up at the mountain. "We have to go up to the cave. That's where he's waiting for us."

Jess turned to her husband and tapped him on the chest to get his attention. "What cave?"

"I think it's the cave Miss Agnes mentioned earlier." I gave the witch a pointed look.

Miss Agnes and Sister Ben exchanged a solemn gaze this time. Resigned.

"I suspect I know which cave," Miss Agnes said. "It's the entrance to the portal. would come through if he/it could. That is if Mullin and Howard have loosened the bonds enough to wedge the portal open."

"Please explain," Iain said in a quiet voice that held way too much pissed off wolf.

Jess gave the men a quick recap of what the older la-dies had imparted to us earlier over tea and muffins.

"So, you think Howard is being ridden by this Mullin?" Iain asked.

"We are pretty certain this is so. It would explain the two scents and the fact that no one knows what or who the other scent is." Miss Agnes smoothed the front of her dress and sweater. I would have said this was a nervous gesture except for the steel in her eyes.

there's a special bit of evil involved," Will said. His lips twisted like he had a bad taste in his mouth.

"Won't the farmer find the message and call the cops? What will happen if more people are dragged into this?" Lottie looked to her alphas.

"I'll take care of it," Miss Agnes said. She turned and strode away in the direction Will and Iain had come from.

"Howard's been taunting us for the last couple days. It's time to take care of this thing," Will caught Iain's "Lottie, please take Jess home." Before Jess could do more that sputter a protest. Iain drew her up against his body, as close has her pregnancy would let him, and rest-ed his forehead against hers. "I need you to go back to the farm, I need to know you and our child are home and you are both safe behind the wards." Immediately the fight went out of Jess as his words and tone penetrated her stubborn protest.

"Yes, Alpha." She sighed and a smile curved Iain's lip before he gave her a deep kiss and released her. "I want one thing in exchange."

He grinned at his wife. "Name it."

"I'll drive myself home with Sister Ben and Lottie goes with you." Jess raised her eyebrows at Lottie in question. Lottie nodded her agreement and bit her lip to conceal a grin.

"Done," Iain acknowledged. "Lottie's good in a fight," he said to Will and me.

"I never doubted it," Will said.

"Alpha, you're going to need a guide to the cave," the witch said, returning to the group. "And Mullin won't be put down with physical force. You'll need a bit of arcane help. I'd like to accompany you."

"Glad to have you, Miss Agnes." her his hand and they shook on it.

I frowned at the witch. "How did you make it back here so quickly?"

Lottie answered for the older woman. "Duh, witch." She patted me consolingly on the shoulder.

"I hear we have a lot to learn," Will said as we turned back to retrace our steps.

"Apparently," I said stiffly.

"Helly, I didn't mean to disparage your dead," Will said, walking next to me.

"I know. The incidents over the last two days are fresher in your mind than events a couple years past." I gave him a weak smile. "Don't worry about it. But what aren't you telling me?" I said in a low voice.

Will glanced back to make sure Iain had Jess well away from where we stood. He was going to personally see her to the car before he rejoined us.

"The message mentioned Jess this time." Will kept his voice low. "The animals that were slaughtered were stalked out and no doubt tortured first."

I nodded in understanding. "No wonder Iain is so in-tense right now."

Howard had killed my brother. I had buried my anger to be able to function. Now was the time to let it surface so I could use it, although I had to keep my anger in check to ensure I would be ruled by my brain and not my emotions.

As much as I felt Howard's death belonged to me. I knew threatening the alpha's mate, in their territory would sign Howard's death warrant. Killing Howard would be Iain's right. Howard was challenging the All I cared about was that Howard would be dead and this Mullin was stopped. Mullin may be the power at work, but

Howard had invited him in. He no doubt want-ed power and the alpha position. I figured Mullin must have promised it to him in exchange for these horrendous acts.

Will's cold eyes met with mine. "We need to stop the son of a bitch."

"Exactly." I knew green rolled over my eyes, but I didn't care. We filed back through the gate and into Miss Agnes's backyard.

Will snagged a muffin off the table as they waited for Iain to return. He was seeing Jess and Sister Ben off with Miss Agnes.

It was decided Jess would communicate the latest in-formation to the rest of the council. She would also batten down the farm. The mages would activate the wards to keep everyone on the property safe until they heard back from Iain.

The blackberry muffin all but melted in Will's mouth. "Which cup was yours?" he asked Helly.

She pointed and Will filled it with cold tea from the pot to wash down the remains of the muffin.

Will hoped they had enough resources and firepower to take on Howard. Or whatever the thing was that was riding him.

Iain returned and Will tossed him a muffin, too, as they made their way to Will's truck.

The logistics of taking his vehicle became all too They had to accommodate four shapeshifters and one witch.

Lottie and Helly clambered into the jump seats in the extended cab. Will would be in the driver's seat and Miss Agnes in the passenger seat up front. Iain hopped in the box in the back. Helly slid the rear window open so he could be kept in the loop of their conversation.

"We'll have to hike most of the way," Miss Agnes

The truck turned into the Kingsview subdivision at her direction.

"The Foggles live in the next street over," Iain said. His tone held menace.

Miss Agnes turned and looked at him solemnly. "Yes, they do. I suspect they were influenced by the evil that is Mullin in some degree. I wouldn't be surprised if he had tried to use them as he is using Geoff Howard. I'm sure he's been looking for viable tools to do his work for some time."

"If you invite it in, evil will find a home," Lottie commented. "It doesn't matter if Geoff Howard was The fact remains the Foggles were tools."

Iain barked a laugh. "Yes, they were."

When Will glanced into the rear-view mirror, he saw the glint in Lottie's eye.

Will accelerated up the steep grade and made a right on Samsum then Salish, as Miss Agnes directed. Finally, he took a left on Kaspa and drove through the park gate.

Iain hopped out briefly to open the road access gate. Will drove up again to head up hill the rest of the way to the summit.

"There are a few stories about Tzouhalem, the man's name that the mountain now holds," Lottie explained. "Some say this warrior or chief of the Quamichan people was a murderer of other men to gain their wives. Some say he was also a murderer of his own wives. However, the legends do agree and my Granny with them, that Tzouhalem was at one point a good leader and something turned him bad. As a result, he was banished to live in a cave on the mountain."

"You think the same thing may have turned him as well as Howard?" Will pulled off the road and parked on the side. area clearly was used by hikers to park their vehicles.

Lottie shook her head. "I don't know."

"Tzouhalem lived back around 1859, so yes, I think it's possible," Miss Agnes said as she glanced back over her shoulder at Lottie.

The head of security for the pack didn't argue.

Everyone climbed out. Miss Agnes waited quietly be-side the edge of the road, as Will broke out the weapons and silver-laced ammo.

Helly had her pistol strapped to her leg with extra mags loaded and stored in her hoodie pocket.

Will offered Lottie Helly's shotgun, but Lottie "No thanks," she said as she shook her head at Will. "I don't want to carry a gun. I'll shift when we get close and use my own weapons."

"What did the message actually say?" Helly asked Will as he loaded shells into his shotgun.

He flexed his jaw and pushed the erupting feelings of rage back down before he could answer. "It said Howard was going to find Jess and find you, too." Will's gaze locked with Helly's. "It said he was going to pull all your insides out. He or it would paint the farm red with your blood if we didn't hand Lasha over to him at the cave by nightfall." Green rolled over Helly's eyes. Will had be-come familiar with how it felt when his own eyes did the same, like now.

The rage wanted to trigger a feeling he was getting used to. It was the precursor to a shifter changing. He would have to keep a leash on that feeling. At least for now.

He glanced over at Iain. The alpha was performing the same task. Loading the shotgun and his eyes were also rolling with color too.

Helly gestured to the shotgun he held. "You won't be able to fire that if you shift into half form," she cautioned the alpha.

Will remembered what Helly had looked like in her half form. Her hands had shifted into large paws with razor sharp claws. They were too large to enter the trigger guard.

Iain gave them a cold smile. "Yes, I know, but when I shift, it won't matter. The shells will have been spent."

Will understood Iain was going to kill Howard. He wondered what it would do to the alpha in the long run. Although, asking Iain if he could actually perform the kill, was crossing a line. He would have to watch and wait. If weapons failed and Iain couldn't do it, Will would step in.

Helly's phone buzzed. She dug into her pocket to pull it out of her hoodie. "Jess?"

"Helly, is Lasha with you?" Will could hear the frantic note in Jess's voice.

The other shifters' heads came up. They could hear the conversation as clearly as Will could.

"No, she's not. Why, did she say she wanted to join us?"

"No, she's just gone. I explained the plan to the others and went looking for her to do the same. No one can find her. She's gone and probably has been for a while."

"Is she at the clinic?" Iain asked.

"No, the site is cleared and everyone is here on the farm property," Jess answered.

"All right. Activate the wards, and we'll check to see if she's in the other parking lot by Saint Anne's," Iain said. He met Will's eyes as Helly hung up.

"Lasha's not waiting for us," Helly said with finality. "She's going to try and take Howard out on her own, I know it. She has something to prove." Helly cursed as she pushed her phone back into her pocket. "Let's hope we finish this before she gets here."

"Should we wait?" Lottie asked.

"We don't have time. Please lead the way, Miss He strode around the tailgate of the truck, and they followed single file behind the witch. She led them off the road and down a narrow trail.

Will could see by the set of Helly's chin that she felt responsible for Lasha going missing.

He figured Helly was right about the former alpha. It was evident to everyone that Lasha Cooper felt guilty. She no doubt blamed herself for her own lack of action over her husband's death. This, in turn, led to the events of last year that allowed her child to be targeted by The man's crazy plan was to put a marker into all shapeshifter's blood to make them easily identifiable. That episode also led to Jess being kidnapped. In Will's opinion, the former alpha had much to answer for and, so far, she seemed to have gotten off Scott-free.

Will was fairly sure that it didn't help that Helly's Lasha must sense this from her sister-in-law.

Then Dylan going to Helly to ask her to train him to fight with a half form must have hurt. It must have smacked his mother's pride and self-respect with the real-ization her own kid didn't feel safe with her.

for the situation, Lasha no doubt felt forced into taking action. Now they had to keep an eye out for the inept alpha on this little trip to "Mordor." He hoped they made it to the cave before Lasha did.

Chapter Seventeen

The team moved along the overgrown trail. They pushed tree branches out of the way, and crushed dried shrubs underfoot.

Their path was hindered with alders and scrub brush. It only got worse when they followed the witch on to the side track she took down the west side of the mountain. Miss Agnes was quick on her feet for a woman of It was evident this new trail was even less well used. Although it might speed things up, the witch showing them the way wasn't actually necessary. The trail was well scented. It reeked of blood, Howard, and the sour rank scent that Will had come to identify as Mullin.

He wished they had been able to track their quarry the first night. That would have put an end to this in a more operational fashion. He had trouble believing the story Jess told them about demons and portals. It was crazy and he couldn't wrap his head around it, so he ignored it. When push came to shove, it was all about taking out a threat. This was the thought Will clung to.

As they rounded a rocky outcrop, there was the dark mouth of a cave in front of them. It was partly screened with willows and the reddish amber limbs of a sickly looking arbutus tree. A breeze had come up and blew the smell of carrion directly at the group.

"This is it," Miss Agnes said and stood to the side of the track. She turned her head, no doubt trying to escape the stink.

The clearing was small and narrow. The western edge ended at a cliff some three hundred meters above a rocky shore. The view would have been heart-stopping enough without the oppressive black clouds. The threat of rain was real. As it was, the panorama took in

Separation Point on the west side of the Samsum Narrows. across the bay and clear up to Arbutus Ridge and the coastal town of Cowichan Bay off in the distance. It all matched the map Will and Ian reviewed earlier, before setting off for the lake.

The darks waters of Cowichan Bay were below. It was slack tide at the moment. The inky water was flat and flaccid in the bay, in the straight, and off the point, As though it all waited expectantly for the confrontation.

To the east and north were more of the close-growing scrub, and south led to a cave's gaping black maw.

"Let me go in first," Miss Agnes said.

Will dragged his eyes back. "No, Miss Agnes, you stay out here, you're not armed," Will instructed and forestalled her with a hand on her arm.

Iain didn't wait. He strolled right past Will, Lottie, and Helly calling into the cave. "Geoff Howard, come out with your hands up."

"Well so much for stealth," Helly sighed as she pulled her Kimber out of its holster and flicked off the safety.

"At least things are moving forward now." Will glanced at her and she nodded in wary agreement.

Lottie dropped her sweats and shifted into her large brown wolf. She padded over to stand by her alpha.

Will stepped in front of the witch and they all waited for a response.

Nothing. All was silent and still.

"As you can see, he isn't going to come out into the daylight unless he has to. Mullin is a creature of the shadows and now so is Geoff Howard," Miss Agnes pointed out sharply as she edged around Will and thread-ed her way past the other shifters.

The witch briskly walked across the cleaning and was almost to the mouth of the cave, when Howard appeared and rushed her. He unfolded as he immerged from the entrance. Howard was in half form and enormous.

"That's the biggest half form I've ever seen," Helly commented in an offhanded tone as Howard came at them. She might have been commenting on the weather for all the emotion she voiced. Will loved that about her, Helly was always unflappable in a fight.

"He never had a half form. as he chambered a round in his borrowed shot-gun.

"This form has to be how he was able to escape his cell at the compound," Will concluded. He noted the enormous upper body of the creature as it lumbered to-ward them. At least it would provide an easy target.

Will chambered his first round as well.

Howard sped up and ran toward them. He went for Miss Agnes first. She had her arms raised, and she shout-ed something Will didn't understand. The witch threw some kind of yellow energy at Howard, but he changed course and her effort went wide.

Will opened up, firing two rounds into Howard's gut.

Boom! Boom!

But the monstrosity that was Howard didn't stop. He was on Miss Agnes. Slashed at her throat and knocked her aside. He turned and charged the alpha and the wolf.

Red eyes glowed from a malformed face. Huge fangs, protruding from his misshapen jaws, and dripped saliva. His lips were pulled back from enormous teeth and his long claws dripped with the witch's blood. He ran at his former pack members.

"Killlllllll you," Howard roared as he zeroed in on Iain. "Youuuu took my place! I will take it baaaack! Lasha is mine!"

A flash of white lightning jumped across the sky be-hind Howard.

"Talk about a bad omen," Helly said. She took a two-handed grip on her pistol, aimed, and commenced firing on Howard.

Will and Iain were right behind her and pumped silver rounds into the monster. They went for the largest target, his torso. But as fast as they fired the silver bullets, the openings healed. The silver wasn't stopping him. The thing kept coming.

"We'll have to bleed him," Will shouted at Iain and the alpha nodded and continued to fire.

The nightmare was twenty feet away across the They took turns reloading. Alternately, they carried on filling the immense abomination with silver-laced rounds.

"We have to wear down his metabolism," Iain called over his shoulder to them.

"We're going for silver overload," Will agreed.

Fifteen feet.

Helly ejected a spent clip and slammed in another. She resumed her straight-arm stance, firing continually into Howard's body as Lottie paced back and forth behind her

Ten feet away.

Iain tossed the empty shotgun aside and shifted. Clothing tore, and he changed into his own considerably formidable half form—he silver, gray, and black wolf head on a man's muscular frame, long powerful arms with razor sharp claws, and fangs the size of spikes.

At a signal from her alpha, Lottie lunged forward and attacked Howard. Biting and ripping at his flank to divide his attention among the four of them.

Will reloaded while Helly shifted into her half form as well. They had agreed to this strategy earlier. Will had asked how they could shift to the half form and found out the answer was again, magic. Shapeshifters could draw on their magical reserve to enhance their strength and speed. Again she changed into that immense cougar-woman extraction. Larger and more powerful than her full human shape, this half humanoid, half animal combi-nation was bloody scary too.

Will liked the sight of her tawny gold fur. It coated her head, shoulders, and arms which ended in finer, more needle like claws. Helly snarled at Howard and the sound seemed to call the thunder. It rippled across the clearing, and Will felt it right in his chest.

Iain was slashing and dodging Howard's swinging fists and claws.

"I'll go for the head, you for the legs," Will called to Helly.

She gave him a thumbs up before lunging forward and attacking with the alpha.

Iain was slashing Howard on his front side. He was fast and sliced Howard's torso diving in and out before the monster could react.

But when Howard did connect it was deadly. Lottie darted in to bite and claw and was met with a slash and a fist that knocked her several feet away, stunning her. The wolf was bleeding and slow to get up.

Will could see the problem was that neither shapeshifter was large enough. Howard was more than half again as big as either Iain or Helly.

Helly went for Howard's knees. She kicked and plant-ed a couple of good ones, trying to knock him down.

Miss Agnes was on her hands and knees. She pulled a handkerchief out of her pocket and pressed it against her neck to stem the flow of blood. She crawled to a tree to help regain her feet.

Will raised his reloaded shotgun and squeezed the trigger, releasing both barrels into the monster's face.

The head snapped back. Howard's eyes were gone and blood oozed out of the horrific face. Still the sockets glowed red and it slowed Howard down only briefly.

The deep roar coming out of the creature was like nothing Will had ever heard before. Blood and spittle went flying.

Howard swiped first at the alpha then at Helly as they coordinated their attacks. The accumulation of silver in his body was starting to take effect. Slashes were opening up in the insane monster's torso from the shifters' Dark blood began to flow down from the cuts. The gashes were not healing as quickly. Some remained open, his healing was slowed, but it wasn't enough.

The shifters in half form at first appeared to be too fast for the monster to grab or hit. Howard either got lucky or timed his strikes better and connected with Helly. It knocked the half cougar, half female off her feet. She hit the ground hard.

Helly rolled with it and came right back up. She aimed another driving kick into Howard's left knee. This time, it crunched under her foot and the monstrosity swayed.

Lottie was crouched down in the grass moving behind Howard to circle him. She was waiting for an opening.

Iain took advantage of Helly's repeated attacks to the knees. torso, like climbing a tree, and sliced at the neck before jumping clear.

The wolf slid in behind Howard and bit the Achilles tendon on the leg Helly was hammering.

The monster's knee collapsed, and it crashed to the ground, with only the upper body vertical. It struggled to regain its feet.

With a vicious snarl, Lottie dashed in and lunged up under Howard's chin. She took out his throat. This caused the head to lull to one side. It was barely attached.

The red glow died in the eye sockets and the huge body crashed to the ground. All was quiet, except for the shifters panting and distant thunder rolling in.

Will was out of ammo for his shotgun. He had emptied the last of it into Howard's head. "That was too freaky." He dropped the empty shot gun and reached for Helly's hoodie.

Up until now he could ignore the pain in his chest and the way his skin wanted to crawl along his bones. Now it was getting harder to ignore so he focused on what he could control.

"Helly, gun," Will called to her as she wiped her clawed hands on a bush. The same one Lottie was Then wiped her sleeve over her face to clear the blood. The gash on her forehead was already begin-ning to close.

Will ejected the partially used clip and replaced it with a full one. He kept the half used one as a reserve and tucked it into his back jean pocket.

"Where is Mullin," Iain called to Miss Agnes.

"Inside the cave, I can feel him." Miss Agnes leaned against the tree she had crawled to. The witch finished tying a sleeve of her black blouse around her neck to keep the handkerchief in place.

Will moved forward and Helly flanked him. Lottie, still in wolf form was at Iain's side and they brought up the rear.

Miss Agnes went first into the cave. It was larger than first visible from the outside. Will and Miss Agnes could stand up right.

Helly and Iain in their half forms were forced to stoop down to enter.

Miss Agnes touched the moss growing on the walls. She muttered something that made the small hairs on the back of Will's neck stand up. The moss ignited with a faint green light, which was more than enough to see the scene inside the cave.

"Nicely done, Gandalf," Will said to Agnes.

She gave him a sour look.

Along the back wall, some five meters away, was a set of complex petroglyphs and pictographs. The designs spanned the wall about ten meters wide. Will had no idea what they meant. The shapes were overlaid with more designs and drawings. The whole of it radiated outward to form a circle.

The pale light from the moss traveled around the cave. It illuminated a shallow trough below the designs. It was freshly dug and the excavated dirt was piled up beside it.

Helly strode forward and came to a stop. She dropped to kneel at the edge of the ditch and leaned forward. in here."

"Don't touch her!" Miss Agnes rushed forward. "Mullin could be dwelling inside her."

"She's out cold," Helly growled at the witch.

"It doesn't matter. Mullin no doubt jumped from Howard to Lasha before sending Howard out to delay us."

"Could this get any more complicated?" Iain dropped down to a knee to look at his former alpha. "She's bruised and bleeding from multiple cuts."

Will stepped up to the edge of the ditch. Howard had tortured Lasha in the same way he had Silas and the animals staked out by the lake. "That's a lot of cuts. Will she bleed out?"

"No, I don't think so," Helly said and turned her cat head toward him. "Most are clotting and if we could get her to shift, she'd be healed pretty quickly."

"Otherwise, she seems okay," Iain said. "She must have shifted at some point, judging from the state of her clothes."

"What concerns me is the amount of blood already painted on the wall." Miss Agnes gestured at the petro-glyphs.

Will could see the drawings in the outer most ring of the circle sported red splotches. It was clear the blood was meant to fill each gouge in the rock.

"Screw this," Helly said. She reached down and tapped Lasha sharply on the cheek with the back of her clawed hand. "Lasha, wake up. Where's Mullin?"

Lasha's eyes snapped open. Instead of Lasha's clear blue, they were greeted with glowing red eyes with split pupils. "I am right here!" A harsh voice emanated from Lasha's bloodied lips.

She grabbed Helly by the neck and tried to pull her in-to the ditch. Helly braced her legs but Lasha was stronger with Mullin riding her. Helly's boot came up as she fell forward and cracked Will in the jaw, knocking him back into Iain.

"She is mine and now you are mine too." It was eerie to hear Lasha's voice cackle and fill the cave. "You have magic and the blood Immundus needs. Lots of blood. Female blood." Helly heaved backward. She and Lasha fell and grappled on the floor, half in and half out of the ditch.

Both Iain and Will hesitated to intervene, not wanting to hurt either woman. Lottie paced behind them and whined.

Miss Agnes narrowed her eyes and stared at the "Her blood will paint the wall. Your blood will fill the alter bowl. The magic will break the bindings. Your life force will open the way for my master!" Mullin pro-claimed.

Helly heaved again. The two female shifters spilled out of the ditch and rolled across the floor. Lasha nailed Helly's jaw with savage punches again and again. The blows were so fast, Helly couldn't respond quickly enough to block or counter them all.

Lasha was not a small shapeshifter, but she had no half form and wasn't even half the fighter Helly was. Finally, Helly got her own punch in on Lasha's jaw stunning the other woman.

In seconds, Helly had her sister-in-law face down on the rock floor. She had Lasha's arms restrained behind her and Helly's knee pinning her in place across the back of her neck. It didn't stop Lasha from thrashing around and howling in anger, but she was essentially trapped. Both males had regained their feet and Iain moved for-ward to grab the possessed shapeshifter's legs.

"We could have done this the easy way, but no, don't listen to the old lady," Miss Agnes complained. She walked up to Lasha and squatted down beside the snarl-ing, possessed woman. "Mullin come out of there this instant."

"No! This is my vessel. I must open the way!" Lasha shrieked but it wasn't her voice, it was Mullin's.

Will had Helly's Kimber pointed at Lasha. If it came down to it, he'd load her up with silver rounds to allow the shifters time to take her out. He hoped it wouldn't come to that, even if Lasha could survive it.

"Mullin, we will not allow you freedom to open the portal. That's not going to happen. Leave that woman this instant." When nothing changed Agnes placed her hands on either side of Lasha's head and began chanting.

Lasha's thrashing stopped. She stiffened, her body went rigid as a board, and then she started to vibrate.

It had to be difficult for Helly to keep a hold on Lasha during all of it, but she hung on doggedly just the same.

Miss Agnes paused her chanting and cut her eyes to Helly then Iain. "When I say, you let her go. If you don't release her in time, Mullin will jump into you."

They both nodded and Agnes resumed chanting.

The volume and resonance began to build. It was be-coming harder on his ears, making Will pant in pain. The reverberations and high pitch chanting was becoming un-bearable.

"Now!" Agnes snapped, and they let go of Lasha.

A reddish, ghostly vision separated itself from Lasha's body and drifted free. It headed toward Helly. The witch flung up a hand and shouted some incomprehensible words.

Agnes fished her handkerchief out of her make shift bandage and shook the square of cloth open. She grabbed the opposite edges to spread the square of blood-soaked cloth wide.

"Come and get my blood. I know you can smell it. There's lots of magic here, you need it to open the way."

The drifting red cloud of vapor hesitated. It shifted in-to the shape of a face with eyes too long and narrow to mimic a human being. They were red slits, below were two holes where the nose should have been above a wide lipless mouth.

"I want it!" the horrible face shrieked.

"Come and get it." Agnes fluttered the handkerchief enticingly.

The apparition drifted over toward the witch. When it got near enough, she reached out. Miss Agnes quickly scooped the murky mist up in the cloth like catching a flailing fish in a net.

"Yes, yes!" Mullin shrieked gleefully.

Abruptly, Miss Agnes turned and ran right back to the designs and signals on the stone wall.

She mashed the handkerchief against a glyph. The witch shouted and then said something that to Will's ear, sounded like profanity. A wash of yellow light flowed out of Agnes's hands and into the designs on the wall.

With the bright light flooding them, the petroglyphs stood out in sharp relief. The details of each design be-came more apparent as the light intensified. He saw the layer upon layer of detail carved into the rock. It was so much more in-depth than at first glance. The wall carvings looked as though they were a foot thick, but it had to be a trick of the light?

"No!" screamed Mullin.

The whole wall glowed and, when Agnes finished her chanting, she gave a final shout. "Cover your eyes!" There was a flash of blinding light. It blazed to white and the shifters and Will averted or covered their eyes as best they could.

The smell of burnt blood and amber filled the cavern. Silence fell again and the oppressive tension permeating the cave was gone.

Black ash drifted down to the cave floor. It was all that was left of Miss Agnes's handkerchief.

The witch turned and staggered. Blood was tricking from her neck again and Iain grabbed her arms and helped her to sit down on a rock.

He shifted back to his human form. "Are you all right?" he asked the old woman, dropping to a knee in front of her. He held her hands in his as he searched her face.

"Yes, yes. Just a bit drained." She sighed. She pulled away from Iain and adjusted her makeshift bandage to cover her seeping neck wound. "Shoving a minor demon across a portal can take a lot of energy. Just give me a minute. Then we can finish up and go home."

Helly flowed back to her full human shape and knelt down beside Lasha's inert body. She tore a strip off the hem of her bloodied and tattered shirt and wiped the grime and blood off her sister-in-law's face.

"Lasha," Helly called her gently. "Please wake up."

"Will she be all right?" Iain asked Agnes.

"I think so." The witch nodded. "She'll have bad dreams for a while but it could have been much worse. Benny can give her a lavender sachet to help with that."

"Benny?" Will said, raising his eyebrows at the name.

"Sister Ben," Helly supplied. She let out a relieved sigh as Lasha's eyes fluttered open.

This time Lasha's eyes were the clear sky blue and she looked bewilderedly around her.

Helly got the dazed Lasha up on her feet and help her outside the cave. The sun had decided it still had some heat to share on this late fall day and the warmth was welcome.

Once outside in the fresh air of the late afternoon, Lottie shifted and dressed. while Iain, Will, and Helly dragged Howard's carcass back into the cave at Miss Agnes's direction.

"He's dead, but he hasn't shifted back to human form." Helly bit her lip. "We always shift back just before death. What's wrong with him?"

"I believe it's because he ceased being human or a shapeshifter some time ago. This would now be his true self." Agnes pointed at the trough under the glyphs. "Place it there please."

"I want a silver shell in each of his extremities. Then I'll incinerate the body and use the energy to finish re-sealing the portal," she explained to Will.

Will swiftly drew, aimed, and fired a bullet into each one of dead monster's head, feet, and hands. The percus-sion of the pistol inside the cave made his ears ring and head ache.

Miss Agnes chanted over the body. Slivers of yellow flame licked over it until the carcass was consumed in a smokeless fire. In seconds, the remains were ashes.

"I'll come back after the embers have cooled and dis-pose of the ashes. I'll check the seal again as well," Miss Agnes told them. "I hope I can get Amelia or Benny to come with me."

"You call me if you want my granny to come here," Lottie called as a warning to the witch.

Miss Agnes took Lottie's words as they were intend-ed. The concern a great-granddaughter had for her elderly grandmother, nothing more. She nodded with respect. "I will."

"Why did you want silver in each of his extremities if you were going to burn the body anyway?" Will asked the witch.

"So, that no one could reanimate him, of course," Miss Agnes said as she shook her head at Will, like he should have known this.

"Haven't you ever heard of zombies?" Helly asked him as she walked at his side and gave his shoulder a playful nudge with hers.

Will wasn't sure if she was serious. If there was no body, how could anything be reanimated? he wasn't going to pursue it.

"How is she?" Iain asked Lottie as they gathered around the former alpha.

"I'm okay." Lasha's voice was shaky but she was sit-ting up. "I don't remember much." She ran a trembling hand through her dark hair.

"What do you remember?" Helly asked, squatting down to be eye level.

"I heard what Jess told Trudy, Guy, and Ben. That Geoff was still after me and I figured this craziness was going to continue until he got me. So, I decided to get him first. I got in my car and drove to Saint Anne's. I took the public trail up the mountain. I was trying to scent Geoff and that thing, Mullin. I got as far as the Cross." She swallowed and continued. "I circled the area until I could smell it, that terrible stink and Geoff's scent. I headed toward it down a side trail and that's the last I recall." She shook her head and flinched in pain.

Helly put her hand on Lasha's head and tipped it down. "You've got a nice laceration here. You need to shift to heal and clean out any infection."

"They abducted you from the trail and brought you here," Miss Agnes informed Lasha. "You were going to be Mullin's sacrifice to open the portal and let through an even bigger evil." She looked down at the befuddled "Shapeshifter blood, especially an alpha, has more than enough magic to activate the portal."

Lasha blinked up at them from her place on the ground. Her mouth opened but nothing came out. Her eyes filled with tears.

Helly was gritting her jaw. She breathed in slowly and stood up.

Will watched as she carefully picked up her She gathered the discarded mags for her Kimber, and her 410 shotgun. She turned to him and wordlessly put out her hand. He placed her weapon in her palm, butt first. She slid the weapon home in to the thigh holster before glancing up at him.

Will looked into Helly's eyes and he could tell she needed a few moments alone to get it together. "Meet you at the truck," he said.

Helly nodded and walked away cradling the shotgun in the crook of her arm.

Will glared down at Lasha. "It's not my place to tell you what a stupid fool you are."

"No, it's mine," Iain said as he stepped up to loom over the former alpha. He turned his own alpha stare on to Lasha. "We'll meet you back at the truck in a few."

Will picked up the other discarded shotgun and turned to the witch. He offered his arm to the older woman. "Miss Agnes, will you walk with me?"

"Thank you, yes," Miss Agnes said, a bit surprised but not unpleased. She glanced uncertainly back at Iain as he stood over Lasha.

Lottie stood at his shoulder, arms folded.

"Come on, I really don't want to be here when Iain rips Lasha a new one." Will led Miss Agnes down the path.

"A new what?" Miss Agnes asked as they moved down the mountain trail.

"Seriously, you don't know?"

"I understand the alpha is displeased with Lasha, but I'm at a loss as to—" Then the witch paused. "Oh."

"Yes," Will agreed.

Helly was sitting on a fallen log, waiting. She turned her head and looked up at him with those pale blue eyes, and he felt everything in him surge to life. She had chosen him. He knew it. She didn't have to say it. It was evident in the way she treated him, and especially in the way she looked at him now—not to mention this mate-bond link they shared. There was caring, empathy, and love in that connection.

Why was he hesitating?

Chapter Eighteen

W hat am I missing here?" Miss Agnes asked as she and Will made their way carefully downhill ahead of me

"To put it mildly, Lasha is a walking screw up," Will said, holding a branch to allow the witch to pass. "She was pivotal in her husband's death, her son's poisoning, and Jess's abduction. Not because she was complicit in any of those plots, but because she was the alpha at the time. She didn't see what was happening around her." Will paused again as he helped Miss Agnes over a fallen tree trunk. "It's been explained to me that as a leader or as an alpha that's dangerous. Her incompetence resulted in one death directly." Will didn't think he could lay the death of the poor guy on the highway or the staff member at the compound on her doorstep. Those were ultimately Howard's crimes. Will hoped the man was paying for them even now.

"You mean Julian Cooper, Lasha's mate and also your brother?" Miss Agnes looked back at me and I nodded. I wasn't ready to speak about it.

"Yes," Will said, taking up my slack. for his own demise. But I'm told the alpha charged with your welfare is supposed to be looking out for you. She didn't do a very good job of fulfilling that duty. Julian was Lasha's mate, and she didn't have his back. I find that the most unforgivable part. I would hope she would take better care of her son and look to his Unfortunately, it appears her need for vengeance outweighed her responsibility to Dylan. What if she had been killed?"

"Wasn't she trying to protect her son?"

"Probably, but she couldn't have fought Howard, even if he hadn't had Mullin in his corner. I know that from merely looking at her. I'm sure the whole pack knows it too. No wonder her kid went to Helly to ask her to train him." Will shook his head in disgust. "It took all five of us."

I was angry at Lasha, too. I also felt guilty and help-less as to how to figure out how to handle this situation. I was no better at the family thing than Will was. When I looked his way, he shrugged. There was no advice he could offer.

"Are you a shapeshifter?" Miss Agnes asked him as they came even with the truck.

"Not yet, but I will be." Will gave me a smile that warmed my heart. I answered it with one of my own.

The drive back down the mountain was quiet for the most part. Everyone was physically and emotionally spent.

Will dropped the three pack members off at the They got into Lasha's car to return to the farm.

We took Miss Agnes home. I insisted on checking that first aid was done properly on her wounded neck.

"So, explain to me how you could snare Mullin," I re-quested as I finished cleaning the slice in the witch's neck.

"Simple, my blood plus potent magic equaled a trap that a mini demon couldn't resist," she said with a shrug. "It was only a matter of reactivating the petroglyphs be-fore it realized it had been taken in, and dispose of the beast." She chuckled and it wasn't in a nice way.

I resolved never to cross a witch, or at least this We didn't leave until the old woman was tucked into bed after she had eaten a bowl of soup and drunk some herbal tea.

Will did the dishes while I left a glass and pitcher of water at her bedside. Hydration was necessary to replace the lost fluid.

Miss Agnes complained we were fussing when it wasn't necessary. But she seemed to like the attention and made us promise to stop by before we left the Island.

We were silent driving back to the farm, both drained from the stress of the past few days. A lot had happened since I watched Will saunter into the Kicking Horse.

I was dirty and bloody and my last favorite long-sleeved T-shirt had bit the dust. I looked down at the shredded material. At some point I would have to find a Mark's Work Warehouse and restock.

Will slid his hand across the middle console to grasp mine. I felt my heart speed up and glanced over at him.

"How are you feeling?" I asked, touching my breast bone to indicate exactly what I meant.

"Not too bad. It aches like a son of a bitch, but it's manageable. As soon as we get a chance, I want to ask Jess to help me shift. I need to feel normal again." He glanced over at me and squeezed my hand.

I chuckled. "Like you have ever been normal."

"There is regular-people normal, and there's our-kind-of-people normal."

"Because shapeshifters are normal, everyday people, right?" I said derisively.

"After the last few days, I'll take whatever normal I can get. We've seen and done some freaky shit over the years, Helly, but this week has moved the yard stick into the twilight zone." He grinned at me. "I was talking about the magic and witches. By the way, why didn't Jess want Miss Agnes's help? Miss Agnes didn't seem so bad."

"Shifters don't trust witches, no sane shifter would." I shrugged. "Maybe Miss Agnes is the exception, I think."

"What aren't you telling me? I'm a shapeshifter too and, as everyone keeps pointing out, I have a lot to learn, so teach me."

"Okay, you're right. I can only tell you what I was taught, though. We may have to get more details from Jess and grant that some of this may be a tad one sided." I paused to figure out where to start. "Okay. Back a couple hundred years ago, everyone knew there were witches. But they didn't know about shapeshifters. Rightly or wrongly, there was a witch in every village. Now I'm talking about a real witch, not a woman that the community was suspicious or jealous of and wanted to get rid of her because she's pretty and unattached." I checked to see if Will followed me, and he nodded. "A real witch can control those types of incidents. If she, or he, found out someone was after them, there is absolutely no way villagers, the local priest, or a witch-finder could capture them—let alone haul them off to jail or the stocks."

"Wait, he? Witches can be men?"

"Of course they can."

"Aren't they called warlocks?"

"No, forget what television taught you." I laughed. "Warlocks are rogue or poorly trained witches."

"Ah."

"Anyway. When the witch trials continued, things got a little too close for comfort. their finger at local shapeshifters. 'Are some of your chickens missing? I saw Fred running around under a full moon, howling and acting weird. I think he was in your hen house. Be careful, if they bite you, you could turn into one of them.' You know how it went."

"It's the same every time anyone is looking for a scape goat. With people it's done by racial profiling." , all right.

"Yes, it is. In this case, witches were responsible for calling out shapeshifters, solely to get the heat off them-selves. It went on for a long time but has died down over the past century. I know people only thought we existed in stories and legends until the pack in California came out."

"That must have been a rude awakening," Will said.

"No kidding—for all of us, not just standard humans. I'm still not sure Nathan Flowers did us a service going public."

"Maybe a witch coven paid him off," Will suggested.

My jaw dropped open in shock.

"What?"

"You could be on to something there. I don't know." I filed it away to think about later.

"Anyway..." Will prodded.

"Yes. It's only been in the past hundred years or so that witches have convinced the general public they don't exist. Except maybe in fairy tales and no, don't even bring up those posers who call themselves wiccans. They're not the same thing at all. True witches are much more than hedge witches. Hence, the fairy tales."

"I understood that most fairy tales had at least a sliver of truth to them or a few facts."

"Of course they do, where do you think Little Red Riding Hood came from? Granny was a shapeshifter and Red was a witch."

"And Red's calling for help brought the wood cutter to the cottage and he cuts the wolf open to allow Granny to escape. That is, if we go by the Grimm Brothers version," Will said as he slowed for the turn that led to the farm's driveway.

"Exactly, but Granny didn't so much escape the wolf, as the wolf shifted back into her human shape."

"The truth has been right in front of us the whole time. Huh?" Will shook his head in wonder.

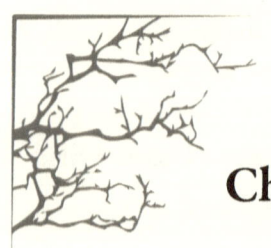

Chapter Nineteen

They were greeted on the front porch by several dozen shapeshifters and their alphas.

Jess ran forward and hugged Helly first, then Will. "Thank you both so much for everything." When she stepped back, there were tears in her eyes.

Will awkwardly returned the woman's hug and stepped back behind Helly to use her as a shield. But it didn't work.

"We couldn't have handled this without you." Iain shook Will's hand and clamped a firm hand on the other man's shoulder.

Iain turned to Helly to give her a hug and thank her.

The other shapeshifters on the porch queued up to shake hands with him and Helly or give them a hug. These people were joined by more that spilled out of the house. Among them, Ben, Guy, and Trudy.

"You'll do," Guy said to each of them, shaking their hands in turn.

They exchanged a slightly puzzled glance. But they had no time to dwell on Guy's words.

Will was a bit shell shocked by all of the attention. He thanked each person as they paused in front of him to ex-press their gratitude. feelings faded, and he exchanged a few words with the adults.

There was a wee girl about five years old with a fall of curly blonde hair and serious gray eyes that looked up at him. She hung on to her mother's hand with her left and offered her right to Will, like the adults around her had. This was what eventually melted his heart completely.

"Thank you, Mr. Conall, for making the bad man go away," she said with wide eyes.

"What's your name?" Will asked. He dropped down to one knee to be closer to eye level with the little girl.

"Matilda Hawking," she said confidently.

"You're welcome, Matilda. I'm glad I could help," Will said as he gravely shook her tiny hand.

He stood again and, as everyone filed back into the house, wondered at the warm feeling that settled into his chest. It almost eclipsed the ever-present ache which had settled in the same spot several days ago.

As Helly ran her fingers down his arm to capture his hand, the pain completely disappeared, and he breathed easier.

Off to the side and alone, Dylan was the last one standing on the porch. He walked solemnly forward and raised his hand to shake Helly's. She shook her head and gathered the kid into a hug. When she released him, most of the tension had drained from the boy. His blue eyes shimmered with unshed tears.

Will offered Dylan his hand and they shook. Will gave him a wink, and Dylan smiled shyly.

"How's your mom?" Helly asked.

"She's okay. Jess put her to bed so she could sleep off the shifting and finish healing," Dylan said, walking be-side Helly.

"Dylan." A call came from the kitchen. It was Trudy. "I need more help here, please."

"Coming," he called back and dashed off.

Helly smiled tiredly at Will. "Let's grab something to eat before we clean the gear."

Will hauled her against him and slipped his arm around her waist. He leaned in and inhaled her scent. She smelled so good, like home.

He kissed her neck, right below her ear.

"Sounds good," he said, leaning back to look into her pale blue eyes.

When her gaze took on a mischievous look, he knew she knew he wasn't thinking about food.

Gear was cleaned, weapons were stowed, and people had showered. After which, the whole crew was fed a roast beef dinner that Trudy had prepared.

For this celebration, she'd pulled out all the stops. A rich, full bodied red wine was served with the perfectly roasted meat.

There was Yorkshire pudding swimming in gravy. Mounds of roasted potatoes, squash, carrots, beets, and salads, and an incredible cherry cheese cake to top it all off.

All Will wanted to do after dishes were washed was have an early night with Helly. Not that there would be much sleeping.

Iain hung up the tea towel he had used during his shift at the dishes. He turned to the other man. "Will, can I ask you to take a walk with me?"

"I'll finish up here, Will." Trudy took the dish cloth from him and gave him a peculiar little smile.

Will dried his hands on the separate towel for that purpose as the sink drained. He followed Iain to the foyer where they each grabbed their jackets. The fall outside air had lost all its heat.

They waved good-bye to Sister Ben as they descended the steps. Lottie was driving the nun back to the hospice that she called home.

Will sensed from Iain's tone, this was going to be a He wondered if the alpha was going to put a deadline on their stay at the farm. He couldn't blame Iain if that was the case. The danger was over and he and Helly were not exactly a stabilizing force.

Iain chose a route to the north barn, and Will fell into step with the alpha.

"How are you adjusting to being a shapeshifter?" the alpha asked.

"So far, there has been lots of discomfort but that's about it. I haven't woken up screaming at the insanity of it all yet."

"Heh." Iain chuckled. "Sorry, it must be weird for you. I can't imagine how strange it must be finding out you're a shapeshifter after believing you were a standard human all your life."

"That part was actually easy to accept. It's the magic thing that's the weird part. I always thought changing shape for some people was like a person having a gift for being good at something. Like some people are good at playing hockey or baseball or have an eidetic memory. I had no idea something like magic existed."

"No one does. That's why we keep it a carefully guarded secret. No doubt you have a good idea what would happen to shapeshifters, if standard humans found out about that aspect of our physiology." Iain stuffed his hands into his coat pockets.

"I don't even want to think about it," Will scrubbed a hand over his face. Man, he was tired and the farther they walked from the house the larger the ache in his chest grew.

"So, what are you thinking of doing now?" Iain asked Will.

Will shrugged. "Helly and I have to go back to work. I guess we'll head back to Vancouver." There was much more to it than that, but none of it was any of Iain's busi-ness as far as Will could see.

"That's not actually what I was asking, so I'll be blunt. Helly doesn't have a pack. I checked." Iain turned his head to meet Will's eyes. "She renounced her ties to Wild Rose when she hired on with SPS."

"Yes, I knew that. All the shapeshifters who work with us renounce their ties to their packs while they're active. Once they retire or quit, they change their status. It's hard to serve two masters."

Iain nodded at this. "That's true, but in her case that means she doesn't have a home base. She has an aunt in Bonneville, but that's it."

"Well, she has Lasha and Dylan, although Lasha isn't much of a draw."

"Tell me about it." Iain sighed. "Dylan, however, is another matter. He's her nephew so she has some clear ties to this pack, to the Vancouver Island Clan." He glanced at Will to see if he was connecting the dots.

"You want to offer her standing in your pack." Will nodded in understanding. "She would have a place here if she needed it."

"That's right. I also want to offer you the same Iain stopped several feet from the barn wall which had once held Geoff Howard's message to Lasha. The message was covered over with bright red paint. The whole wall had been redone.

Will turned a frown on the alpha. "Why would you of-fer me standing in your pack?"

"I have a few reasons, actually. One reason is whether you choose to acknowledge it or not, you are attached to Helly. You have a mate-bond link with her that is broad-casted loud and proud every time you two are in the same vicinity."

Will opened his mouth to protest, and Iain held up a hand to forestall comment. "Don't take that the wrong way. Jess and I were in the same boat last year before we could openly claim each other as our Chosen and get married. It happens with alpha males like us and alpha females like those women." Iain grinned.

"Yeah, I guess you're right," Will said as he returned the other man's grin.

"Can you see yourself without her in your life?" Iain asked with a speculative tone.

"No, not at all. Not now." Will shook his head and he didn't, he couldn't. He may as well stop breathing as give up Helly.

"That's why I thought I'd talk to you before I made the offer to Helly. I'm hoping she'll ask you about it." Iain left unsaid that he hoped Will would accept, if Helly did.

"What's your other reason?"

"I could use another strong male alpha around here. I don't know if you noticed but males are sort of Another male under ninety-five years old would be a bonus," Iain said with a dry smile.

"Aren't you worried I'd challenge you for your "No, I'm not. If you think you would make a better al-pha than me, I'd like to discuss it. If I agree with you, I might hand the job over to you."

"No, no, that's not what I'm saying." Will held up his hands to fend off the offer.

"I know what you're saying. I'm just screwing with you." Iain chuckled. "Times have changed and the packs have to adjust with them. Most North American packs have easy succession processes now. We hardly ever fight to the death anymore."

"Unless the shapeshifter is crazy and possessed," Will reminded the alpha. He thought about Howard and Helly's theory. Mathieu might have had an agenda. If so, his plan had gone as far sideways as it was possible, "Well, yeah, there is that."

Will understood where Iain was going with this "This is a job offer."

"Yes, essentially," the alpha agreed.

"And how would that work?"

"Guy is currently the alpha for non-wolf shifters. He's looking to retire. I need someone, a non-wolf, to take on that role. You would be looking after several different shapeshifter species. Their wants and needs have to be brought before the council and the ruling alphas. If you accept, both you and Helly would sit on the council, too. Jess and I think you'd both be a good fit. So does the sit-ting council."

This explained Guy and Trudy's attitude. "You must have other locals that can handle the job."

"Not as many as you'd think. the big picture and can handle leadership with-out the power going to their head. Then to find a pair, hopefully a mated pair—" Iain gave Will a steady look. "—one who could fill the positions and work with Jess and me."

"Are you planning on taking the pack public? Do you need Helly and me to swing the council votes in favor of your plan? Is that it?" Will asked, frowning at Iain.

"Partly. It is inevitable we will at some point, just not yet, we aren't ready. This last couple of days has shown me that. I need someone who understands the risks and the benefits. I need someone who will challenge me to make the right decisions. Jess does that, but she could use some allies sometimes. Apparently, I can be fairly stub-born, although I don't see it." Again he chuckled. "The pack also needs more young blood to sustain it and make it grow. You'll come in with new ideas and a different perspective. We need those things, too."

Will gave Iain a considering look. These people had trusted him. Iain and Jess had shared things they didn't normally share with anyone outside their pack. Will There was a particular piece of information he shouldn't divulge. But he knew how these things went. There had to be give and take. "You do know that your pack isn't secret, right?"

It was Iain's turn to frown. "What are you talking about?"

"SPS isn't the only security organization that knows about the packs. The other two, CSIS and CSE, know as well. We all report up to the Prime Minister's office. That also means everyone inside the inner circle knows as well."

Iain closed his eyes in resignation. "Then the cabinet and other ministers and their staff know."

"It gets worse. The military brass know, and are actively recruiting shapeshifters, as does any civil servant that handles the intel or data pertaining to shapeshifters. The only ones who don't know their secret is out are the packs."

"Two people can keep a secret if one of them is dead," Iain said, nodding. "My old mentor always said that."

"And your mentor is right," Will said. He knew how hard this was for Iain to hear. But there you are." Will spread his hands.

"Thanks for telling me. Does this mean you'll accept my offer?"

"It means I'll think about it," Will conceded.

"That's all I can ask," Iain said.

I tracked Lasha down after I contributed to the dish washing and clean up. The former alpha was in her room wrapped in a pink terry towel robe and fuzzy pink This was not exactly the way I had pictured Lasha.

"I'd like to talk to you. Can I come in, please?" I asked my sister-in-law.

"Yes, of course." Lasha held the door open wider and allowed me to walk past her before closing it again. "Have a seat." She gestured to the two winged backed chairs in front of the bay window. It was dark outside now so there was no view to appreciate.

I dropped into one of the gray chairs. The whole guest room was done in white and gray and seemed to suit Lasha's mood, I thought, as I looked the other woman over. The cuts and abrasions she had been subjected to were almost healed, although her eyes were shadowed and she still looked pale.

"I'd like to ask you a few questions, mostly to ease my own mind," I said, as I rested my hands on my thighs. This was going to be a difficult conversation.

"Sure, how can I help?"

There was no reason not to get right to it. "Before yesterday, had you ever heard about Mullin or the evil that is sealed in Mount Tzouhalem?" I watched her expression carefully.

"I'd heard the stories, like anyone else that's lived here most of their lives." Lasha shrugged. "Everybody knows about how the mountain got its name and some of the grizzly stories that go with that. Then there was my dad's master's thesis. He has his degree from the University of Victoria for indigenous history. He wrote a paper on Mount Tzouhalem."

"So, your dad is an expert on Mount Tzouhalem's "Yes, I guess so."

"What about Mullin and the portal? Did you know about the minor demon and its relationship as an "My mother told me a story once about Lottie's great-grandmother. There was an evil that was running loose in the valley. People were killing each other and there was chaos. Because of that, no crops were planted. There was no hunting and no trading. The people were starving."

"When was this?" I asked to get a bearing.

Lash a shook her head. "I don't know exactly. Amelia has to be close to a hundred and fifty with her shapeshifter blood adding to her longevity."

"It's probably the same for Sister Ben and maybe Miss Agnes. I have no idea how long witches live."

"Me neither," Lasha said with a shrug.

"Sorry I interrupted, please go on."

"Amelia was the shaman and she tracked the evil. Everyone was affected, it didn't matter who you were, what race, or where you lived, the evil would find you. Amelia put a name to it, Immundus. I don't know how Amelia did that. We would have to ask her. Anyway, she was determined to try and stop it by binding Immundus into the mountain but it didn't work. He got out once more. She knew it would take more magic users to do the job. Amelia had to find a witch and a mage to help her bind Immundus. When she did find the help she needed, it took them two days to build the bindings and then banish Immundus back into the underworld."

I remembered that Sister Ben and Miss Agnes listed the local sites that anchored the bindings. I wanted to mention the Butter Church, Paddy's Mill Stone, and the others. Then I decided it was better to let Lasha tell me what she knew without tipping my hand.

"Someone had to keep watch on the mountain and check that he is still bound behind the petroglyphs. My dad would walk up the mountain to see the cave. He was studying the petroglyphs. I would ask to go with him, but he always said it was no place for me. It was too dangerous."

"Did he take anyone else with him? Did he ever take Geoff or Julian?" I leaned forward in my chair and rested my elbows on my knees.

"Yes, sometimes he would take them both until Amelia ran him off. He never went again after that." Her eyes met mine and narrowed. "What are you getting at?"

"Geoff Howard and my brother were both directly "So? The site has to be watched."

"It is, by a witch and a mage and probably a shaman. Your father is none of those things," I pointed out. "He visited the site numerous times with Howard. Years later, Howard is possessed by a minor demon that is linked to Immundus. You don't think that is at all odd?"

Lasha blinked. Her eyes tracked back and forth like she was only now processing the information.

"And now Geoff is dead, just like Julian." I waited to see what she would say.

"But Geoff killed Julian." She shook her head at me. "Julian wasn't—" She cut off her own words.

"Julian wasn't involved in anything bad?" I voiced the question for her. "Maybe not, maybe he rejected whatever plan Geoff was hatching, and that's why he had him killed. He did confess to using the Foggles to kill my brother. He rode the Foggles the same as Mullin rode him."

I sat back in my chair. I could see her slowly Lasha scowled at me. "You think my father is in some way responsible for what happened? For Geoff becoming possessed?"

"I don't know. I'm merely looking at the information and sharing it with you. It isn't up to me to judge I figured it was time I left. I stood and walked to the door. I paused with my hand on the lever and turned back to her one last time. "Keep in mind who your main priority should be, and that's Dylan. He's your blood and part of the future of this pack. Of everyone involved in this mess, he's innocent."

"You need to leave," Lasha said through clenched teeth and rose to her feet. She was vibrating with rage.

"You need to look after your son and put him first I nailed her with my gaze and allowed my own alpha magic to blaze forth. I knew green was rolling over my eyes.

I could see my words penetrated as her shoulders dropped along with her eyes.

"You're going to tell all this to the alphas." Her remark wasn't a question.

"Absolutely, they need to know, in case they have to take action." I dialed down the intensity of my magic so she could breathe again.

She closed her eyes in resignation and compressed her lips. "What do you want me to do?"

"I'll give you a chance to speak to the alphas before I do. Answer the alphas' questions with the truth and step out of the way when they figure out what needs to be done. Your father's actions are not yours." I hesitated to let her off the hook, but I had my nephew to think of. "Continue to be a good mother to Dylan. He needs you."

She opened her eyes again. There was a touch of relief in her expression and maybe a hint of gratitude.

I nodded once and left, gently closing the door behind me.

It was quiet when I took the stairs back to the main floor. When I concentrated on the link, I could feel that Will was still out for a walk with Iain. I was sure they were having an interesting conversation. I knew I'd hear about it later.

The light was on in the dojo so I wandered toward it. I would have to figure out a schedule to start teaching Dylan the art of half form before he hit full puberty. After that it would be more difficult. I'd probably have to teach Will too, because I doubted he would be happy about not having the same skills I did. Now that was going to be difficult, to say the least.

Jess was in the dojo on a thick mat in a modified yoga pose to allow for her exceedingly huge belly.

"So, are you having twins or what?" I asked as I stripped off my shoes and socks. "Don't make me laugh. I know I'm huge." She smirked as she stood up. "No, it's just one baby, a huge baby boy, but there you go."

"Maybe you look so big because you're so short," I said, raising my eyebrows at her. We changed positions to go into a straight leg stretch.

"We can't all be amazons." Jess gave me a haughty look down her nose as we raised our arms over our heads. We both snickered.

"How much longer do you have to go?" I asked as I moved into the next stretch.

Jess flowed down gracefully to the mat and parked her bottom, looking up at me. "Another three weeks," she said with a sigh.

"It must be tough, but still kind of exciting," I said as I finished up the last stretch. I turned to look at her and hiked down my T-shirt. She was giving me a steady look with a slight frown. I wasn't sure what she was thinking, but I could see she had an unvoiced question on the tip of her tongue.

"So, this is where you are." and paused to remove his shoes. He strolled over and stopped by my mat.

tossed and his face was flushed from the cold. He smelled like fresh-cut cedar, and that wonderfully personal scent that was all his own. There was a definite sparkle in his eyes when he looked at me. I slowly smiled back, I could guess his agenda.

Jess glanced between us then settled on Will. "Do you want to start learning how to shift, Will?"

Chapter Twenty

Yes, that would be great," Will said and grinned at his half-sister. "I'd like to get rid of this It's distracting."

"We can fix that fairly quickly," Jess said as she I leaned forward to offer her my hand to help, but she waved it off. "I'm okay, if just a bit Let's move over here so I won't have to do that again."

We followed Jess to the back wall where there was a small wooden bench and a couple of metal chairs.

She dropped a cushion on the bench and turned to Will. "I'm going to sit here. Grab one of the chairs and put it in front of me. I need you to sit down close enough to me so I can physically reach out and touch you."

"All right," Will agreed, and did as Jess instructed. He placed the chair in front of her and sat facing the bench with his hands resting on his thighs. He had on his black track pants and a T-shirt, the same as I did. Our clothes had been taken away to be laundered after we returned from Mount Tzouhalem.

"Do you want him to strip?" I asked Jess. I was a bit uncertain how this would work. Will was an adult and, up until a few days ago, he considered himself a standard human. Getting naked in front of a new half-sister might be an issue.

"What? Why?" Will glanced up at me with his eye-brows raised in surprise.

"When we walk people through shapeshifting, they're usually nude," Jess explained to Will. She was keeping her expression and tone professional which was more than I could have done. "However, they're already used to being nude in front of others.

Shifting shape requires it, and we've been doing it our whole lives. There's nothing taboo about the nudity side of it." She watched Will care-fully.

I knew she and I were both picking up on Will's So, I stood behind him and placed my hands on his wide shoulders. I glanced at Jess and she nodded. I began a slow, muscle-penetrating massage that Will immediately leaned into.

"For now, since you aren't used to it, you may want to strip off your shirt and down to your underwear. This is so you won't feel so restricted. To make her point, Jess turned her back to him and folded her arms. "It's all right, I won't blush."

Will laughed as he grabbed the hem of his T-shirt and pulled it over his head, exposing a smooth broad back. He dropped the shirt over the back of the metal chair, and I couldn't help but straighten it. The fabric was still warm.

He peeled off his socks and track pants, exposing his black boxer briefs. They were made of a soft knit material that clung nicely to his butt. He caught me looking and winked at me.

I mouthed the word "later" at him and was gratified to see his pupils dilate.

"Behave," Will said as he dropped the pants on his socks and sat down again.

I stepped up to restart the massage, and Will let out a rumbling murmur of pleasure.

"Don't make me get the hose, you two," Jess teased as she turned around and sat down on her cushion. I wasn't sure why she turned her back. But the illusion of privacy dropped Will's level of discomfort considerably.

"Sorry," I said contritely and widened my eyes at her, feigning innocence.

"You're the experienced one here, I expect you to show a good example." She wrinkled her nose at me and I grinned. "Okay." Jess turned to Will and her features sobered. "I'm going to share some information with you that if you were a part of a pack since you were a kid, you'd know. Stop me though if you already understand what I'm about to tell you."

"No problem."

"Cats have a higher degree of control over their She dropped her voice. "Just don't tell anyone I said that."

"I won't," Will said, and I could hear the smile in his tone. He liked his half-sister and I was happy for him.

"Once you have your shifting under control—you may need some practice on that by the way, although the pool of magic you carry is considerable—keeping your form should be fairly easy for you, too," Jess said as she Will rubbed the heel of his hand over his chest. "How do you know I'm a cat?"

I dug into the hard ropy muscles, trying to get him to relax.

"With this," Jess tapped her nose. "And with touch." She brushed Will's hand away from his chest and re-placed her own.

She closed her eyes, and Will went very still under my hands.

"This is where it could get complicated." Jess sighed, opening her eyes and locking on Will's. "When I couldn't shift, a more powerful mage helped me. She essentially unlocked my shifter potential and aligned it with my mage abilities."

"Sister Ben, of course," I said and Jess nodded.

"What did it feel like?" Will asked.

"Like the last puzzle piece sliding into place."

"It must have been a relief. If I can shift, will the pain go away?" I was relieved he was asking Jess questions.

"Oh, yes. You'll need to shift at least once every few days or the stress will build up. If you don't, because you are new at this, shifting will come at a moment you aren't prepared for."

"In other words, do it regularly, like brushing your teeth," Will said, closing his eyes and leaning back into my hands and the massage.

"More like having sex regularly," I commented.

"Exactly," Jess agreed.

"So, that's what I am, a release of tension for you?" Will glanced up at me with an amused glimmer in his dark eyes.

"Boy, are you ever," I said with an exaggerated sigh.

Jess laughed. "Way too much information," she said, holding up her hands as if to ward off our risqué humor.

Will sobered as he turned back to the mage. "Do you need to call Sister Ben to help you with me?"

"I don't think so. I can see your magic and the barrier plainly. I think I know what has to be done."

Will frowned. "Barrier?"

"Yes, you have an obstruction built around your It constrains it and that's probably why you're in pain," Jess explained. She held out her hands, offering them to Will, and he automatically grasped them. They were only inches apart with their knees almost touching. "Do you trust me?" she asked, looking him directly in the eyes.

"Yes," he said, looking straight back at her.

"No, you don't." Jess shook her head at him. "But you do trust Helly, don't you?"

"Yes, I do, with my life." Will's voice was steady and hearing this admission made me feel warm all over. It wasn't "I love you," but it was close.

"Good." Jess nodded. "Helly, place your hands on Will's shoulders only touching him to show support."

I stopped the massage and did as she asked me.

"Will, Helly will keep you safe. I will keep you safe. You are in the pack's house with a couple dozen shapeshifters that would also protect you if need be. after what you and Helly have done for us.

You fought for us, and with us, to protect our pack." She paused and he nodded in acknowledgement of her words. "You can be yourself here. We know you, and we know what you are. We support you completely. If you chose, these shapeshifters would be your pack and die for you if need be. Do you understand?" Her hazel eyes were locked on his face with an intensity that I could feel.

Magic was building.

I had wondered how Jess was going to get around the barrier that Will had erected. I could understand that Will might not know that he was a shifter if he had only lim-ited magic. But that wasn't the case.

It was puzzling because he actually had an incredibly deep magical reserve. He shouldn't have been able to prevent his body from shifting, even as a kid. But then he had the potential to become an extraordinarily strong He also had tendency to be unreasonably head-strong. This could be part of the reason and, so too, as Jess said, not feeling safe enough to be yourself.

It all could have played a part in building the barrier around his magic. , Will had gone in the other and been as standard hu-man as it was possible to be. This was odd since most of us shifted as easily as we breathed. Will's shoulders eased as Jess spoke to him. I could feel she was making progress and cracking open his barriers. She was reassuring him that he was accepted, wanted, and part of this pack if he wanted it. It would be wonderful if the last part were true. I could feel the change in his mood and feel the yearning to belong in the bond between us. He wanted everything she was saying to him. He had to open up and allow her in, allow me in, and everyone who cared about him.

"Close your eyes," Jess instructed Will, and he did. "Reach out and touch your magic. It's right there inside you. It's wrapped around your heart and your organs. It's in your bones and in your blood. Let it flow through you."

Will sighed, and I felt the shimmer of his magic. and flowed through every artery and vein. He vibrated with it.

"Do you see your animal?" Jess gently prodded him.

"Yes." Will's answer was a soft response, like he was a million miles away.

"He wants you to let him out, doesn't he? He wants to have his turn to run and hunt. Do you trust him?"

"Yes, he's me, he's my other half," Will answered, in the same far away tone.

My cougar sat up and took notice. My awareness sharpened along the mate-bond. I could feel Will's cougar just below the surface. He was stretching and pushing. He wanted out.

I couldn't help it. I stripped off my clothes and rested my palms on his bare shoulders. When Will shifted, I would shift with him.

"You're right. He is your other half. Together you will make a whole, William Conall. I'm going to help you let him shift your shape. We're going to go slowly at first so you can see and feel what I do, and then next time you can do it for yourself."

"Yes," he said.

I could hear the yearning in Will's voice and feel it sing across our bond.

"Helly will shift with you, Will." Jess flicked her eyes to mine for a moment, and I saw that hers glowed with a blue light.

So that's what mage power looked like.

"You'll feel her shift with you through the bond. to breathe. Are you ready?"

"Yes." His eagerness washed over me.

"Here we go." Jess inhaled and called on the magic she had built up around us. I felt the thick wave of power she called flow into Will. "Shift, Will, you're safe with us."

I leaned down and brushed his back with my chest to increase the physical contact between us. "Shift with me, Will," I breathed into his ear.

His body arched and I felt his transformation happen at the same time and in sync with my own. It began from our heads down: first hair and face, then skull and neck, shoulders, chest, and spine. Our organs shifted and then the torso, hips, genitals. Legs and arms were last.

I stood on all four paws. My pads pressed into the in-door-outdoor carpet, and I sank my claws in I looked over at Will and lashed my tail.

He had knocked the chair over and was lying down at Jess's feet. He shook a large tawny gold head and looked over at me with the same whisky-colored eyes.

That's my Will, I thought.

He stood up and sauntered over to me. Will's cougar was larger than mine, and taller. He pushed his broad flat nose against my cheek, butting me. I returned the greeting and pushed my own nose into his thick corded neck, breathing him in.

He smelled wonderful. He smelled like mine, and I purred my happiness.

I felt his ease and satisfaction over the bond between us as I nipped him under his chin with my sharp canines.

"Well done!" Jess clapped her hands together and covered her mouth. She was so proud of him. I could see it in her eyes as they glistened with tears.

Will paced over to her and butted his head against her leg.

Jess placed a palm on his head and smiled.

All three of us looked over as the door opened and the alpha stepped inside the dojo.

"So, this is what you've been up to." Iain paused with his hand on the door handle.

"We got Will to finally shift." Jess wiped tears from her eyes. "Wonderful, isn't it?"

Iain walked over and pulled his wife into a hug. "I'm proud of you, Jess. This is amazing." He let go of her and dropped down to his hunches to be eye level with Will. "I figured that eventually Will would take the stick out of his ass and let you help him." He laughed when Will shoved him off his feet with a paw the size of a dinner plate.

I stilled in alarm, but the alpha didn't seem to be I dropped my butt down to sit and wait, meeting Jess's eye roll.

"Here we go." I rolled my words into a growl, but they were distinct enough for Iain and Jess to snap their heads up and stare at me. "What?" I shrugged a tawny shoulder. "I can talk in all my forms."

"That's...pretty awesome," Jess said carefully. "I have only ever heard of shifters like Iain—alphas capable of speaking in their half forms, not as their animal. Can you teach it?"

"Yeah, probably, I never tried."

"That's something to discuss later then." The alpha marked me with his gaze. "But for now, we shouldn't waste Will's first shift." He stood and, as he stripped, he transformed into his huge silver, gray, and black wolf.

The massive alpha wolf looked at his mate, and she shook her head. "No thanks, I've tapped enough power for one day. I don't feel like a run."

She did follow us out to the main doors with an arm-load of our clothing.

Iain had the front doors open. There was a reason all the doors had levers versus round door handles.

My nose twitched with a myriad of scents that drifted in on the night air. The darkness awaited us, and we should join it.

I glanced over at Will and nudged him with my He was so solid he didn't budge an inch but he did look back at me, and I saw joy in his eyes.

The alphas had a brief moment where Iain pressed his massive head against Jess's side. She hugged him and then Iain led the way out across the porch and through the yard.

I glanced back at Jess as she dropped our clothes in a pile on a chair by the door.

"You guys go have fun," she said and grinned at us. "I'm getting another piece of cheese cake." She laughed as she closed the front door.

I chased after Will and Iain. They were well up a path that led east. When I caught up, Iain emitted a rough yelp and took off. Oh, ho, a race! Will bunched his hind legs and sprang after Iain.

dug into the soil for traction and the tree trunks I used as stepping stones. It had been a long time since I had run in my cougar shape for the fun of it, and I loved it.

My muscles warmed and my heart pumped faster, I was gaining on the males. I decided that catching them didn't interest me all that much. I wanted to outsmart them instead. So, I paid strict attention to the other scents that crossed the trail and moved parallel to the males.

There was deer scent that ran a different course. It cut across the trail on a straighter angle than the meandering track. I shot up it. If I remember right, this was Mount Richards and part of the pack lands. uphill, so the summit of this mountain must be the goal.

In minutes, I gained the summit and the small clearing that was lit by a sliver of the new moon. There was an arbutus tree close to the center of the clearing. Its trunk was more horizontal than vertical. It was nothing to leap up and sink my claws into the soft wood. I draped myself across the trunk and watched the trail while slapping my tail against the tree.

I could smell the ocean, but couldn't see it, now that it was well after dark. A ferry's red and green lights on the dark expanse were visible. I could also make out the yel-low lights that studded the darkness from houses in Crofton, a good five kilometers away.

I ignored the scent of squirrels and deer. I wasn't here to hunt, only to enjoy the night.

Not long after, Iain and Will came charging up the trail, almost side by side. As they gained the summit as well, I let out a rumbling snarl. I had to let them know I had bested them.

The male wolf and cougar cut their eyes to me. I would have laughed if I could. That was something I couldn't do in my cougar form so I settled for looking smug. Something all cats were good at.

The two males paused to look at me. I gave them my most haughty pose.

The pack alpha froze for a moment and lifted his head. The massive wolf let out a somber and mournful howl.

then charged back down the trail. I leaped off the tree, and Will and I followed Iain down the mountain. The wolf alpha wasn't playing. There was urgency in his stride. Something had changed.

Chapter Twenty-One

We descended the mountain trail much faster than we had ascended. We passed other wolves who watched us go by with alert interest, but didn't follow us. If their alpha wanted them, he would have called to them.

outside wrapped in a thick green sweater waiting for us. "Sorry I had to call you back," she said to Iain as we all shifted back to our human forms and sorted out our clothing.

but, his shifting to human was seamless and fluid. The blockage was well and truly gone and I hoped his inner demons were gone with it.

"What is it?" Iain asked as he pulled on his jeans.

"Lasha is very agitated, and she wants to talk to us," Jess said gravely. Her eyes took us all in.

I paused from stuffing my arm in a shirt sleeve. "Good," I said and continued to pull on my T-shirt. "I was hoping she would do the right thing."

"Then you and Will had better join us," Jess said and opened the door. She and Iain went in.

"Now what?" Will mumbled as he pushed his head through the neck hole of his T-shirt.

"You'll see," I said as we followed the alphas inside.

Lasha was pacing in the foyer. She was now dressed in jeans and a sweater. She looked relieved to see Iain accompanying Jess. That made me hopeful that I had done the right thing in letting her go to the alphas instead of reporting what I knew.

Will raised his eyebrows at me in query, but I shook my head as I detoured first to the ground floor washroom to clean up a bit.

As I entered the washroom, I heard Will thanking Jess for helping him with his shifting. That brought a smile to my lips.

It might be the cat in me, but I didn't like to have dirty hands and feet. I wiped off my muddy feet as best as I could and washed my hands. Then I bound my hair with the ponytail holder I had stuffed in my pocket before I shifted.

When I came out, Lottie was coming in the front door. From the grim set of her mouth, I knew she was here for the same meeting.

"Did Jess call you?" I asked, falling into step with her.

"Yep, Lasha strikes again," Lottie said dryly. "She's such a drama queen."

I shrugged. "I like having all the loose ends tied off."

Lottie raised one eyebrow at me speculatively as we entered the conference room.

We seated ourselves around the table and Jess closed the door. Iain, Lasha, Lottie, Russell, Will, and I were the only ones in attendance. There were no older or other pack members.

Interesting, I thought.

"All right, what's going on?" Iain's tone had a touch of impatience. He was probably tired of Lasha's drama too, but the pack was stuck with her. Even so, this was information he and Jess needed to know.

I sat back and folded my arms. I wouldn't contribute unless asked to. Or unless Lasha was telling it wrong and leaving out important points.

The former alpha sighed and rubbed her forehead, "Where to begin?" Lasha seemed to take hold of herself as she leveled her gaze at both alphas. "All right then." She swallowed, decision made, and continued. "Helly came to see me earlier and asked me some questions that got me thinking. As Helly helpfully pointed out to me, evil like Mullin doesn't just pop out of nowhere. There has to be a cause." She swallowed again. Admitting this must have been difficult for her.

"I swear that last fall, when my dad took Geoff up north, he wasn't possessed. He didn't radiate the pure evil that he did today."

"That's true." Iain nodded. "When I answered his Challenge, it was nothing to beat him. He didn't have a half form then either. He stayed in his wolf until he was taken to the compound for judgement."

"Yes, that's right." Lasha glanced at me.

I shook my head and gave her my thousand-yard stare, because this wasn't my story to tell.

My sister-in-law turned back to Iain and Jess and She told them the story her mother had shared with her, and then she also went one step further. "I called Sis-ter Ben. No one, not Miss Agnes, Sister Ben, or Shaman Amelia thought at the time that my father was up to no good. No one said anything, or accused him of trying to use the power the evil represented for anything. They thought he was only curious. After my mother passed away, it became his full-time hobby. We thought his re-search about the history of the mountain was harmless. It helped him deal with his grief. Even so, the petroglyphs hold power. Sister Ben confirmed that Miss Agnes fig-ured out my father was still going to the cave regularly. To stop it, he was instructed by Amelia not to go near the mountain again. They were afraid he would disturb the bindings. He could inadvertently allow something nasty to get out." Lasha threaded her fingers together to stop their fidgeting. "I know he didn't listen. I think my father was responsible for Mullin getting through the portal, and for Geoff's possession. Whether the evil that leaked out affected him or if he actively went seeking it, I don't know." She shook her head and looked back up at her alphas. "I think my father spent too much time up there, and it affected him." She swallowed but continued. "I do know Geoff was power hungry and maybe my father promised him something. But none of that matters. The results are still the same. Silas was hurt and two more people were killed by Geoff. I think my father also bears some responsibility for those acts. I am responsible, too. You took injuries because of my stupidity in thinking I could stop Geoff on my own." There were tears glistening in her eyes. "I am so sorry."

Iain was quiet for a moment, as he studied Lasha. He turned to look at his mate and reached out to grasp Jess's hand to give it a squeeze. He was rewarded with a nod from Jess.

From the nonverbal communication, it was apparent that the alphas were united, their opinions matched.

I glanced at Will and saw his grave expression. He looked at me and nodded. He was telling me he agreed with the theory I had posed to him when we were travel-ing to the compound. Was that only two days ago?

"Have you spoken to George?" Iain asked.

"No, I wanted to talk to you both first. I don't think I should talk to him until you decide what should be done." Lasha looked miserable but resigned.

"Good. Don't call him. We need to go up there and speak with him. I would prefer he didn't have time to construct some new plan." Iain glanced at Jess, and she nodded again. "I'll go up to the compound first thing to-morrow. Russell—" He pinned the younger male with his gaze. "—you'll go with me."

"Yes, Alpha." Russell was trying to contain his He all but bounced in his seat. Then he winced. Lottie had kicked him under the table.

"Lottie, I'd like you to stay here and keep an eye on things with Jess. If the baby comes early, we'll need you here to take over running the pack."

"Yes, Alpha." Lottie nodded and glanced at me and Will, but her expression was unreadable. I wondered what she was thinking.

"Lasha, you'll go with Russell and me. We'll take Ben along too. He will round out the team."

"It wouldn't hurt to take one of the senior "Good call." Jess turned to look at her former alpha. "Lasha, this doesn't remove the fact that you disobeyed a direct order to stay on the farm property. There will still be repercussions because of that."

The warning was clear in Jess's eyes. Lasha had better toe the line.

"Yes, Alpha." Lasha dropped her eyes and nodded at Jess. "I'll talk to Trudy about looking after Dylan while I'm gone," she said, standing.

"I'm here," I said, looking up at my sister-in-law. "I'd like to get to know my nephew a bit better."

She stared at me, nonplussed for a moment.

Was she surprised I would help her out? "We're still family," I said.

"Yes, of course, that would be great. I'll go talk to him and let him know you'll be keeping an eye on him." Be-fore she left she handed her cell phone over to Iain. "I don't want to be tempted to call him," she said and left the room to hunt up her son.

"Russell, we need a vehicle that is up to the trip and gassed up. Take care of that please."

"I'm on it." The younger man jumped to his feet and hustled to do as he was asked by his alpha. The door closed behind Russell.

Iain leaned back in his chair with a sour look on his face.

"You were going to tell us about all of this, weren't you?" Jess said as she looked at me with somber eyes.

I unfolded my arms and leaned on the table. "I was," I confirmed. "I figured I'd give her until morning to do the right thing. If she didn't, I'd physically bring her to you and ensure you got all the facts. I know your history, and I know this pack's history," I explained.

"I know Iain was sent away for seven years, and that's not normal. George Mathieu was responsible for that and for pushing you two apart. He was trying to manipulate who would be the next alpha. While Lasha did do the job, she didn't do it particularly well. She should never have been handed the reins of power, just as my brother should never have been an alpha.

"It's so obvious that you both should have been the ruling alphas years ago. Lasha wasn't capable of anything more than an interim leader, but that's not how George Mathieu wanted it." I shrugged one shoulder. "After he retired, Mathieu could still control the pack through Any decisions that were made during Lasha's tenure as alpha may need to be re-viewed, but that's a side issue. The result was Mathieu lost control of the pack when Lasha stepped down in your favor." I included both alphas in that statement.

"She knew she couldn't handle being alpha. She was hanging on by her fingernails as it was," Lottie interject-ed.

"So I understood when I came back last year," Iain agreed. "If George killed, or severely injured, one or both of us, it would destabilize the pack again. Then he could manipulate Lasha into stepping back in as alpha. Possibly, retake the alpha position for himself. It wouldn't matter which plan he picked, he would have control again." He frowned in thought.

"What's Mathieu's motivation for retaking control of the pack?" Will asked, speaking for the first time.

We all looked at him. "Power, money, for the sheer hell of it, does it matter?" Iain asked.

"He could also take another mate and continue his line," Jess said. "More likely though, he would groom Dylan for the role like he did Lasha. exchanges from other packs. Keep the way clear for Dylan to be ruling alpha when his grandfather felt he was ready. Again, like he did with Lasha. want to take on the headache of being in charge."

She rubbed a section of her belly. It was evident their son was kicking and doing summersaults.

"We'll sort it out," Iain said as Jess took his hand and placed it over her belly. Immediately the squirming under his hand ceased.

"Your touch works every time." Jess smiled at her husband. He patted her belly with affection.

"We'd better go talk to Ben," Iain said.

"Do you need any help?" Will asked both alphas.

"I think we've got this, but I would appreciate it if you both hung around a day or so longer until I get back." Iain met my eyes and Will's in turn.

"Of course," I agreed.

"No problem," Will said.

"I'd also like you to think about my offer and give me an answer when we get back." Iain stood and helped Jess to her feet.

Will nodded. "I can do that."

Iain and Jess left the room.

"I'll go bring Trudy and Guy up to speed," Lottie said but paused by our chairs. "I'm glad you guys are staying for a bit longer. I was afraid you were going to run off to Vancouver, now that all the fun was over."

"Not yet." I smiled at her. "What offer?" I asked Will.

The radio on Lottie's hip crackled. *"Lottie, this is Silas. We have a visitor at the front gate."*

"Do you have a name?" Lottie said into the mic.

"George Mathieu."

Chapter Twenty-Two

H old him there a minute," Lottie said, striding out of the conference room and down the hallway.

Will and I glanced at each other. "I guess the fun isn't over yet," Will remarked as we exited the conference room too, and followed Lottie to the kitchen.

"This doesn't change anything," Iain was saying as we entered. "Tell Silas to escort Mathieu to the north barn and wait there. We'll come out."

Lottie relayed Iain's instructions over the radio. "I'm putting out a Call," she said to Iain.

The alpha paused a moment. "Good idea," he said. He turned and headed toward the side door with Ben and Lottie close behind.

"I'm going with you," Jess said as she elbowed her way through the other shifters. Her tone said there would be trouble if anyone argued.

Iain studied her face with a closed expression. He probably wanted her to stay back at the house, safe and sound. Pregnant or not, Jess was done letting her mate meet threats solo.

Iain held out his hand, and she strode up to take it. They jointly led the way out the door and down the steps.

We followed close behind the group. If back up was needed, Will and I would provide it.

George Mathieu was a grizzly bear, and it was never a good idea to underestimate a grizzly. Plus the fact that he held alpha magic in addition to shapeshifter speed and strength. All these factors would make Mathieu a lethal threat. And who knew how this was going to go down?

Silas stood a few feet away from a brown half ton. He looked relieved to see his alphas coming down the path from the house.

Katherine, however, had a deadly glare trained on Mathieu. She didn't for a minute look intimidated by the old alpha.

Mathieu slowly opened the driver's side door of his truck and climbed out. His height hinted at the size his animal form would be if he decided to take offense.

I frowned, why did I think he would fight? We could maybe have a friendly conversation with him, and he would apologize and go back home.

Sure, that would happen.

"I was hoping for a cup of coffee and a slice of Trudy's pie. Why would you ask me to meet you here?" Mathieu chided Iain like he was a kid and not half of the ruling pair of the VIC pack.

"The fighting ring is in the north barn, George, you know that." Iain came to a stop and stepped in front of Jess. Her eyes flashed but she stayed back.

"Silas, Katherine, who's got the front gate?" Jess asked.

," Lottie said, answering for the younger wolves. She had it covered. No one was going to surprise her crew.

"You guys can head back to your post," Lottie said. "I put out a Call." She said it like a warning she aimed at Mathieu.

I wanted to ask what a Call was, although I was pretty sure I could guess.

"So, you want to fight me, do you?" Mathieu's tone was fairly dripping with condescension. "For what "How else will we stop you from meddling with the pack and the alpha roles? I was thinking it may come down to a fight. You're too stubborn to take advice." Iain's tone was even but hinted at repercussions.

"I have no idea—" George began.

"Cut the crap, Mathieu," I said. I bared my teeth at him. "We know you were responsible for letting Geoff Howard escape from the compound." I couldn't help my-self. All the anger I had bottled up was starting to leak out as I stared at the cause of my brother's pointless death and the deaths of at least three others. I included Howard's in my tally. "I think you've destroyed enough lives."

I felt Will's hand on my shoulder briefly. Whether it was to calm me down or show me support I didn't know and, at the moment, I didn't care. I trusted he had my back either way.

Mathieu's eyes widened when I threw out my That was always a good indicator the opposition didn't think you were smart enough to figure them out. It worked in the field, and it worked right here.

"What Helly said is correct." Iain moved to the barn door, swung it open, and then turned on the interior light. He looked back to look at his former alpha. what you were up to on Mount Tzouhalem, and you must know by now that your puppet is dead."

This last seemed to take Mathieu by surprise, although he hid it quickly. He hadn't known Geoff Howard was dead, even though as soon as he saw Iain and Jess, he must have known that his plan had failed.

If Mathieu didn't know about Howard's demise, he must have come down from the compound with the thought he would finish the mopping up and ensure the correct alpha was installed over the VIC pack.

"Please, after you." Jess gestured for Mathieu to pre-cede us into the barn.

I could see Mathieu was rapidly rejigging his story on the fly by the way his eyes were darting around. To stall, he walked slowly in front of us into the barn.

The fighting ring set up on the far side. It looked like any regular practice ring I had seen in a few different gyms. And yet there was no platform, it was all at floor level. It was square with three sets of ropes, at a low, These made up the sides of the ring and were tied off to four fence posts.

Mathieu moved slowly past Iain and stood in front of the ropes. He made no aggressive moves. "I don't know what you're talking about. I'm here to visit Lasha and my grandson. I was worried Howard was after Lasha. He said he blamed her for all his disappointments."

None of it rang true. Why was he even trying to lie to us? Did he think his force of personality would actually make us believe his words?

"Seriously?" The question was voiced from behind me, and I looked back to see Lasha advance toward her "And you never tried to fix his thinking? You let him continue to blame me? For your machinations?"

"Now, girl, you need to calm down. You don't under-stand." Mathieu was trying to be placating but all he did was piss his daughter off even more.

"Do. Not. Call. Me. Girl." Lasha enunciated each word slowly and with force. "I could have been killed. Geoff assaulted me and dragged me off to that cave." Her voice was going up with each sentence, and she was vibrating with rage. "He was going to sacrifice me to bring over some bigger evil than the one you encouraged to possess him. If it hadn't been for my alphas and my pack, I would be dead and Dylan would be an orphan."

"I am your alpha," Mathieu corrected her harshly.

"You're not!" Lasha screamed at him.

"Lasha," Iain said in a quiet tone that contained steel and alpha magic.

She cut her eyes to him and met his stare, immediately dropping her gaze, and took a deep breath. Her shoulders slumped, and I sensed relief that she didn't have to Iain was the alpha. It was his responsibility, and he would take care of it.

She stepped back behind Jess's shoulder and brought her head up to level a glare at her father.

During Lasha's tirade, other shapeshifters had trickled into the barn. It was a large open space, and it could Ben took a position behind Iain while Trudy and Guy stood behind Jess. Other shifters were crowding in. Some I recognized, some I didn't.

I scanned their faces to gauge where their support would go. To a person, male and female, each had their eyes pinned on Mathieu. There wasn't a friendly expres-sion among them. That's what I had expected, and I was glad to see I was right.

"You're not strong enough to run this pack," Mathieu was saying as he rounded on Iain.

"You think I'm not strong because I choose to ask for consultation from my pack members before making Iain was relaxed. He clearly credited Mathieu as a real threat, and he watched him like a wolf watches a lone deer.

I glanced at Will. Our eyes met and, as one, we moved slowly out of the cluster of people and along the walls. Will went along one side, I went along the other. He did that thing where he could blend with the shadows. I so had to get him to teach me that skill. We would cover the exits to ensure Mathieu didn't run.

"You're weak. You don't know how to lead." Mathieu scowled at Iain now. "You're not fit to be an alpha."

"Because you say so? Is that all you've got?" Iain grinned at Mathieu as he moved forward. Mathieu took one step backward. He was too close to the fight ring to move farther away. "Of course, I know how to lead. I was taught by some of the best alphas from three different packs over seven years. Or did you forget you sent me away for that long?" Iain glanced at Jess and she stepped up to her husband's side. They faced Mathieu shoulder to shoulder.

"There's a problem with sending away alpha She looked at her mate but the remark was aimed at Mathieu.

"That's true. I received training and mentoring from some of the best. The same as Jess did." Iain turned to look calmly back at Mathieu. "You are banished."

My skin prickled. Power was building.

"You don't control the pack territory. I can go where I will." Mathieu's face was turning red with suppressed fury.

"Yes, we do. I control the territory. I'm linked to the land exactly as you wanted." Jess folded her arms above her expanded stomach. "Just as you tried to force my mother to do, but she resisted you. Didn't she?"

"If she'd mated with me like it had been contracted, the pack would be three times as strong as it is now. I wouldn't have to put up with babysitting snot-nosed, spoiled city kids." Mathieu's expression was sour, and he pointed his finger accusingly at Jess. "It's your fault. If she hadn't been expecting a child when she got here, this would have all been settled long ago. But your mother had to be difficult. She didn't want to mate with me. She was spoiled and self-centered. She should have been thinking about your future and the future of the pack that took her in."

I saw the surprise in Jess's face as her lips parted and her eyes widened. Her lip curled in disgust at the thought of Mathieu as her stepfather. Or maybe there was some-thing deeper?

"You are banished." Jess said the words slowly and distinctly. There was another surge of power with Jess's words. Banishment meant he didn't rate a quick He would be a lone shapeshifter, with no pack and no support.

I looked around to see if anyone else noticed. Every-one was intent on the scene being played out between the old guard and the new alphas.

Jess looked at Iain, and he took his cue.

"Shapeshifters and pack members of the Vancouver Island Clan." Iain addressed the room with a thunderous voice. "What is your judgement upon George Mathieu, former alpha?"

"Banished!" included me and Will, even though we weren't actual pack members. Mathieu would die a slow death on his own. No other pack would touch him when this information got out.

"So be it!" Jess raised her hands. "George Mathieu you are banished from all VIC pack territory!" And she brought her hands down sharply, releasing the gathered power. The energy signature echoed and rolled across us all. "Will you accept the judgement and peacefully enter into custody or challenge the our decision?"

In answer Mathieu's clothes and skin split. His enor-mous grizzly emerged. His mouth opened wide to display giant teeth and fangs as he roared his defiance. The huge shaggy gray body had front and back legs that were well-muscled. Each massive paw ended with razor sharp claws.

He charged Iain. But in the fastest shape change I had ever seen, Iain met the charging grizzly in his massive wolf half form. He must have been hoping Mathieu want-ed to fight and been ready

The nightmare creature that was the alpha connected with the bear. He must have weighed five hundred pounds, and yet the alpha used the momentum of the at-tack to flip the grizzly over the top rope of the ring. The bear crashed to the floor and raised clouds of dirt that were flung into the air with the impact.

As soon as the bear was down, the shifters surged forward to encircle the fighting ring. I rode along on the tide.

The bear jumped to his feet as the alpha wolf cleared the top of the ring with a leap. Then the fight was joined as they slashed with claws and landed punches. In his half form, Iain was as tall as the bear was on his hind legs. I wouldn't have thought it would be an even match in theory, but I was wrong.

The crowd shouted abuse at Mathieu and "We are no longer under your fist, Mathieu!" hollered Trudy Tremblay.

"We will choose our own mates!" shouted Jerry Greenwood.

I had forgotten how rabid shapeshifters could be en masse. No doubt there was deep-seated anger against George Mathieu. Even if he won, there was no way he would be allowed to retake the alpha spot.

The bear was trying to grapple the wolf, to crush his opponent's chest if he could. Iain was too quick for the old bear. He slid in and landed two slashes, opening up wounds on the bear, and danced away smoothly.

The bear's agitation was growing. He wasted energy on roaring and spraying spit instead of going after his I saw Jess among the crowd. She was flanked by Lot-tie on one side and Ben on the other. No one was pressing in on her. She was quiet with her hand over her mouth, waiting for the outcome to be decided.

The bear got a shot in that knocked Iain back, opening a cut above his eye and down the right side of his face, although, it was more a muzzle in this half form.

The blow appeared to decide things for Iain. He crouched and, instead of leaping, he swept the bear's legs out from under him, sending him crashing to the floor in a cloud of dirt.

Iain was on him in an instant, his claws were sunk partway into the bear's neck, and the grizzly froze.

"A bit more pressure and I'll slice your jugular. I'll make sure you bleed out right here, right now." Iain's voice flowed from the monstrous jaws. "Yield," the alpha commanded. "Take your punishment and our judgment."

The bear paused, frozen. Then he shifted back into his human shape. Iain's claws were still sunk into his neck. He moved swiftly against the razor sharp edges and slashed his own throat.

Blood shot up and coated the wolf and the ring, splattering some of the pack members who jumped back in surprise. Both carotid artery and jugular vein were slashed open. This was too much for a shapeshifter's metabolism to handle.

"I knew you were too weak," Mathieu whispered right before he went limp in a pool of his own blood.

George Mathieu was buried in the pack cemetery in the shadow of Mount Richards. It was done without No prayers were said and probably no forgiveness, at least for a while.

I stood behind them as the two had a moment of Will and I volunteered to assist with the burial. The person who was responsible for my brother's death was gone. I felt a weight I'd been carrying for some time slip off my shoulders.

Four steps to the left and I stood over at Julian's grave. This was the first time I had visited. I laid some wild grace ward on the mound. The blue flowers were still vibrant, even as we left fall and edged into winter.

"I wish we had talked more," I said to my brother and let out a long sigh that seemed to clean out the last of the anger. "I'm sorry I wasn't here for you."

A warm presence was at my back, and Will's arm slid around my shoulders. He hugged me to his larger body, and I nestled in against him.

We didn't speak for a while. Lasha had taken Dylan back to the house and let me have my privacy to morn my brother. It was only Will and I in the well-manicured clearing.

The grass was still green and the cedars always so. The sun had risen and was pushing through the branches and light drizzle with a watery light.

"What are they going to do about explaining Mathieu's death?" I asked idly.

"You can't shut off your brain, can you? You're al-ways looking to tie off the loose ends," Will commented.

I shrugged one shoulder under his warm hand.

"I took care of it. SPS will assist with issuing a death certificate. The document will read heart attack. George Mathieu had one after he arrived at the farm last night."

"Good."

"We should go. Iain wants to have a word with you."

Will released me, and I fell into step beside him as we took the path back down to the farm.

"When you start teaching Dylan the art of half form, can you teach me as well?"

"Of course," I said. "It can come in handy."

"I can see that." We stepped over a fallen log and skirted some prickly blackberry bushes.

"Can you teach me to talk in full and half forms?"

"No." I shook my head and glanced at him to see him frown.

"Why not? Don't I have enough magic to achieve that skill?"

"You have plenty of magical capacity. I just don't want you to be able to argue with me in your other forms," I said then sprinted away.

Will grabbed for me, and I shrieked with laughter as I slid out of my clothes. I shifted into my cougar form to run and run hard.

It wasn't thirty seconds before I felt Will behind me, gaining. Then he was there beside me in his cougar form, and we chased each other through the trees and scrub. When we tired, we lay in the sunshine until we decided it was time to head back to the house.

Dressed and in human form, we walked back side by side. We were both much more relaxed and incredibly dirty.

Iain was crossing the yard as we got closer, and he paused when he saw us coming. He stood waiting, and I got the feeling he had something on his mind.

"Do you feel better?" Iain smiled at me, for it was probably fairly apparent I had been running with Will in animal form.

"Yes." I nodded. "It's good to be able to run when you need to."

"That's something I wanted to talk to you about." Iain's eyes briefly touched on Will before he returned his gaze to me.

I tipped my head to look at the alpha. "What about?"

"I'd like to offer you standing in the VIC pack," Iain said. "Jess and I discussed it a few days ago, and I also mentioned this to Will. We would like you both to join us, even if it's only part time. You need a pack, and we need you, both of you."

I was stunned. at being offered this opportunity. "Thank you," was all I got out. I blinked back tears. What the hell was wrong with me?

Iain grinned at me. He seemed to understand. "We'll talk about it later. Will, have you thought about my "Yes, I have," his eyes slid over to me. "I still need to talk to Helly about it."

"Ah. Okay, see you at dinner," Iain walked away to continue on his original path.

"What offer?" I asked.

"I'll tell you about it upstairs," he said as he took my hand.

The intense look in his eyes communicated that he wanted privacy. And not just for conversation. I was game for that so I closed my fingers around his. We made it all the way to the third floor and behind the door of our room.

Then I gave into the impulse to feel his mouth on mine.

I opened myself up to him with that kiss. I opened my heart and let him feel how much I wanted him. I showed him my hope that we could make this thing between us work, if he was willing.

He was different now than the man who walked into the Kicking Horse. He knew himself better, but I could help him know himself completely.

"Have you got the first idea how intense that was when you whispered to me to shift with you?" Will asked me when we finally broke for air.

I gave him a smug, knowing smile. "Of course."

"Helly," Will said seriously as he stroked my cheek. "I was afraid to let you in. I was afraid to let anyone in. I knew there was something about me I couldn't trust, something that made me dangerous. I didn't know what that something was."

"You had to unlock who you were, who you are. You were denying half of your identity. Anyone trying to do that would think they had issues. I'm glad I could help. I'm glad it was me."

He grinned. "Me too."

"I'm also glad you're a cougar, like me. It explains why I've always been attracted to you. me something my brain wasn't picking up on." I slid my hands up his torso and over his shoulders to wrap them around his neck. His hand slipped around my waist and drew me to him.

I took a breath and locked my eyes on his. I was going to do this.

"Will, I love you. I have for a long, long time but even more so after this week. If I go back with you to Vancouver, this is the type of relationship I want."

I saw a flame ignite in his eyes. "Thank God." He ex-haled harshly and crushed me against his chest. He buried his face in my neck and breathed in my scent. "I love you so much, Helly, it hurts to be away from you. I almost went insane when you disappeared last year, and I drove research crazy until they found you."

I leaned back so I could see his face. "So, we're good?"

"No, not really." He gave me heated look with an intensity that made me weak. "We have a lot of decisions to make, but right now I want to make love to you. We can talk about the rest of this later."

"Good, because I want you so bad, I can't think straight." I pressed my mouth against his and teased him with my tongue. He growled deep in his throat and I felt a primal need to see if I could turn that into a purr.

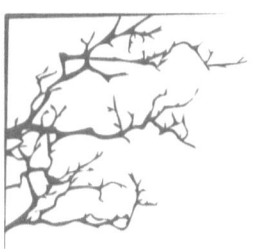

Epilogue

"H elly?" Will asked cautiously.

"Mm?" I answered. I was so relaxed lying next to Will. I could trail my fingertips across his chest as I lay on my back. I enjoyed the feel of his hands on my skin. "You know if you go higher or lower, it would be more fun," I pointed out.

We had made love fiercely. Each of us desperate to show the other how much we needed to touch and be touched. Afterward, we'd showered and climbed into bed.

Only that time, we went slowly and painstakingly to savor each other to the fullest. But a third time was the charm, right?

"Why has your scent changed?" His dark eyes met mine and his tone made me frown slightly. "A few days ago your scent was more distinct. It's become more com-plex and I can feel that your magic reserve has expand-ed."

"I don't know. I can't detect a change in my scent."

His eyes searched mine and I read a deep concern in his eyes.

I placed my hand on my breast bone and probed my pool of magic. It was true, it felt expanded and there was a deeper texture to it. to rest on the slight curve of my belly. I relaxed and let my senses absorb the state of my body.

Ah, yes, there you are.

I looked up at Will as he leaned over me. I could see the unasked question in his eyes.

"No, Will, I'm not possessed by Mullin," I said with a grin. I took his rough hand and placed it back where he initially had it on my stomach, cradling the slight curve.

"This is our baby," I whispered and waited.

Will took in a slow shaky breath and I could see a myriad of emotions cross his face.

He shook his head "I can't be anyone's father."

I raised one eyebrow at him. "Why is that?"

"I don't—" He swallowed.

I knew what he was thinking. Will's father and mother—Jess wanted to look up his genealogy. What could he tell her?

"All I know about my parents are their names." He swallowed and exhaled sharply through his nose. "I have no idea how to be a father. I have no experience or the first clue what to do."

I realized I was seeing fear in his eyes for the first time, ever. Well, I'd put an end to that.

"Are you kidding me?" I said. I placed my hand over his, over our baby. "You have more caring and empathy than any man I have ever known. Besides, what makes you think I know anything about being a mother?" He was gently rubbing his fingers over my skin and I wondered if he even knew he was doing it.

"You had parents."

"Yes, for a few short years. I don't have them to ask for advice or direction."

"I don't know how to be a father. I never had one," Will said desperately.

"You know we'll be in this together, right? It will be a learning curve for both of us." I rolled toward him and slipped my arms around him. He drew me to him, and I rested my cheek against his shoulder.

"Yeah." He nodded. "I guess this is a good time to tell you that the alphas want us to stay with them and run the non-wolf shapeshifter side of things."

"We could use a little group support. to trust and accept us."

"That was my thought as well. Plus, we're only half an hour away from the office by float plane."

I blinked in surprise. It was true. I smiled. "You've been giving this some serious thought."

"Even more so in the past three minutes." He gave me a strained look, but it changed as a thought occurred to him. "You're my mate now and the mother of my child."

I could sense the protective side of him ignite, and it gave me a warm glow.

"Yes, I am, and you're my mate and the father of my child. I think I'll have to marry you to make an honest man out of you."

He grinned at me. "I like the sound of that."

"Please remember, like every other mission, we're a team, and I have your back." I could see relief and acceptance gradually wash over him.

Will kissed my temple and hugged me close. "And I have yours."

More Titles by Yvonne Rediger

VIC Shapeshifters Mysteries

The Shape of Us
Hell Cat
Trusting the Wolf
Into the Wood (short story collection)

Musgrave Landing Mysteries

Death and Cupcakes
Fun with Funerals
Condo Crazy

Adam Norcross Mysteries

The Wrong Words
The Right Road

Diving In Heart First
The Common Touch

About the Author

Yvonne Rediger was born in southern Saskatchewan. She lived and worked in northern Manitoba, New Brunswick, Alberta, and Vancouver Island. She now resides in central Saskatchewan with her husband. She has two grown children.

Read more at blackyvy50.wix.com/yvonnerediger.

www.ingramcontent.com/pod-product-compliance
Lightning Source LLC
Chambersburg PA
CBHW020650030726
47498CB00002B/446